To Jo

I hope you w...
enjoy the story
X

D1826246

The Ninth Cross

J. Karst

Karst

Published by New Generation Publishing in 2019

Copyright © J Little 2019

First Edition

ISBN
Paperback 978-1-78955-823-4
Hardback 978-1-78955-824-1
ebook 978-1-78955-825-8

www.newgeneration-publishing.com

New Generation Publishing

Dedication

To my boys:
        Paul
        Martin
        Benjamin

Prologue

'When you turn off the main motorway into the small village called Nine Crosses you will shortly end up at a T-junction overlooking eight crosses. The ninth cross, despite many repairs, never stands still due to the rotten soul lying underneath, waiting to be called upon.'

Book of records, town folk and history, written by a Benedictine monk.

14th July 1540 – The unthinkable has happened, just a week ago our Lord all Almighty has shown us what greed, lust and want can do to us humans. Massacre, that is the crime, pure souls have been murdered. We buried them one next to another. I am unable to speak of the terrible events in details for it pains me greatly. I can still see their dead eyes looking upon me to say what they could not speak aloud; hence I must stop here and hope in my heart that I will be able to forget just as the rest of us. I shall place my quill down and pray.

Summer 1541 – It has been almost a year since the terrible wedding massacre last summer. The locals feel that we have been cursed by an invisible peril. A joyful occasion, a new young wedding was to happen, which was to be the first wedding since those dark, unhappy times. The family could wait no longer otherwise they would have lost the place for their much-loved daughter in this family of high standings and riches. Yet the happiest of time can turn fast. The invisible peril, the curse has come to claim this young bride too. This poor child of god has been taken by the evil one. Has it been her broken heart that gave her away or was it something else? We pray for us all who live so near to the crosses.

Summer 1542 – The summer months are upon us and another bride, who seemed happy at first, has been claimed by the dark force. It has been said that her heart had stopped beating due to being broken, because it had always belonged to another man. Had she really died of a broken heart? We need to pray yet again and hope the dark one isn't coming back for more. The people of the village are asking for us to go and place holy water beneath the one cross where pure evil and innocence lies, side by side. Twas the Bride that has been seen wandering through woods, weeping. The local people want to help her, to cross into the arms of God so that no more brides are lost. We shall gather and pray for we hope that she will never come again.

Summer 1543 – It has worked. Villages that attended the wedding massacre joined the townsfolk in celebrations. The apparitions that plagued our town for so long have seemingly vanished. The Bride has not returned this summer, and no young hearts have been taken. We give thanks to the Almighty for hearing our prayers and lifting this curse. Praise be to God!

Summer 1560 – I returned to the crosses just as dawn was setting behind the tall pine trees. I went there, during evening hours, to put holy water down as I did before. I had not understood why the locals would not go there at such hour as surely the curse has been lifted. Though I apprehended only too late why, for she has appeared before me. I looked upon her dead eyes and listened to her whispering voice. She told me of the evil one's insatiable thirst for the souls of the broken heart and warned me that others would share her fate. I didn't believe her for we ensured that the evil one has gone to join the fallen angel in hell. We now pray twice as hard to God Almighty to remove this wicked trickery. It's the hope that remains.

Summer 1572 – Though I have been enjoying the time given to me by our lord all mighty, and not heard of any sadden moments since that summer of blood, it has come to happen again. Another broken heart – another bride lost. This time it was a young man who was smitten by his beautiful new bride that lost his life. Town folk say that she, the one, has come back to haunt us, but she is not alone. It has been told once more that she is wandering the woods again. It is as though history will repeat itself, just as she said that day when she appeared to me. Why had I not listened? I have gone to travel to the village once again. What I saw was sadness and despair that has been placed upon the local people like a wall of black and blood. I have placed some holy water upon the cross to see whether I can stop this from happening, though I don't feel that it will work. We shall see next summer what shall become. Our brothers, who were witness to the first bride's passing, have all but left us. Only brother Maynard remains, but his mind is rotten and plagued by demons. He screams in the night and calls out to the Almighty to save us from this evil.

Summer 1690 – Since 1572, the chronicle was left alone, not a note was placed in after the sad death of the last Benedictine priest who wrote into it so religiously. He died soon after the last record that he wrote in, his brother Maynard, died a day after by his own hand. He has not been able to cope with the demons in his head. We are the replacements sent in to ensure that villages know that God has not abandoned them. We ensured that we go frequently to place holy water to the crosses to keep the evil one at bay. The villagers are worried as they have seen many young brides taken by this wicked force. There have been many sightings of the rotten soul, near the nine crosses. A dark shadow hangs over us, but God will protect us all. We are all going to stop now, no more on the matter, ever.

Brno, local newspaper, letters to editor, 28th July 1980

Response to the accident report on D1 – 'I am writing to you regarding the D1 accident article in your newspaper. It seems to suggest some sort of apparition being responsible for the crash. It has been known in the past for the public to blame their reckless driving on the appearance of the Bride. I'd imagine there may have been the alcoholic spirit involved rather than the "floating" one. This local legend seems a convenient excuse for drunk drivers to try and escape punishment. This made up story is sadly kept alive by mad (entrepreneurial?) gypsies keen to sell their protective nick-knacks to gullible tourists. I've lived in this area for over 20 years and have never met this Bride, nor do I ever expect to.'

Brno, local newspaper, "Fatal traffic accident after 'ghost sighting'", 18th July 1983

A driver responsible for the deaths of three people has claimed that he crashed his car because of a ghostly apparition. The infamous stretch of the D1 motorway near the town of Nine Crosses where the accident occurred last month is said to be haunted by the Bride who appears to the unsuspected drivers.

Robert Palach, 39, claims to have seen the Bride appear in front of him on his way home from a social event. As he moved his car away from the apparition that appeared before him, he has clipped the car driven by Ivan Rouskal, 51, who died in the crash with his wife and their young daughter, Sofia.

Mr Palach was breathalysed at the scene by police and found to be within safe limits. A passenger in Mr Palach's car also corroborated his claims that he has seen her.

The family of the deceased have dismissed Mr Palach's claims as "the ramblings of a drunkard that cannot accept his responsibility" in the three deaths and are pressing ahead with a civil case for compensation.

The police officer in charge of the investigation, Detective Terberk, has refused to comment officially on the possibility of a spiritual apparition causing the crash, but sources close to him have revealed to us that his 'mind remains open' to the story and he will not stop till he finds the truth.

Brno, local newspaper, News Headline – "Our brightest football star Petr Kocman passes away", 25th of July 2000

A spokesperson for FC Brno has announced that promising 19-year-old footballer, Petr Kocman passed away suddenly yesterday evening. Mr Kocman had a heart attack at approximately 21 50 hours as he cycled past the nine crosses.

His coach commented that: 'He always gone cycling post training, but we are unsure why he deviated from his normal route to pass through Nine Crosses.'

FC Brno's doctor has said that Petr was 'probably one of the fittest players at the club' and had no history of any heart problems.

Mr Kocman, 19, played as an attacking midfielder for FC Brno and was already considered one of the brightest young players the club has ever produced.

Petr's family, including his fiancée, have thanked the public for their support and asked for their privacy to be respected in this difficult time.

March 2019 –

'…And as the panel agrees, you are to retire effective immediately. We thank you for your services.'

Vavřinec Terberk threw the desk contents into his box making sure everyone was looking. Slamming the drawer shut with his foot made the key clatter across the floor. He'd had enough, nobody listened; the superiors won.

'One day you'll regret this,' he said as he left the office. 'You all know that there is more to this than just what's in front of our noses. You are all narrow-minded fools, you will never solve these.'

He threw his arms into the corner of the room at the pin board labelled 'unsolved' and with that he left.

Chapter 1

'They call it sleep paralysis. We've gone through this so many times, Abigail!' The older woman leaned forward in her chair before taking a deep breath.

'The pills won't harm you. Just take one before bed, to relax.' There was a pen in her right hand; she rolled it between thumb and index finger.

'Try to tell me about what has been bothering you over the last month.' Her gaze made the little girl fidget.

'Especially … What made you so anxious? Anxious enough for a full sleep paralysis episode?'

'It was the lady again; she came to me. It was so scary! I couldn't move! All I could do was breathe.' She closed her eyes at the memory.

'I knew it because my whole body went numb as the door slowly opened.' The shivers ran down her body now, so much she wrapped her arms around herself.

'That's when she walked in from the dark. I was so scared.' She paused. 'But when I could see the face, I knew who she was. And then she asked how I was and then she told me that she missed me.'

The little girl talking raised her face closer to the adult as if trying to keep the secret just between them.

'She is alone, you know. She can hear my thoughts. That's how we talk: I don't have to shout it out, I just think of the question and she hears it. Luckily, she can't stay long because bad people are always about, and they can also come through the opened door. That's what she told me!' Abigail clenched her hands into little fists that drained the blood from her knuckles.

'But when she's gone, I can finally move again! That's what happens!' The psychologist shifted in her seat, making the wooden frame squeak as that musty odour rose from the olive-green upholstery.

'Abigail, we've gone through your dreams in detail, and they're always the same. You go into your episode and then you can't do anything apart from breathing. And each time it's Josef or Dina that enters your room and then leave, and then you can move again. We know this doesn't change and we don't need to work on it. We've been over it so often, and you know it's not real. Tell me, do you remember the little science drawing we did together? The one where we talked about the difference between deep sleep and a light sleep? You remember the special REM sleep pattern?'

'I remember but it's no good. I don't like it.' The heat rose in Abigail's face. 'You're wrong because she's real; she says stuff that nobody knows! I don't care that it's scary, because she wants to be there for me, she wants to be my mummy!'

'Abigail, the woman in your imagination doesn't exist! It's your creation only. We went through this last time. That's why you got all the tests done, remember? It's just sleep paralysis; the things you think you're seeing aren't real.' The psychologist smoothed over the navy-blue fabric of her trousers.

'And that's why we meet up to see how you're getting on with the treatment. It's unusual for someone your age to have this condition, so it's critical you just do as you're told and record anything that makes you anxious during the day.' For a moment she looked at something on the carpet, a crushed leaf, maybe, or a thread of moss.

'You must concentrate on this as we need to identify the triggers. Have you been doing the bedtime relaxation exercises? And can you explain to me,' and with that she reached out an upturned palm to Abigail's scraggly mop, 'why you have cut your hair? What made you so angry?'

'I didn't.' Her little voice shook as she wiped the tears that had collected at the tip of her nose. She patted the side of her head. The hair was all over the place, jagged bits of different lengths, but Abigail was aware how Gran found her sad little face irresistible, and she hoped that it would work on her psychologist now. But no such luck.

'Was it him again?'

'He said he'll make me pretty and that I'm his special girl.'

The tears turned into a flood and her little shoulders shook as she cried. Her clothes were getting soaked.

'Abigail, I'm going to speak to your grandma again. We must make sure she's aware of these "friends" and helps you deal with their visits. Do you have any other friends? Any real living friends?'

The psychologist shot upright wide-eyed as Abigail jumped up from her seat and punched the armrests of her chair with her tiny clenched fists. Despite her tiny frame the chair scattered quite a distance from the force of her standing up.

'They are real! You silly woman!'

'Abigail don't give me that attitude.' The psychologist had composed herself, although Abigail could tell from her flared nostrils that her breathing had sped up.

'I'm here to try to help you because your grandma is very worried for you. She told me there is a lovely little girl living next door now who has shown interested in playing with you. You should be more open and approachable to other people, otherwise you'll never recover.'

Abigail stared at the wall as if she was looking at someone else. When she spoke, her voice was low and flat: 'Ring a ring of roses,' she sang. 'A pocket full of posies. You all shall die."

The psychologist stared ahead, her face utterly unchanged.

'Abigail, I can see you aren't very responsive today. Our appointment is at an end. You haven't made any progress. Could you call in your grandma please?' She pointed at the large melamine door behind Abigail.

***

Behind the door with its 'Psychologist' sign sat the old lady. She shifted uncomfortably, but the rosary in her hand gave her some distraction. Slowly, one by one, she worked through the beads with the wiry fingers on gnarled hands that spoke of decades of hard, physical work. Each count deepened the lines on her face. Rays of sunlight coming in through the window reflected off the silver hair, perfectly combed as always.

As she made her way through the rosary, Mildred Slante thought of the daughter she had lost when her husband decided to pretend the girl had never existed. No choice but to stand by her husband, never mind that Rosie was their only child. There was nothing they could do when the girl fell in with a bad crowd. Wild parties, raves as they called them back then, attracted her like the sun attracts a sunflower. On countless nights Mildred drove around trying to find the right field or park, hoping to find her daughter in a conscious state. She seldom did find anything, so upon her return her husband would give her a good hiding for wasting petrol looking for the druggie their daughter had turned into.

For him, his own daughter no longer existed, but for Mildred it was different. She never gave up on her, while he dealt with it by denying her and using his fists as a release. It peaked when the girl turned up at their doorstep, a big pregnant belly straining against her jumper. No matter how much she pleaded to stay, her father threw her out. There wasn't the time for her to explain to him that she was clean. That she wished to be a good person, a good mother. After that day she disappeared, and they lost contact until the heart-stopping phone call came. So many times, Mildred had kept thinking that she would see her daughter again, but that wasn't her destiny. That call was from a hospital: their daughter had given birth, but things were touch and go for her.

The memory of running into the car was so strong she remembered the smell of spring in the air, the fresh scent of daffodils and new green foliage washed by rain. On arrival at the delivery suite she was told her daughter had suffered a stroke from pre-eclampsia: blood pressure, water retention, all the water from her body pressed into her head, brain compressed, then the stroke.

The feeling of being completely useless never left her. After that she straightened her spine and made herself a promise. She wasn't going to fail this baby as she did her daughter. So instead of planning a leisurely retirement, she arranged a funeral, an adoption and filed for divorce. Yet, even before the divorce was through, the years of alcohol abuse killed off Mildred's husband in the form of an aggressive liver cancer. Still, she got on with her life without the guilt in a better environment for Abigail to grow up in. It was Abigail that kept her alive, this little baby that now depended on her in every single way.

Then the door opened, and Abigail's dimples deepened at the sight of her gran. 'Oh Gran! You're the best!' The skeletal arms flung around Mildred, squeezing into her plumpness.

When Abigail let go, she looked up at Mildred. 'The special doctor wants to talk to you. She doesn't believe me about my two special friends. Tell them, Granny, that they're real!'

'Of course, I will, darling.' Taking a deep breath, she pulled her cardigan tighter around her chest. 'Now sit and read your magazine. I'll only be a minute.' She walked into the office with dread. The psychologist welcomed her with a handshake before pointing to a chair. Mildred nodded and took a seat.

'Mrs Slante,' she began, 'I'm here to help you. I know that it's been incredibly hard for you. First losing your daughter, and then out of the blue you had a baby in the house. Not to even mention the husband troubles.' The woman pulled her lips into a straight line, drew a deep breath and looked at the floor, her long lashes momentarily casting a shadow across her cheekbones.

Mildred's shoulders shook, and she started weeping. Losing her only daughter still hurt. It didn't bother her a bit that she was single; she couldn't stand having a man in the house again. She was too frightened of what it would mean for Abigail.

'I am sorry.' The other woman shook her head and held out a box of tissues. 'We don't want Abigail to know you're upset. Listen, what we need to do is to try to get Abigail interacting with other children. You told me there's a new couple that moved in to the street, and they have a daughter, don't they?'

'Yes, that's right. The girl's called Natalie. A lovely little dear. So wild and full of laughter.' She dabbed at her eyes with a tissue. 'I've invited her over for a playdate next weekend.'

The psychologist sighed. Was that melting of her feature's relief? Mildred's fingers caressed the last bead on her rosary for surely the tenth time that day. Maybe this Natalie would be the answer. Maybe Abigail's invisible friends would finally leave.

***

The weekend came so fast that Mildred hadn't planned on how to deal with the butterflies in her stomach. How would Abigail take to having a real friend around? But her worries dissolved as soon as she opened the door to Natalie.

'Hello, Mrs Slante! So nice to see you looking so fresh.' The child's face was one big smile. Then she turned more earnest. 'Where is Abby? I brought my dolls. What do I call you? Do I call you Mrs Slante or an old lady?'

Mildred smiled at the little bold blondie who had brought life to her house.

'You can call me Mildred,' she answered with a laugh.

From behind Mildred, Abigail poked out her little face but seemed too scared to shake Natalie's hand. That didn't put Natalie off her stride, though. The wild little thing had courage in spades.

'Don't worry, I don't bite, silly! Come on, this is my dolly, her name's Stacey and she has a huge secret! She has an invisible friend!'

Abigail's brown eyes widened. 'She has one too?' Natalie curled up her pretty pointy nose and giggled.

'Of course, everyone has one.' After that the two girls played, laughed and chatted to each other all day. Abigail was in such a happy place that she wasn't afraid to open her heart. Mildred pottered about the kitchen and later sat sewing in the lounge, from where she could hear the girls.

'That one's a lovely lady, but the other one's a horrid man. Still, before I had you, I didn't have anyone else. They were always my friends, but you are the best!' Mildred felt the warmth spread in her chest as she heard the smile in the child's voice.

'I don't want that man to talk to, though. He has horrible teeth! He probably eats too many sweets before bed time.' Natalie must have been listening carefully, in agreement, Mildred thought, because the girl was quiet except for the occasional affirming murmur.

'Definitely sweets. One of my friends had hole this big in her teeth because she ate lollies in bed.' Mildred looked up. When she craned her neck, she could see Natalie with arms flung as far apart as if she was going to hug a whale but then threw herself onto Abigail.

'I'll make sure that the horrid man never comes again. Promise.'

'Really? Promise? But how?' Abigail whispered the last words.

'Well, I have the power. My mum and dad told me so. Every Sunday we go to a church to listen to a lovely priest who says that it's God that has power over everyone else. I will make sure that next Sunday I'll ask God to make sure that the horrid man doesn't come to see you ever again.' Natalie emphasised the 'ever'.

At that, the two shot off, running around the house pretending to be fairies. They played with their toys so excitedly that Mildred could no longer keep up with their conversation. That evening, Abigail seemed changed.

'You know what, Gran?' she asked. Her cheeks were rosy, almost unlike Mildred had ever seen them, and the dullness of her eyes had been washed over with light.

'What, my darling?'

'Today was the most wonderful day in my whole life.'

'So was mine, precious, so was mine.' Mildred kissed the little forehead as she always did but today it felt so much sweeter.

***

Over the next several months, Natalie helped Abigail to turn into a more mentally stable individual, no longer requiring her invisible friend. It was as if Natalie turned the 'happy' switch on. Mildred knew that Abigail doted on her even though sometimes she felt a pang of jealousy despite the love she had for Natalie. Only once did the two of them get into trouble with her. It was the time they got too boisterous and broke her favourite vase. Both stood there before her with pursed lips, hands on their hearts, swearing for life that the vase had been like that forever. Natalie shook her golden hair in agreement with sparkly eyed Abigail.

'We swear, it was that way!' Mildred knew she had a better chance of running a marathon than getting the truth out of those two when they had both decided on what the truth was. And in this sincere friendship the two of them stuck together all the way to their teenage years.

***

Though Abigail tried not to care that she lived in a two-bedroom terraced council flat with one bathroom and a tiny kitchen, it did bother her that Natalie always seem to have so much more.

It was the vast bedroom that always made her feel insignificant: decorated in pastel pinks with little splashes of purple. It was a proper princess-themed bedroom sporting four-poster bed with a large canopy that made you feel like you were floating in the clouds. An oversized rocking horse was always standing by should any prince want to scoop you into his arms and take you away as his bride. To Abigail, this room, this house was a fairy tale dream. The opposite of her drab home. It was rare to have a Christmas where she got more than two presents, and neither would match the quality of Natalie's. Natalie's life was better in every single way. She had one wall decorated by evidence of her own achievements: show jumping champion, ballet star, the best actress in school, school prefect, the best of all this and that. If you tried to judge the two by the way their walls were decorated, you would have never thought Abigail had her own merits. Abigail's wall was a humble white-washed affair with an old tattered black and white photo of her mum, the strange woman she never met. Though each visit was exciting, more and more they left Abigail with sour taste in her mouth.

'Gran, why does Natalie have so much compared to us? Why does she deserve a mummy more than I do?' The small red Corsa swerved towards the edge of the road. Mildred was a good driver, but the question startled her.

'Darling, nobody deserves a mummy more than you.' If she weren't trying to drive, Mildred would have rubbed the child's back.

'Sadly, some people aren't lucky and lose their parents a lot sooner than others. I can tell you that she loved you dearly.' The car windscreen misted as Mildred exhaled. 'You know, I would love to give you all that Natalie gets but I am not as clever as her parents. I can never earn as much as her parents can.'

Abigail turned her head away from Gran. She didn't want her to know how much it hurt. Natalie had it all, the family, the big house, lots of toys, the dream bedroom and all the success in the world. She felt as alone as the tree they were passing. It stood there alone in the middle of the field, battered by all the weather until broken midway down the trunk. Abigail was that tree, she wanted to know so much why.

'One day when you are ready, I promise you, darling, that I'll tell you everything. Just not yet.'

Years passed, and Abigail wondered if her gran would ever realise how anxious she was to hear about her past. One day after school Abigail returned home and started making the whole house spotless. She wanted so much to have Gran in a talking mood so if all the chores were done it would remove any excuse of not sitting down for a chat. By the time she finished the hoover was full. The pine smell of the furniture polish reminded her of that tree she saw on the way back from Natalie's. She moved to do the lounge which had in places gaps around the window rim where the weather eaten away at the concrete. The dust always blew in through these gaps, so it was one room that got particularly dirty. A gust made her hair stand up on her arms. Once she'd finished cleaning, a quick inspection satisfied her that all was up to Mildred's standards. As Abigail stretched her back she realised the only thing missing was the smell of freshly brewed tea. A glance at the clock confirmed no more could be done apart from put the kettle on. Gran was due home soon and there was still come tidying to do in the kitchen.

Thankfully the kitchen wasn't a mess but as it was very old fashioned, it never looked properly cleaned. The old sixties tiles on the wall had that a huge orange flower pattern that made the room smaller than it was. The only other work surface apart from worktop was a little drop-leaf table Mildred used as her 'office'. She would neatly place all paperwork into a pile to tackle each Saturday. Abigail knew the piles of paper were out of bounds, so a quick wipe was all she could do before putting the kettle on.

While the tea steeped, Abigail did a quick walk about to check the flat one last time. Though not as stylish, the pink 60s lounge suite had regained some lustre after its clean. Mildred's bedroom was in great state apart from Abigail forgetting to replace the cushions onto the bed, which she corrected promptly. This was the room where she would go to cry in secret. She would curl herself in the only wardrobe that smelled of mothballs and lavender. No sooner than she returned to the kitchen to check the tea, Mildred walked in through the door.

'Abigail, darling, what is that I smell? My favourite!' Mildred's face broke into the gorgeous warm smile that made Abigail's heart skip a beat. It was a pure pleasure.

'Oh, my goodness,' fussed Mildred. 'Abigail, did you notice? The cleaning fairy came over. How am I to say thank you to her?' Abigail beamed.

'I know you are the fairy, love, thank you. My back pain returned so I wouldn't have had the strength to do it. I'll make us supper and then I suppose I'd better start talking. Don't think, young lady, that I don't know why you're making me so comfortable. I haven't forgotten. I owe you an explanation.'

***

They ate in silence until the clattering of cutlery against porcelain broke the soundlessness as they washed up.

Midway, after yet another cup slipped past Mildred's fingers clunking at the side of the bowl, Abigail looked at her. The atmosphere crackled between them with the excitement of a thunderstorm building, rumbling in the distance and sweeping closer until it brought down gushes of wild water, leaving the air smelling electric.

'Abigail, please don't think worse of me when I tell you.' Mildred placed the cup on the draining board to let it drip.

'Let's get out the photo albums. I think it's time to have our chat.' Before leaving, she downed a shot of a whisky from the bottle she retrieved from the kitchen cupboard. The ring of the empty glass upon the worktop was the boxing bell, announcing that finally, the game is on.

Abigail was going to find out everything. Midway through their talk, Abigail couldn't explain how the whiskey bottle had made its way onto the coffee table neither how the amber liquid managed to keep disappearing in such a short time. Neither of them could hold their emotions at bay. Abigail just couldn't get her head around how her mother had been treated so badly by her own father.

'How could he?' Abigail whispered the question over and over. 'Why didn't you stop him?' She gritted her teeth until her jaw hurt. 'Why didn't you stand up for your daughter?' Abigail dropped her head into her hands.

There was no answer, though the bottle emptied steadily each time the question was asked. Once Mildred had told the whole life story, Abigail could only sit there. The only sound was the rush and blare of traffic outside, the bustling of the street, a police siren, people going about their business. The deathly silence between them was only broken after Mildred downed the last shot. The smack of her lips brought Abigail back from her trance.

'Abigail, I have been honest with you, now it's your turn. I know I'm not perfect and I regret all I should have done. That aside, I have a different burning question I wanted to ask for a while.' Her voice remained steady. 'Last night you were speaking to someone in your sleep again and … you had a right giggle. I tried to listen, but it didn't make any sense.' She paused. 'Abigail, has your sleep paralysis returned?' It was the old woman's face that gave her away. The grey eyebrows raised like arching caterpillars, and the grooves on her cheeks and the side of her mouth made her look twice her age.

'Gran, don't worry. I learned a lot about sleep paralysis and the worry was the man, remember? The lady friend is harmless. She just sometimes pops up to catch up, that's all really, it was just her.'

Abigail could tell Mildred wasn't convinced. To change the subject, she grabbed the old leather-bound photo album and opened it. After some page turning she found it. An old black and white photo with a little baby chewing a book corner. 'I would like to remember the good stories. Tell me again, what did she do when she was a little girl?'

***

Since Abigail turned sixteen, Mildred took Abigail along to help her with her usual weekend cleaning jobs. This helped Abigail realise how important was to have a good job, though she knew some people are just luckier than others. Natalie was just one of those who had opportunities falling into their laps on a regular basis. It was Natalie who got the degree and managed to land a fabulous job in the accounts department where an admin position opened. So, Abigail applied. Abigail turned up for the interview with grumbling intestines. It was Natalie who greeted her at the company door.

'Darling, don't worry, you'll like it. Just be yourself, be honest.' After it was all over they went for lunch.

'I think I totally conked out. I'm so stupid, Natalie. Why can't I just be like you?'

'You don't want to be like me, Abby, you're different, you're special. Don't worry. I'll sort it out, but I think you'll be just fine.' Natalie's positivity was charming. So many nights Abigail spent in front of the mirror thinking how she could be more like her. What if she used eyeshadow, or brow pencil? Natalie always used them to define her eyes. Somehow these tricks made Natalie look beautiful, whereas Abigail got the opposite result. She looked like a monobrow monster. The darkening of her bushy brows turned them into one huge dark brown mess. It all had to come off, the eye liner, mascara and the gigantic brows. As the wipe swept away the make-up it also took away the dream of being more like Natalie. With a shoulder shrug over the realisation she'd never be anyone other than herself, her posture returned to that of a humble donkey.

It surprised her when the firm called back with the news that she'd got the job. Mildred was over the moon and organised a special day out. With as much as budget allowed they dressed to impress. Natalie recommended some styles and looks but in the end Abigail chose out what she had seen Natalie wearing previously.

She worked hard and after couple of months felt like she belonged. She did feel like she was always in Natalie's shadow and was sometimes little jealous of Natalie's higher position and her nice fancy office.

Then, when Abigail finally felt content that maybe the future could be better, the worst happened. One day she walked into the lounge and caught Mildred sobbing. Something wasn't right.

'Sorry about that dear, something upset me today, never mind, life goes on.' It was that behaviour that made Abigail suspicious. The constant weeping followed by the secretive shuffling of papers gave it away. Once alone, Abigail decided to act. She approached the paperwork tower on the small kitchen table. It smelled musty but then what wouldn't if it was exposed to this damp environment.

Their kitchen was north facing so it never fully dried. The letter she was looking for was at the bottom of the pile, the little white envelope with the large 'CONFIDENTIAL' stamp. Abigail pricked her ears. What if Mildred decided to come back? She held the envelope a long while before opening it. The word 'cancer' in the letter felt like something electric plugged into her brain. Her heart pumped heavily as she tried to control the emotions swarming through her body, as if she was a volcano trying hard not to erupt. 'Cancer' bounced off the kitchen cupboard like a bolt of lightning that rebounded and struck her in the chest. Mildred was dying.

Despite her pretence of ignorance, Abigail's behaviour must have given her away. Neither of them said the word as they tried to keep it together. At the end, Abigail couldn't hold it anymore. It was when Mildred had a little stumble and was left breathless on the floor. The cancer turned Abigail's steel-haired mountain of strength to a skinny Golem-like creature that found it hard to get on with everyday life.

Eventually, Mildred's skeletal figure was a picture of what cancer does to your muscles. No longer could the disease remain hidden. Abigail had to step up in running the household as well as listen to Mildred on what her funeral should be like.

'Darling, I can see you're getting more and more distant. I know you're trying to be strong, but you have to let your emotions run.' The worry in Mildred's voice turned Abigail's anxiety on. She had been home for only five minutes and the talk turned morbid again.

'I just don't want to talk about the coffin, I want to ignore it, OK. You're the only thing I have. You and Natalie, actually.' The answer hung in the lounge with Mildred as Abigail fled into the kitchen. The clatter of a dropped teapot strainer echoed as Abigail's shaking hands found it difficult to grip, the knuckles white from trying to retain some control. It was pointless, the anxiety took a deep bite off her insides.

'I'd love to make sure you'll manage when I'm gone.' The sound of shattering glass and sloshing milk carried back to the lounge along with Abigail's whispered swearing.

'What happened, love, do you need me to come to help?'

'NO!' came the answer coming from the kitchen that had turned into a milk bath. Each piece of shattered cup had to be carefully picked up. Easier said than done with shaking hands. 'What would Natalie do?' Abigail asked herself. She wouldn't have been a pathetic, shaking figure, she would have got on with it. Been there for Mildred as well as being strong. 'I must be like Natalie!'

'Darling, you don't have to be anyone else. Be yourself!' Mildred had been able to hear her muttering all the way to the lounge.

'Natalie isn't as perfect as you make out to be.' There was a pause. 'I did notice that recently you've started to comb your hair like hers. You've even started to extend you eye liner just the way she does! Your eyes don't suit it, love, you're prettier than Natalie. Please promise me you won't change when I'm gone.'

The whole flat became deathly silent apart from the sploshing of a wet cloth on the kitchen floor. That was the last conversation they had that day.

***

As Mildred lay in hospital she realised there were two sides to Abigail. Her subconscious was confirming that Abigail's dark side was taking over her mind. Abigail was like the weather in spring, going from warm to freezing within seconds. Mildred tried to ignore it, but when you're lying in a hospital bed with a failing body thinking was the only thing left to do. The end was near, that was the only certainty. The bleeps of a machine continued beside her rhythmically. Her blood pressure was dropping. Only the previous night the occupant of the bed neighbouring hers had died. As the wheezing suddenly stopped the whole thing became real. That's where she was, in the final stage of her life, at the absolute end.

The geriatric ward was full of painful moans, the constant reminder of a path they all shared. None of them was going to leave this ward alive. Her mind was the only fit thing she had. It was racing from one worry to another until she begged the nurse to give her something to stop her thinking. The only interruption to her thoughts now was the familiar voice. 'How is she today? Any change?'

Shortly after Abigail walked in dressed in the same suit Natalie wore to their last visit. The make-up was more prominent, mimicking Natalie's to the final detail.

'Abigail, it's lovely to see you, thank you for being here for me. You are the most   wonderful granddaughter. I love you for all eternity.'

'Gran don't be silly, I'll be back tomorrow. OK, I'll sneak in your favourite chocolates, how about that?' Her voice gave way a little at the end of the sentence followed by a tiny sniffle as they hugged tightly.

'Abigail, I feel like I have to say this but there is heaven, you know. I will be always with you.' Mildred held tight onto Abigail whose chest shook with the sobs that had been trying to escape ever since she walked in. The nurse didn't need to say that it wouldn't be long before Mildred was gone. Abigail knew it so it didn't need to be said.   She decided to pretend that nothing was happening, that everything was fine. An anxious nurse run past, causing the curtains to flutter open for a second. Abigail loosened their hug as she turned her eyes to the movement. To Mildred it was as if Abigail had seen someone in the gap in that moment.

'I can't talk to you! I should be with her!' Mildred tugged at Abigail's hand to grab her attention. 'Tell me, how was your day today? Any news?' A couple of blinks later, Abigail turned back to Mildred.

'Yes, Gran, actually I do have something to tell you. There is a new boy in the office. Dan is his name. He is so handsome.' Her eyes closed with dreaminess which was welcome as it helped her to focus on something other than death.

'I can tell you're fond of him but try to be yourself. Today you could be confused for Natalie. Try to impress him by being who you are, darling, promise? You don't need to be anyone else.' That was the last time Abigail and Mildred spoke.

When Mildred did not wake up the next morning, it was Natalie who kept coming to see Abigail, who stood next to her at the funeral and helped her to get up and get on with life again. It was Natalie that now had all she had ever wanted. But apart from Natalie, Abigail was alone. Natalie, who had it all: family, confidence, looks.

Chapter 2

BRRZZZT … BRRZZZT. Bloody alarm! Abigail's hand smacked the little machine at the top of her bedside table. As the little red numbers shone into her face she muttered underneath her breath. 'I really dislike you!' No matter how much she wanted to stay in bed it was time to get up, someone had to go to work to earn money, to pay the bills.

As she sat up on her bed she tried to convince herself that it was worth it. It was difficult to be excited to go to work to earn money when so little was being spent after the bills were out of the way. Her whole bedroom wasn't worth the struggle. The curtains were still the same old shabby old sun bleached out cotton that her gran sewed up. Her feet went very cold once they touched the floor. The spine clicking got louder the more her arms stretched. The cold went through her toes like a bolt of electricity. The instinct reaction was to hide the feet back underneath the duvet. Nope, it wasn't the time to get out yet. As her head hit the pillow, excuses came bouncing into her head on how she can prolong the stay in this cosy warm heaven.

'I could have faked a cough and rung the boss: "Sorry I'm just not feeling right today … yes, it probably is better that I stay home, I'd hate to pass this on", yadda yadda yadda …' The same context message was typed into the mobile phone with recipient being the boss. The real reason why getting out of bed was so unappealing was that news which ruined her weekend. Abigail wasn't ready to face it. Midway through the message, the phone Facebook update receipt flashed green. There it was beaming at her from the worldwide web. Natalie changed her profile from single to engaged. There it was, black and white, the reason for her miserable weekend.

'Hello, Aby, I have some fabulous news for you!! Call

me when you're free asap. Xx'.

Ignoring the text message, Abigail gone through the secret photographs she secretly took of Dan. There, in the privacy of her phone, she scrolled through snaps she took of him unaware. He was that much further away from her having him than ever. The bed comfort became too constrictive as if a large python was crawling upon her blanket to strangle every single last breath she held in her lungs. The feet had to take the cold; it was time for the mind to get busy with work rather than self-pity.

Her feet made a little slapping sound as she walked bare footed to the bathroom. The bathroom was colder than her bedroom, but it was time to put on the war paint – or as they call it make-up. From the mirror there was a face looking back with miserable large bags underneath cried-out red eyes.

Natalie's voice kept ringing in her ears. The very high-pitched happy voice that turned her stomach. 'Oh, Abigail, I am so happy you rung. Guess what, he proposed! I can't believe it but it's the happiest day of my life.' Abigail had to grit her teeth not to say her thoughts out loud.

'Are you going to tell him about Henry? The best thing is to reject the proposal because if you don't tell him then I must. Henry is so much better suited for you, he is the typical handsome full of himself type, a perfect fit for you.'

Instead, through the gritted teeth she managed 'Well done, Natalie, I am so happy for you.' It was this conversation that ruined her weekend and made her resemble a red blotchy blobby fish.

Enough of considering the mess, it was time to hide the truth. The problem with that was that most of make-up was hand me downs from Natalie. Each eye shadow opened, each mark of eyeliner made her face to look like Natalie's. To avoid this, the make-up got piled up which resulted in a clown creature gazing back from the mirror. Despite of all that cover, it couldn't hide the pale red blotchy face.

'Arghhhh, there is no point looking like her, move on, find a different man.' The last sentence was drowned by the warm soapy water as she dived into the sink. The make-up had to come off. There was still some residue on the towel after wiping. Glance into the mirror reflected her face. The eyes were redder due to the soap that got in thanks to the scrubbing.

'Maybe if I curl my hair I might look prettier? Maybe then I can try to find a different man?' Her face became black and from nowhere her throat gave a large grunt of anger. Her fists tightened right before her white knuckles met with the mirror.

'No, I don't want a different man! I want him!' The white, stinging knuckles helped to focus again. It was the bleeding that needed attending to. Thankfully the first aid kit was in the same room, so it didn't take too long to stop it.

'Why did I ever fell in love with that sad short git,' was the sentence rolling about in her head like a marble in a circle. He showed interest right at the start of his career at Finsco. It was his chin dimple paired with the beautiful smile that made his face sparkle. Despite his hairy, slightly squishy belly with receding hairline he was embodiment of perfection to Abigail. He was a real man with a magnificent body. Each morning he strolled into the office with his gym bag smelling of testosterone. Even though after each shower he must have applied a ton of aftershave to mask the body smell, Abigail could always sense he just came in. Never was she able to resist to glance at his top shirt button hoping that it was opened just a smidgen to reveal his chest hair.

'Enough, no I won't stand for it, I will go to work. I must expose her for Dan's sake. She must return the ring to Dan. Once he is over the break-up he will run into my arms for comfort.'

With that thought she left the bathroom to get a fresh pair of knickers and a bra from the washing basket. It took ages before the water got hot in the shower, so it was turned on before leaving the bathroom to get the clothes. There was a little saving pot filling up with change for a new boiler, but somehow it kept depleting rather than growing. The boiler had to wait.

On the way back, Abigail caught another glimpse of herself. 'What a pathetic sight!' Her hair was still a mess with one side curling into her face and the other side curling the other way. That was soon going to be fixed as after a good scrub the hair would be burned to its place by a good blast of the hairdryer. The bathroom steamed up nicely as soon as the hot water hit the skin. When finished the shower curtain rings made a swishing sound once thrown open. Before Abigail stepped out onto the bath mat she noted that the steamed-up mirror revealed a large heart shape written onto it. A little puzzled she wiped the mirror clean, so she could apply some mascara to highlight her long lashes in the hope that it might distract the attention from her blue eyes that were currently beaming red. Thankfully there was some of the waterproof mascara left over. The last thing that was needed was to end up with panda eyes after some serious crying. The mascara was yet another one of Natalie's hand me downs.

'Abigail, you have beautiful blue eyes, they are your best feature, you must emphasize them!' It wasn't a night out without Natalie saying it at least once. 'You can't wear that with the eyeshadow! Don't you know anything? Go on, you are naturally beautiful, you are so going to pull tonight.'

For Abigail going out with Natalie meant that there was always one of her rejects who would be happy with second best. It was painful watching a nice-looking man approach only to ask for the name of the pretty blonde friend wearing a tight skinny strappy dress revealing just about enough to tease. Natalie's perfect long natural blonde hair would be flowing from her perfect Barbie doll face. Her large green eyes dressed in perfect long lashes worked like a pretty moth attracting its prey. Her small full lips and pixie nose just finalised the picture of beauty. There never was a spot on her perfectly smooth skin gleaming under the disco lights.

Only after all men got the cold shoulder they would turn to Abigail. The bland, size 14, square face brunette with squarish jaw underneath a medium size nose. The only thing going for her was her brown eyes with naturally long eyelashes. For that the men had to be close enough to notice, which was impossible as they gone off on their merry way once Natalie's name was given. Still, that didn't matter, as if the time of the month came, her face would be sporting at least three sprouting spots that she tried to hide.

'Abigail, you are such a silly girl, you should really think of yourself better, you are gorgeous if you just smile a little.'

That was advice ringing inside her head she gone into doubting overdrive. There were some short-term relationships proving that she wasn't a bad looker. They chose Abigail because of her smile as it made the whole face to lit up. Her kindness was the second strongest point that her boyfriends cherished. Still, none of them stayed long enough. Why couldn't Dan be one of these men that chose Abigail over Natalie? How could he go for Natalie when he always vouched for the natural look rather than the Barbie doll lookalike.

The thoughts disappeared as soon as the hunt for the hairbrush began. The place where the hairbrush should be is anywhere apart from the place where you expect it to be. Abigail skipped across the cold floor to the only carpeted bedroom in search of it. It was helpful that her mind no longer was stuck on how Natalie was prettier in every way. The brush was on the bedside table next to the one cuddly bear that Abigail could never part from. Now it was her and this bear all alone, the only reminders of when once they were all happy.

Mildred was gone forever. That memory grounded her as if a large stone was placed upon her head. The only thing to do was to hug the bear tight. Her whole body curled up in the foetal position underneath the duvet.

'Dyna, are you here? Please speak to me.' There was always Dyna to speak to, the imaginable secret friend Abigail had to hide. No longer was she comfortable to share her secrets with Natalie.

'Dyna, please answer. I really need someone here now, I need to listen that I am special, your special little girl. I need you to open that door where all the dead are, I need to talk to Gran, please help me.'

The screeching of the opening door made Abigail's head to pop up from underneath the duvet. 'Dyna?' There wasn't anyone at the door neither in the room.

'Fine, I knew that in the end there is nobody!'

Abigail didn't notice the shadow in the room corner as she stomped away back to the bathroom. The steam hit the skin as soon as Abigail walked in. It was hard to see anything.

'Bloody boiler, that's it. I can't touch that bloody savings pot.'

That is when the noise started. A little squeaky noise as if someone pressed against the steamed mirror and words begun to materialise.

'I can help.'

'Am I going mad? Dyna is that you?' The squeaks started again and 'No' appeared on the mirror.

The door started to slowly open from behind her, but nobody walked in. Abigail's head shook drastically from left to right.

'Nonononono, I can't start this again, I can't be going mad. It must be me just seeing things.' Abigail retrieved the towel and wiped the mirror. Then pushed the door shut. This time she took her pill as prescribed without hesitation. Ready, the nostrils enlarged as with lungs they took a large deep breath.

Abigail walked out of her flat. Her war paint on, ready to smile and pretend that she was happy about Natalie's engagement.

***

On the way to work Abigail had to battle through the other work-goers on the narrow pavement. The rain from the night before left large puddles on the road so each car driving past resulted in a good soak. Nobody wanted to be that person so they all walked as far away from the edge. For Abigail it was took too much effort to avoid people, so she chose to get soaked. At least her look would be matched to what was in her mind. Natalie just seemed to occupy every single cell in her grey matter cells. It was her that recommended Abigail for the job. On her first day at work Natalie ensured that she doesn't feel lost.

'Don't worry about your boss, he looks scary, but, he is a purring kitten. Just be yourself, he likes that.' That was the first advice which was well received as the boss was a man with a very serious outlook.

Natalie was always there as the only best friend but after Mildred's death things had changed. There were hints of change during growing up, but the critical turning point was the death. Natalie was there to help to deal with losing Mildred. Abigail remembered how Natalie made her giggle over the 'bad chat up moments' and her hidden code words she used for men.

For example, there were some permanent chasers after Natalie's attention which she classed as 'rabies' because they blatantly foamed at the mouth any time they approached her. Her sweets theory was a cracker.

She would say, Abigail, 'Men are like sweets. For example: a sherbet lemon would be a nice young blond, masculine German guy; chocolate buttons – hmm someone sophisticated like Thierry Henry; marshmallow – nice and squishy, gummy bear – the English chap but don't forget the Werther's originals – the older bloke otherwise known as "the silver fox".'

It never failed to bring out a laugh when Natalie would announce that there was a yummy marshmallow at six o'clock. Or when she sent me a message at work on Friday afternoon – 'shall we go sweetshop tonight to get us some M&Ms or bit of something else???' M&Ms in translation meant Mushy Marshmallows which she always thought was Abigail's type.

After Mildred had gone, it was as if there was a black hole present, swallowing all happy thoughts. The laughter got sucked in till it was silenced.

'Abigail, you can't carry on like this, go on, snap out of it! You can't get this upset, remember what that ends up with, you don't want them coming to you again. Please, just try for your gran's sake, she wouldn't want to see you like this.' Despite of all the help and emotional support, Abigail grew further away from Natalie as the time went by.

The walk to the office wasn't pleasant. leaves heavy with rainfall were dropping water onto Abigail's head. Inside the big glass-styled office building, she dripped all the way to the carpeted part of the building past the reception. Their office was designed with an open plan idea in mind. It consisted of lots of airy space with glass everywhere, tidy desk policies and unrecognisable paintings on the walls. The problem with that style of office was that no private discussion is ever private. Everyone knows each other's business. Walking through the door was no longer a happy occasion, a joy of a new job, now it was means to an end; a salary at the end of each month.

Once Abigail climbed up one flight of stairs her ears pricked up with recognition of Natalie's voice. Natalie was already in the office which was unusual as she was the last one in. The only time Natalie would turn up early was if she forgot to change the time on her clock.

Abigail picked up her pace so she could sit at her desk to re-organise her thoughts. As soon as she opened the door the bustle of the office overfilled her senses. The only inviting thing was the fresh coffee someone just made, the rest was Natalie's overpowering squeaky voice. The main admin gossip team surrounded Natalie. Everyone knew the gossip coven group members, as they just couldn't keep out of another people's business. Natalie used them as the distributor of any announcement that needed to be faster than email. Abigail cringed at the thought that Natalie didn't find them threatening in any way and would always find the time to chat to them. She was also one of the admins, but she made sure that if they started to gossip, she would be too busy or on her way to get another round of drinks.

'Abigail don't you know the key rule of office etiquette? Keep your loved ones close but your enemies even closer' she would say when Abigail wondered why it was important to Natalie to talk to them.

'Nobody is your friend, Abigail, they are just work colleagues, so give them a piece of information but never show them who you really are. Otherwise they'll rip you apart.' Those words were Natalie's 'office gospels' so despite of dislike towards these girls, Abigail tried to pretend that they were the best of friends.

Susan, one of the chief witches, ran up as soon as the door shut behind Abigail, gesturing frantically with her hand to come closer. 'Come up, you have to hear this! Natalie is engaged! Isn't that great news! Office love ends in marriage!'

All Abigail could think of was that Susan would have to be off for a couple of days with a sore throat if she carried on screaming like that. The same feelings came flooding back into her already clenched stomach. The act of pure calmness had to be preserved.

'Yeah, I heard, Susan. Natalie told me on Friday night. She told me the great news just seconds after he proposed, isn't it wonderful?' Susan and her coven giggled and squeaked.

'Yes, it's wonderful! This is like something out of a romance novel.' Abigail's mind started to spin as Natalie came towards her holding out her hand.

'Look at the ring, Abby! Isn't it beautiful!?' Natalie's ring was the size of Africa. It was huge, just like Dan's bank account.

'Not bad for a badly, right?' interjected Susan with a little spite in her voice. They all suspected that the true reason why Natalie caught herself on the hook was the little gestures. Paying for lunches, chocolates with flowers deliveries each time Natalie had a 'bad day'. Everyone noted that his attention turned fully towards Natalie. The turning point was the flooding of random presents with huge price tags. Then Dan turned up to work in an Aston Martin DB9. A very sexy car that his dad bought him for birthday. Somehow over time Natalie's affections grew, and they would flirt with each other like mad. The muppet fell for it, ignoring the fact she was still seeing Henry.

'Don't worry, darling, I will split up with him, he is just a nobody,' she would sweet talk in his ear so often he forgot about it.

Dan fell madly in love and after numerous flowers, gifts, chocolates and expensive dinners Natalie got far enough to discover that he was also great in bed. The attention was easy to get hooked onto as it was the sweet overpowering drug of wealth. Abigail had to take to her escape.

'Girls, anyone want a drink? Sorry but due to the lack of champagne dispenser availability, it's coffee or tea?'

It was greatly received that nobody paid any attention to her as they were so engrossed into talking about the ring. The little voice inside her head spoke.

'That's how it goes. That's the story of my life; the gorgeous women can choose whomever they like and leave scraps for the rest of us. Natalie is the prime example of a "used to be" best friend that has changed with time to be someone completely different. Every time she clicks her fingers, a man would appear and do whatever she asked. Any man would eat from her hand like a tamed lion in couple of weeks after she made her mind to have him. Men are pathetic.'

Thankfully the workload for the day was repetitive boring stuff. Dan came in a little late but had not even broken a sweat. He sat in his chair like a king upon a throne. Natalie giggled about something and a message popped up on Abigail's screen via internal message software.

'I am so happy, Abigail. I know I took him away from you, but I promise I will find you an even better man. After all, friends stick together, and I won't stop until I find you a replacement. It was you that opened my eyes that love is only skin deep.'

Abigail's face froze with spite when her fingers got busy with a response. 'How do you have the nerve to add a stupid smiley face at the end? How can you feel that this response is going to make me to say, "oh thank you"?' After a small sip of coffee, she decided to delete the whole lot and start again.

'Nat, I am not interested in another man. I have to think things through, just leave me alone, okay?' The little bell sound echoed in the ear drum as an immediate reply was received.

'Abigail, I am so sorry but really, we cannot stop talking to each other! I need you! You are like a sister to me. I can't afford to lose you.' It was difficult to control the red mist that started to close in front of Abigail's' face.

'Then don't marry him! Or at least tell him about Henry!' was typed in such force that it was louder than the phone ringing. The message stayed beaming at the reply messenger, unsent.

'Jesus, Abigail, I hope that the keyboard is still alive? I hope that the email wasn't sent to me,' giggled Susan from the office next door. It was what was needed to try to calm a little. It was deleted, and a politer version was sent back.

'Look, Nat, it's very difficult for me now. I will get over it, but I need some time. Just leave me alone. But make sure you split with Henry or I will tell Dan!'

Even though it had been a long time since Abigail had the need to smoke, this was the day to start the habit again. The desk drawer had some last year's cigarettes in hidden for emergency. This was that day. Once found, Abigail walked away from her desk and didn't look back despite having that burning feeling as if someone is watching your every single step. There wasn't the need to check as Natalie knew Abigail well enough to understand. The cigarette pack in her hand was the indicator that things weren't as calm as she wanted to make out. She watched her leave the office trying to hold back the tears of disappointment.

Anyone who is an occasional smoker knows how this works. If the nerves are shot there is one cigarette that can help to stop the thoughts flowing. It was Dan that she craved more than a cigarette but only one craving was readily available.

The bench outside was an easy spot to use for some personal time. It was so hard to hold back the heartache, but at least on this spot where the back was facing the office, she could have an easy cry without an audience. Abigail savoured the drag on the freshly lit cigarette. The birds were hoping around the bench hoping that some scraps of food would be left over by the human. They were frequent visitors who usually provided entertainment but to Abigail even their little faces couldn't bring a sun into her doomed face.

'I want him, I really do. You are a stupid bird but at least you don't have to share your loved one with anyone else. If you win, they are yours and I am sure that I would beat Natalie in a fight. She has got her claws deep into him. How could she do this, she is supposed to be my sister.' The bird hopped away uninterested in having a discussion with the stranger who didn't bring any food with them.

Abigail took another drag, pulling her shaking hand close to her lips. As she flicked the cigarette butt onto the floor she noticed Dan watching her through the blinds. He was wearing his 'I am so sorry' face.

'Crumbs, I hope he hadn't seen me falling apart.' Her thoughts were full of the feelings she had for him.

'Why can't you know that I need you, I love you?' her eyes were pleading into his direction. The gentle breeze caused her to blink. There was a man standing right next to Dan. Her hands gave way and the cigarette pack went scattering down to the floor. Her bottom lip opened in disbelief, is it him? Is that really him? Abigail was asking with her eyes of that man who he truly was. As if the man understood he mouthed a reply.

'Hello, Abigail.'

Abigail blinked multiple times in succession as if she tried to wipe away what she saw.

'You can't be back, go away!' The picture was so clear that the only thing was to close her eyes very hard. Afraid of the outcome, her curiosity got the better of her. When her eyes opened, he was gone.

'Natalie can't know that he is back! Only her and the psychologist knows about him. No way am I letting anyone that close ever again!'

With that the pack of cigarettes was picked up off the floor. It was time to return to her desk. Instead of having it easy, the day just dragged. Abigail had to bite her tongue when Dan kept visiting Natalie's desk, stealing kisses in full view of the whole office.

'I know what you are feeling, sister, your face says it all. If the boss was here they wouldn't have been able to do this so blatantly.' It was one of the coven members whispering behind Natalie's back.

'Suze, you are so right! They are so lucky he isn't in

today!' The email message popped up on the email screen.

'Oooh, look guys, now they are misusing the office email. That title – 'we're getting married' is so cheesy!' Susanne pulled a long face but as Natalie turned her body to face them, all of them changed their tune.

'Well done Natalie, it's wonderful news!'

Abigail wasn't impressed by their two-faced persona. 'Why can't they be just honest. They all know like I do why Natalie had decided to go for him.'

The situation game changer was when Henry walked in in his usual 'tense muscle' body movement. He whispered something to Natalie who then followed him to one of the meeting rooms. It was obvious that their discussion was an uncomfortable one. Henry was waving his arms around in anger. Natalie just stood there with her arms crossed over her chest. Most of the walking was done by Henry as his voice echoed through the glass wall. The whole coven waited in anticipation. As soon as he stormed out they launched themselves off their chairs to join Natalie in the meeting room. Abigail didn't want to go in. Between the small door opening some of the conversation got through.

'But he is as poor as a church mouse! No way am I going to be involved with anyone who takes me to the cinema by going on a bus!'

'Oh, Natalie, you are so right, he isn't a marriage material. I completely stand with you on the decision, Henry isn't the right man for you. He is just trying to spoil your wonderful day.'

Abigail felt sorry for Henry as he really looked hurt. Still, he wasn't the first. There were many men who Natalie was involved with during her working life in Finsco. There was one manager that she went out with even though he was married with kids. Despite disagreeing with this, Abigail stuck by her because, at the time, she desperately needed a shoulder to cry on. It was Abigail that in the end had to pass on messages to him to slowly get him used to the idea that there wasn't future in that relationship. For that he took it against her, she still remembered the moment that he stood up in a meeting and told her off in front of everyone. At no point Natalie stood up to say something, she just gave her 'I am so sorry' look but sat there quiet as a grave. Poor Henry, he probably would have preferred to be hit by a bus. How could she be so heartless? How can Natalie think that playing with people's feelings is a good thing to do? Abigail's head was full of sorrow on Henry's behalf even when walking back from work.

Birds chirped all the way to her home. 'Shut up, stupid birds!' Abigail's surprised shout scared the lady walking her dog in the opposite direction. The old lady just tut tutted as soon as their shoulders met. Abigail didn't care less, her whole body was strained by hate, by the unfairness in her life, even the birds were showing off their happiness that she never can have. The door of her flat paid the consequences. It nearly shook off its hinges the way it got slammed. All inhabitants of the flat knew that the owner of a flat 4 was at home. Abigail paced her small premises like a caged leopard.

'I hate you Natalie, I really, really, hate you!' It was when pulling the knife out of her kitchen drawers that Abigail stopped. The clunking of the knife came down in a noisy metallic whack. It was impossible to think what the hell was going on.

'Jesus, Abigail, what were you going to do with this?' The knife lay there on the floor reflecting the light like a mirror. /It reflected her shameful face, after all Natalie was the only one she had. It was her that came to Abigail when she was full of cold. It was her who brought the chocolates to get rid of the sour taste of loneliness and sickness in Abigail's mouth. It was her forcing the chick flicks onto Abigail as that was the way to get one more hopeful. The knife lay on the floor as a sign of betrayal.

'How the hell did I get here? Why was Dan more important than my sister?' Nobody answered her question.

Abigail picked up the knife so she can scrub away her shame.

Thankfully the whole situation stopped her pacing, her breath calmed down and she could think rationally. Though it was her stomach that re-structured the motion of her thoughts.

'Shit.' Abigail pulled out of the cooker the supposed lasagne that now resembled a burned blob. Her fingers got a little burned because as she was pulling out the pan her mobile rang. Abigail reached for it, but as it was Natalie calling, she drew away as if the phone was as hot as the pan.

At that moment, her face darkened and the dark blob she was pulling from the oven changed shape. It turned into a coffin revealing Natalie's pale face thorough a small opening. Then, it turned into a dark, blackened pathology slab. Abigail shook her head to try to rattle out these beads of hate out of her head. With a fast motion she threw the lasagne into the top of the worktop. By now the raindrops were hammering onto the window creating a pitter patter. Abigail glanced at the black and white floor tiles to convince herself that the knife wasn't there. The kitchen cupboards were still the originals from the sixties, a pale yellow the colour of old butter. Still, no matter how bad the lasagne looked, her stomach kept bringing her back to the present. The tugging at her insides helped to see that even though it was burned on the outside, it was okay to eat. Her fingers slowly peeled the burned bits to reveal the tasty part. Soon all nicely placed on the plate it was time to tuck in. It didn't taste too bad and soon the dish was nearly empty. Once the table was wiped and dishes were put into the sink to soak in the large bubbly hot water bath, it was time for a little sofa telly time.

It was hard to find anything worth watching. After some channel flicking Abigail stopped at the *Embarrassing Bodies* programme. It was mildly entertaining to see that some people secretly lived with embarrassing illness for years but then decided to flaunt it on a TV show. Quickly bored, Abigail decided to catch up with her chores and grabbed her ironing pile. The attempt of ironing her silk shirt ended just like the lasagne – burned. The recent bout of forgetfulness claimed yet another victim.

A slightly burned shirt was nothing compared to the time the kitchen cleaner was used instead of the furniture polish on the antique bedside table inherited from Gran. It ruined the last thing Abigail treasured from the one person she missed so much. At least the shirt can be replaced.

There was time when she sat on the sofa with closed eyes trying to pretend that Gran was still there pottering about the kitchen, talking. Even when it was obvious that their roles changed due to cancer, the talking never stopped. It was the chatter that filled the place with warmth. It was great to inherit some money but what Abigail wanted now was to have a little chat about the programme. The option of calling Natalie was out of the question. It wasn't that bad that Abigail would have to talk to the self-absorbed boyfriend snatcher.

In these moments, it was Gran, Mildred that would always make things right between her and Natalie if they argued. As a child, Gran would try to buy anything that Abigail asked for despite of being a low earner. It pained Abigail watching Mildred getting up in the morning, moaning in pain unintentionally as she tried to straighten her back. The memory of her clicking spine was one Abigail wished she could forget. Still Mildred carried on working, despite having cancer. It was the weakness of her body that put a stop to it at the end.

It was Gran that tried to explain to Abigail why Natalie had so much more than her. Mildred was gone, now there was nobody to explain why. The *Embarrassing Bodies* ending tune woke Abigail from her thoughts. Somehow, she gone into her little world where she tried to disappear too. Now she was sitting there by herself, nobody to fall back on. A small sniffle came out of her as she tucked her feet underneath her body. The remote was thrown onto the worn navy carpet as soon as the TV was turned off. Her sniffles were drowned by someone's argument outside the flat; that's exactly what Abigail wanted to do with Natalie.

'I am all alone,' flowed the pity out of her heart. When the eyelids closed to wash away yet another tear, a small whisper came to her.

'You aren't, I am with you, always.' Abigail stood up from the sofa to look around. Nobody was around. The lounge was a little colder. The room was as it always was, a little shabby but functional. The remote still lay motionless on the carpet. Abigail bent over to pick it up before, yet another accident caused her to stand on it unintentionally. As she bent over, the light flickered on and off.

'Are you here? Can you talk?' Abigail knew who it was. Since her childhood she had 'friends'. Only Mildred and Natalie knew about her visions. Now talking to Natalie was out of the question and the only way to speak to Gran was to find her in the huge space of nothingness, of the place where the dead go.

'Is it you, Dyna?' The lights flickered with a little cracking sound coming out of the lightbulbs which tried to retain the extra charge of electricity.

'I know it's you, only you are this cheeky. Do you want to talk? I would love to talk, but it's been a long time.' From a young child, Abigail was able to speak to them but only when asleep. This was little different as she was awake. Still, her heart skipped that she wasn't alone.

'I am so happy you are here. Give me a minute, I will try to get to you.' Abigail turned the light off in the lounge and walked towards the kitchen. By now the lights flickered in each room she stood in. Even the fridge light was flickering as she opened it to retrieve the bottle of wine.

'I must have fallen asleep. I promise you I won't be

asking about you, I remember your life. You are like me, I know. You have also suffered because of love, you also died for love. I promise I will behave and listen.' The lights went off at the same time Abigail tipped the bottle down her throat. The darkness grew in the corner of the kitchen by the table. A shape was crawling from beneath the table.

'Is it you?' BANG slammed the door by itself. The kitchen was engulfed in darkness.

'I promise I will keep the door shut after our talk.' Remembered to mention Abigail as Dyna was very adamant to ensure to 'close the door' when she leaves. With that promise, the light flickered back on, the kitchen door opened out again. With the help of the wine Abigail made her way to her bed, she was ready.

'Are you here Dyna, can you speak?' The darkness surrounded Abigail's body which had gone completely stiff apart from the small movement of her chest that took calming breaths. The darkness grew and from within shadows crawled out of until there were figures surrounding the bed. The door was still shut. As each figure took a closer step towards the bed, the door started to open. They all turned their heads towards the opening door. Within seconds, not glancing back they floated out of the open door.

'Yes,' was the answer that was so long overdue.

'Oh, Dyna, I feel so betrayed, I hate myself and everyone else around me. I hate this world! I was thinking of taking my life as this one is not worth living. I want to join you. Tell me how you have done it. I want to be with you and all the others you are with. I want to come back as a presence for a little while. I Lost Dan so have nothing else to live for. That's what I want. Please can you help me?' Dyna sat down by the feet and answered with her wispy voice.

'This life is one of suffering, but worth living. You must not fuel anger, you must not hate. More is to come should you not listen. Do not call on me anymore as I sense a difference in you. Do not speak in this manner for your life will be in danger.'

'What do you mean by that?'

A huge scream escaped from the door that suddenly opened. After it circled around the bed it disappeared back. Dyna moved closer, her hand clasped Abigail's. The duvet moved as she sat nearer. Abigail's hand started to throb as if someone just put it in an icy water. The ghostly shroud brushed past Abigail's cheek as she spoke, nearly touching her face.

'You are now open for the wicked ones, ones that prey on weakness, your heart is shouting out to be exploited, you must stop, you cannot speak to me anymore, leave us, leave us…' She stood up and released the hand clasp. At the same time some warmth started to flow back into Abigail's veins. Dyna's silhouette slowly floated towards the door.

'Don't go! You're the only one that I can talk to! Don't turn your back on me! You are abandoning me at the time when I really need you? Are you a true friend? Answer me!' For a second Dyna's ghostly apparition halted her movement towards the door. Then the screech of an old hag came out as she turned her face towards Abigail. The lines in her face were thick as if someone had cut her face into bits with a knife, her eyes were glowing a deep maroon colour. Her hand reached for the door handle.

'You'll need to leave us! Keep this door shut!' Then with a loud bang the door slammed shut behind Dyna. As soon as she was gone Abigail's movement returned. Maybe it was the emotional exhaustion or the alcohol that made her fall asleep, but she kept being haunted in her dreams. It was Dan happy with Natalie that kept popping up to tease her even at the time when she should sleep in blissful ignorance.

***

Abigail's mind was full of storm clouds the following weeks making her mood to deteriorate. Even workplace was full of wedding discussion rather than work.

'Jeanette, did you hear about Henry?' Susan's nose crinkled with fresh gossip.

'Jeez, go on tell, what happened? I am all ears,' playfully responded Jeanette putting hands behind her ears to indicate she was ready to listen.

'Well, apparently Henry has been really aggressive, and he has been seen punching the cabinet door!' They noticed that Abigail was also listening.

'What do you think about that, Abigail? Henry is totally inappropriate, right? It's the company property he has been damaging.' Abigail moved her mouse to open an email. Trying not to give up her emotions she composed herself.

'I think you two should just keep out your noses out of his business. Of course, he is annoyed, who wouldn't be?' Abigail sunk into her chair whilst Jeanette sniggered.

'Wow, hold your horses, we know how much you liked Dan.' The emphasis on the last two words were put there on purpose. They knew where to hurt her. Abigail locked her screen. Her face was giving away what Jeanette wanted. It was there: the enlarged nostrils, flush in her cheek, the clenching of teeth. Through gritted teeth, Abigail mumbled she had to get a drink. Then she stormed off away from the quiet, heated, hushed conversation that Jeanette led.

The judgment was wrong. Usually empty small kitchenette was full. In the middle was Natalie talking about Henry. Abigail wanted to sneak out as soon as she realised but was dragged into the conversation.

'Abigail, did you hear? Do you know what Henry is saying, apparently he wants to have a fight with Dan. Isn't he totally idiotic?' Sadly, for Abigail, there was no chance of escaping the gossip. No matter where she tried to run away to, if the secret chat wasn't about Henry, it was about Natalie and her wedding.

Friday that week was the turning point. Yet again, Jeanette and Susan were gossiping, each day of gossip was like water dripping onto Abigail's head. It was hard to explain why and what did it. Maybe it was the hushed conversation that purposefully wasn't quiet, maybe it was Natalie posing again with her ring, or it was Henry storming in slamming doors. It was impossible to explain but even if the boss was in, nothing stopped the poisonous chit chat.

'For fuck's sake, shut up, just shut you, all of you just SHUT THE FUCK UP!' Abigail's voice carried through the office. With the force of her standing up the chair was thrown into the desk next to her, hitting Jeanette's back. The mouse flew across the room in Natalie's direction. The keyboard clanked against the glass wall of the manager's office. Finally, all the talk stopped. The only sound little later was the shout from the boss.

'Abigail, I need to have a word with you, can you please come in to my office?' By then Jeanette was pulling up the back of her shirt to show Susan the bruise that the impact had caused. It was complete over-reaction. Abigail stomped her way to the office. Their boss was a lovely chubby guy with the heart of gold. Still it didn't mean that he was a push over. Being Indian, there was always the spicy smell of his aftershave. Somehow, the exotic background never left him despite living in the UK for over a decade. Each time he went to visit his family he would bring some native nibbles. This chat wasn't going to be about his visit nor anything pleasant at all.

'Can you explain your behaviour, please? I will have to raise this with Human Resources but before I do that I need you to explain why. I want to hear your part of the story.'

'I am sorry that it seems my behaviour is inappropriate, but what I believe is inappropriate is that people who wish to work and do the job are interrupted by those who wish to gossip about rubbish. I just can't take this crap anymore.'

'Abigail, language, please! We aren't in a pub.'

Abigail shifted uncomfortably on the swirly chair. No longer were the floods of self-pity contained. Her shoulders shook with sobs.

'I can't take it anymore, it's so unfair, there isn't anyone I can speak to normally. Everyone is talking about Dan or Henry or Natalie and her stupid wedding. I just want them to stop, I don't want to gossip, I don't want to hear it. I have no one.' The word no one tugged at her boss's heart. He knew the sensitivity she carried. He also knew her history and that the death of the only person in her life, her gran, was raw.

'Abigail, I suggest that you take a week off as sick leave. I am happy to sign you off, so please take the offer. Go now, clear your head and come back next week. I suggest that you go and see your GP to seek out relevant help. We also have a company programme where you can talk to someone free of charge. Here, take this.' After going through his drawers he presented Abigail with a card. Abigail examined the card, nearly cutting herself on the sharp cardboard edge.

'Thank you.' She slowly took her leave. By the door, before it was opened, she faced him again.

'See you next week.' Her boss was a good man with good judgment of character. Abigail quietly closed the door of his office. Like a guilty teenager she picked up the keyboard. It was Natalie that run towards Abigail helping to find the missing alphabet off her keyboard. There wasn't any conversation, but actions speak louder than words. Abigail avoided eye contact whilst Natalie was pulling a begging puppy face. Abigail took the keys off Natalie's opened hand. Natalie tried to stroke her hand, but she immediately pulled her hand back. Carrying the broken cargo, Abigail made her way to her computer. She didn't need to look at her neighbours. Their burning stare was felt on Abigail's back. Her spine, though chilled, had burned holes caused by them.

Once her handbag was taken out of the drawer, it was impossible to ignore Jeanette or Susan. Abigail moved slowly towards them ensuring that she couldn't be seen. The shorter the distance got the closer both sat. Both looked as if they tried to huddle together from the bogey man. Jeanette no longer held her back where the chair hit her, she held Susan's hand tightly. With a precision of extending their fright, Abigail chose her timing and sharpness of her voice well. The targeted words were accompanied by the spit which showered their faces.

'You back-stabbing, gossiping bitches. Should you cross me once more I make sure you both will be drinking from a straw for the rest of your life!' Her knuckles tightened by the way the handbag was pulled. Neither of them moved even though Abigail already departed through the office entrance.

Dan caught up with her in the atrium right by the main door. 'Abigail, wait!'

Abigail turned around with raised chin, hands on hips. 'What do you want?'

'Please, don't be like that. This isn't you. You are a kind person, not who you are now. I know I hurt you and I never meant to do that. I've always had a soft spot for you. You must have known that. This thing with Natalie, I never thought I had any hope with her. Natalie really needs you, Abigail, she wants you to be her chief bridesmaid. Please, think about it.'

That was the last straw. Abigail turned around and walked out of that door so fast that some passer-by got elbowed.

'You don't know me! Nobody does!'

***

It wasn't only one passer-by that got some attitude. One lady walking her little sausage dog got little more than she deserved. As the cherry trees were opening their flowers, the fresh spring air was too sweet to not enjoy it. The lady was taking her time leisurely walking the way the little dog led her. The little dog kept changing lanes making it impossible for Abigail to pass.

'Argggghhhhhh, for god's sake, you old dear, make your mind up where you're going!' It made the lady to stop in her track and finally Abigail passed her disapproving stare.

Abigail was still fuming when she reached her flat. As soon as the main door shut, the handbag flew into the corner of the tiny hallway. Her back pressed against the door as if someone was trying to get in. By this time her handbag was beeping like mad. It was the familiar sound of text message received. Once she had on that funny 'you got message' alarm but now she was glad that she changed it to the normal beep beep sound. Nothing would irritate her more than having that going on and on. With one foot extended, the handbag was dragged back to the door. The mobile was fished out but there wasn't the need. Abigail knew who would have been messaging. She was right, there were multiple messages from Natalie and one from Dan. Reading them would mean that an answer should be written. The only thing that seemed like a good idea was to turn the thing off.

***

It was good that the boss gave Abigail the whole week off. At least that's what he thought was a good idea but for Abigail it was an extension to hell. No matter what she did, her mind was running overdrive. Her thoughts were like a large furnace fire burning intensely. Any positive thinking was engulfed by the flames. It was exhausting which is why most of it was spent lying on her sofa. When there wasn't anything worth watching, she would just watch her reflection in the turned off TV. At one point, after staring into the empty TV screen she thought she saw a figure standing by her sofa, but it was probably just exhaustion.

As the thoughts kept gathering, the more clouds entered her mind. Abigail was motionless, staring into the empty black TV screen with shapes popping up from behind the sofa. Then as if the world started to spin, the walls were closing in. A panic set in. It was what was needed, spurring Abigail to stand up from her stagnant state. The fridge sadly revealed that hot chocolate was out of the question unless someone walked to get some milk.

Instead of talking the heavy handbag Abigail retrieved her purse. She put it in the pocket of her favourite musty smelling coat. It needed a wash but the way things where she didn't want to do any damage to it. At least if she smelled of her own body odour, it was less likely that people would stop to talk to her. The dusk was already set in, bringing in the chill. The shop was thankfully empty apart from the owner behind the counter. On the way back, it had gone nearly completely dark. The streetlighting turned itself on causing white circles upon the footpath in between darkness where there were none. Most people were at home making their dinners, so it was surprising having a figure of a man walking towards Abigail. It was hard to make it out but when he hit the light spot his whole body disappeared. Then the figure stopped by the cherry tree that was engulfed in darkness. When Abigail walked past she glanced back at the tree trunk. There wasn't anyone. Maybe it was her mind playing up again or just maybe he was someone rushing back home, making his way through the grass.

At home some warm hot chocolate was made, providing Abigail with some mood elevation. What was needed was a good movie. Without hesitation her favourite movie *Aliens* was put into the DVD player. With a little buzz of mechanism, the 20th Century Fox intro surround kicked in. No sooner than her lips touched the warm rim of the cup the loud knock coming from the hallway forcing Abigail to leave the taste of that lovely warm sweet liquid for a little bit longer.

Not being in a much of a mood to talk Abigail wanted to find out who was the owner of that inconvenient interruption. Quietly she crept towards the front door and placed her ear upon it. The familiar voices were recognised immediately, though it was hard to make out the discussion. A loud exhalation left her lungs at the same time as another knock. Abigail opened the door to shout out 'get out' but when he curry scent entered her nostrils, she changed her mind.

'Chicken curry, egg fried rice!' said Natalie pointing at the bag, smiling.

'Yeah, you got that right Nat, thank you.' Natalie was positively beaming, a crooked smile on her face, while Dan was standing there smiling but with his arms stiffly at his sides. The longer the hesitation, the stiffer his arms became. Abigail blinked, arose out of the fog and stepped back to swing open the door. It was more of a reaction than a thought that made her to open it. 'Come on in. I wasn't expecting visitors, um, so it's messy.'

'Oh Abigail, you've got some rubbish on again. Why do you watch these movies!' Natalie pointed at the flat screen telly, the only lavish thing that Abigail spent money on.

'You know why I love them. I relax watching them.' Natalie turned the DVD off before the movie could properly start. Dan raised his eyebrows at Abigail. Their movie taste was similar, and *Aliens* was the movie they rather watched.

'Leave it!' shouted Abigail from the kitchen as she was putting the food on to the plates.

'Too late,' chirped Natalie back. Another intro sounded out of the speakers but this time, what followed was some mushy music.

'Yep, it's a chick flick,' commented Dan.

'Oh dear, Natalie. I do prefer Abigail's choice, put it back on.'

'No way, I'm not watching that rubbish. It's scary! I'll put on a proper movie.'

The raised eyebrows accompanied by rolling eyes was an agreement of what would be the better choice. Abigail couldn't help but notice that Dan was wearing his usual aftershave. It felt natural to lock into his smell rather than the overpowering smell of spicy curry.

***

Despite the bad movie choice everyone enjoyed themselves. Abigail managed to forget about the clouds in her mind for the last two hours. At around 9.00 p.m. ish Dan excused himself and took his leave.

'I think you two need to have a lovely girlie chat without me. If I stay I will turn into a he-male testing make-up, asking if my butt looked big in these jeans.' His cheeky grin made both girls giggle. In the hallway after putting his shoes on he put a small peck on each girl's cheek. Abigail was happy, it was just like old times.

The atmosphere of the flat changed a little when he departed. It was during the washing up that Natalie cut through it.

'Abigail, I know you are hurt, but I don't want to lose you. You are my sister. That will never change.' The wiped plate was put on the pile of others in the cupboard.

Abigail scrubbed the last plate in the sink so thoroughly that it created more bubbles on the surface. Once it was put in the drainer, Natalie retrieved it to wipe. The bubbling sound of the emptying sink was to Abigail like the drain she opened in her mind. The more water disappeared the more she wanted to acknowledge that she really needed her sister.

'Let me make you the usual.' Abigail's wet hands reached for the secret alcohol cupboard. Once the Amarula was pulled out, Natalie's eyes shimmered of naughtiness.

'Do you remember last time we had this?' Abigail's cheeks flushed.

'Do you remember how cross Mildred was finding us completely drunk on "special milk" we found? It was hilarious, us laughing non-stop at the Road Runner whilst spinning around? "Meep Meep".'

Abigail poured the cocktail whilst Natalie kept reminiscing how poor Mildred used to fret. After so much giggles fuelled by Amarulla, it was time to get ready to try to get some sleep.

'Let me make the sofa up for you.' Abigail moved the small coffee table to expand the sofa into a bed.

'Do you remember when we had the boys around?' Natalie pointed at the sofa bed. Abigail broke out with nervous laughter.

'Are you by any chance referring when we had that particular party ending with the drunken snuggle on the bed with…. Blimey, I can't even remember his name!' It was Natalie's turn to break out in a roaring chuckle.

'I can't remember either! The only thing I know is that it was one of the earliest kisses with Dan. It was in the toilet right after I vomited!'

'God, Natalie, that's absolutely gross. You forgot to give me that tiny detail.' Natalie's face became a little more serious.

'Abigail, would you mind being a chief bridesmaid to a vomit kiss couple?'

'Yes, I would love to be the bridesmaid, Natalie. I really appreciate you thinking of me.' Natalie dropped the pillow and rushed to Abigail. Her squeeze was the same as when a child hugs their mum, thinking the harder they squeeze the more they love her.

'Abigail, it means so much to me that you are prepared to do that. I really look forward the hen night trip. It is a secret that I only know snippets of from Susan. She has taken it upon herself to sort it out. I hope you have a passport – I think that we are travelling abroad. It will be so much fun!'

'Okay Natalie, now you can let go before you break my rib cage. I did hear some small information about the hen night, so I bet it will be wicked.' At about 1.00 a.m. both were completely exhausted. Abigail couldn't explain how she got to her bed, neither why now she was awake in her bedroom. It was still early in the morning as it was dark. She tried to reach her phone to check the time but her arms weren't moving. Her eyes tried to make out the surroundings especially as the floor creaked nearby.

'Natalie, is it you?' Though the question was asked no noise left her mouth. Her throat was dry, her legs limp, arms motionless as if they were full of lead. The creak got closer. Small beads of sweat were making their way down from her forehead ticking her skin slowly on its way. Even that little itch was too much to ask her motionless hands. The floor creaked again but this time the maker of the sound became visible. There was a figure in her room, making a slow approach towards her bed. Panic set in.

'Help, anyone help.' In the end it was useless. Her usual instinct kicked in.

'Who are you?' The shape tipped its head to the side.

'An old friend,' came a manly, throaty, gargled response. He took a step closer. The small hair on Abigail's skin stood up, as with his approach came a slight gust of cold as if someone had just opened a fridge.

'What do you want from me?'

'I want nothing from you, my dear, but you want me. You need me, you need my help. I can do it for you, you can have him.' He came even closer. It was too hard to make him out but thankfully he moved to where a small strip of moonlight made its way through the curtains.

Abigail's pulse quickened. A scrawny figured, yellowed teeth man was right before her. Words escaped her mind through her clamped mouth which was still paralysed.

'I don't need anyone! Especially not you, I don't know you, go away.' Only now Abigail noticed that something was wrong. In the back of her mind she knew thing was missing. The door. It was shut. He could sense her thoughts, read her mind. A sniffling hoarse gargle escaped his throat.

'If you don't need me then why am I here? How do you think I made it to you without opening the door?' His scrawny finger pointed towards the closed door.

'Now I have your attention I need you to listen. I know the deepest needs that you store in your heart. I am the only friend you ever had. The only one that can help you. There is trip to plan. If you want what your heart desires then you must go to Europe, travel to Brno, in the Czech Republic. I will be there waiting for you. Once we make a physical connection I can help you to get what you want. I will give him to you.'

Then, without waiting for an answer, he wafted to the door. Before opening it to leave, his head cocked once more towards her as if he was going to ask a question, but nothing more was said. As soon as the door closed behind him, the movement returned, and Abigail jolted upright. With a speedy action, she skipped to the door and held it shut. Then the exhaustion kicked in again. Abigail allowed herself to slump against the door where she fell asleep, happy that her bodyweight was enough to block the doorway.

***

It was too late to regret the drinking in the morning. Abigail's spine was in so much pain that it was impossible to stand up. Her buttocks lost all feeling as she slept sitting down on the hard floor against the door. When she finally made it to the kitchen, Natalie was already there.

'Abigail, what did we do last night? I think we're getting older. I am more sensitive than I used to be.' The hot water from steamed up the cupboard as she poured water into the cups. Abigail took one cup and began to drink it like she had just came back from desert. Sadly, the coffee wasn't cutting it and a headache descended.

'I shouldn't drink. It doesn't agree with me, Nat.' The sunlight filtered through the bedroom's net curtains, casting patterns on Natalie's face where she'd just sat down at the foot of the bed. Both were in a sorry state. Their grey skin didn't look right in the morning spring sunlight. Both made it with their coffees to the lounge. Once the sofa was pushed to its sitting position both slumped into it. Natalie's breath was awful.

'I am no better, Abigail. I am sorry, I chucked up in your loo and made a bit of a mess of the bathroom. I better go home before my mum sends out a search party.'

Abigail grinned at the idea of Natalie chucking up at her toilet just like old times. The short gain was followed by longer self-pity. She didn't have a mother who would care to look for her if she had not turned up. Natalie was so lucky.

'Damn it!' cursed Natalie. 'We need to be at a viewing at Garden Close in two hours. I must pack and move on without helping you to tidy up. You don't mind, Aby right, you know what Dan's like with timekeeping. You see we are looking at houses to start our lives together.'

Abigail didn't mind that Natalie left quickly. Once she had left, the place was quiet again. Abigail was back in her dark place. She was alone, left to tidy up all the mess Natalie left behind. Her mind was running into overdrive. *Maybe last night the man is really trying to help?*

'Sod it, if I am mean to go then I will at least make it worth my while.' Despite the lack of desire to speak to Susan, Abigail dialled her number.

***

During the rest of the weekend not much happened apart from noting that Abigail's anger had been building again. Calls to Dyna were unproductive. When finally contact was made Dyna gave the same answer in her whispery voice repeatedly 'Leave us, leave us....'

She wasn't ready to listen, but the man kept whispering into her ear: 'let's meet, I'll give you what you want.'

Eventually Dyna stopped coming. Abigail got bitter and as the man kept coming, she needed to talk to someone. After some time, she knew a lot about him but his name pronunciations was strange. The way it spelled was of non-English origin.

'Where are you from, what year did you die?' Abigail asked during one of her episodes.

'That is not necessary to know. My name is Josef.'

'Why do you want to help me, why me?'

'Because you are special. I was there with you when you were young. I was with you all the time, watching you grow. I am the only person that knows your most hidden secrets. I understand what's it like to lose a loved one, I know how much it hurt.' The knowledge that this person knew Abigail since birth made her feel at ease. If he was with her all this time, then he could have hurt her long time ago. On a positive side he also knew what it felt like to lose a loved one.

'What do you mean that you lost your love? What happened?'

'I was a soldier, a trained killer sent to fight. I did my duty well, but that resulted in me being away from home a lot. My love had been pressured by her family to marry and when we were sent off to train on how to use the new weaponry, she was wed without my knowledge. It was her family that made her, those vicious snakes, laughing at me when I turned back to claim her hand. They weren't laughing when I used the new weapon on them. The power it had, the ease of use, the way it got heavier when you filled in the powder into the cold steel. Maybe harder to aim but there was no other thing that can gave you that pleasure when you aimed at your target. They went down like a felled tree. Their limped bodies lay upon the floor glaring at me with their upright turned eyeballs. What a power.'

The pleasure he put into that sentence made her uncomfortable. 'You mean you killed them?'

His presence made the room little less home like as Josef brought in the cold of death. He moved his face away when responding.

'I hadn't really killed them, I helped them. They were rotten, they only married their daughter for money. They didn't care that she was beaten every single day by her new husband. That night he pushed her off the stairs and her neck broke, I was so full of anger that I just reacted. I filled the guns that I stole, all four of them. Nicely ready, tucked underneath my belt I walked to visit both households. Her husband was the first. He got his medicine first, right between his eyes. The parents were next. Don't call me a killer, I am the angel of mercy, I am the one that provides justice. That's why I want to help you.'

***

The time had gone so fast that Abigail hadn't realised that her whole weekend was spent speaking to Josef who was answering all her questions. He had become the friend Dyna should have been. Josef was always affectionate when they spoke about the whole Natalie situation. The smacking of his lips made it clear that he completely disapproved of how badly Natalie treated her. Abigail was so happy to be listened to that she completely poured out her heart.

'A true friend would not do such a thing. It is only a mere suggestion but us, those whom have not yet parted with the material world, can guide such unfortunate souls such as yourself, to provide justice. I can help, but to do that I need your complete permission.' He cocked his head towards Abigail.

'On a serious note though, I can't do that unless you give me your full commitment. Should you wish to give me your belief I will be guiding you in achieving what you want. I do not want to raise your hopes, but I really can give you what you want the most. Think about it because if you decide you want me to stay I will never leave. When the time is right I will give you what your heart desires the most.' This small demand to seal the deal was sprung on at Abigail on Sunday evening. Her inner self was screaming the opposite to what came out in her mind.

'Yes, yes, yes, yes, yes, I am ready to do anything.' That answer came out before her mind was able to put both arguments against each other.

'Ahhhhhhhh.' His ghostly gargled voice made a pleasurable siren sound.

'That's like honey to my ears. You have made me a very happy man.' He sat on the bed stretching his neck towards the ceiling, taking breaths in with his long pointy nose. His hands were on his thighs.

'Our agreement is now completed. You must listen; do what you are told. I will establish a connection with you when you are in Brno and soon my presence will be known to you as your desire will make me stronger. You must believe. I thank you. I will be in touch and who knows, you might be helping me too in the future.'

The conversation gave Abigail the oomph for the week ahead. By the end of the week her flat was tidied, just like her mind. After so many months of wanting to do it, she got out her paintbrush and decorated her lounge a nice gentle cream colour.

***

Abigail was much more positive the following weeks at work. The conversations with Josef gave her the confidence that Natalie's engagement was only temporary. The only dark cloud in her subconscious was the question as to why Josef would not say what he wanted in return. Her positive mood was well received. Even the boss noted the difference giving her a little wink of an approval. She didn't get wound up by constant kissing between Dan and Natalie. To her, each kiss, hug will eventually belong to her.

Not all was rosy, as since Josef came into her world some adverse effects came with it in form of a strange repeating dream. The same story over and over, slowly escalating, growing in detail with main character in a wedding dress. Abigail interpreted it as premonition. . But as the woman started to whisper, more details appeared and they turned darker.

The surroundings in which these dreams were happening were also unfamiliar. In each dream there stood a man of Josef's proportions in the background. There wasn't much time to try to interpret the dreams as it was easier to live with them. Abigail did try to call Josef to ask about them, but he hadn't come to talk since the time they sealed their agreement.

Abigail worked well to hide her jealousy. Though scary, the dream must be the future, as the Bride never showed her face. It must have been her, ready to be Dan's wife. It all fitted. Dreams were coincidences of feelings, or of the following events to come. The positivity gave her the status she needed as a chief bridesmaid. She delved into organising the hen night despite Susan's constant pushback. Susan originally wanted to go to Amsterdam, but Abigail managed to turn the decision around. The cost analysis she done had served her purpose and everyone agreed with Abigail.

***

When the day came to go to Brno Abigail no longer cared about her dreams, despite that they frightened her. Afterall she woke up the next day without harm. The more annoying thing was that so far nothing had happened to stop the wedding. A pang of mistrust set its seedling roots inside her. It could have been the anxiety or frustration, but a blanket of doubt has been placed over her.

She spent the night before the trip thrashing about in her bed. Nothing was helping her to fall asleep. Thankfully she still had some of the over-the-counter sleeping pills. One pill later she was dozy like a drunken cat. Her sluggish brain tried to keep running into overdrive, but the pill won. The winter duvet of 16.5 tog warmed her whole body fast that soon she was in deep sleep.

This time the only change was that the usual 'bride' dream turned a little different. It was the same white dress but this time the woman had a wildflower band upon her head like a crown. Her face hidden by the veil, she stood in the distance. The only indication of her talking was the small movement of the veil where her lips were. Then from behind her Josef appeared. He raised his hand, pointed one finger with which he made a gesture underneath his chin. With this crude movement he made the gesture of cutting someone's throat. Abigail woke up on the floor. The dream caused her to thrash about. It kept rattling around her head like Smarties in a box. Picking herself off the floor gave her some time to align the thoughts. Doubts about Josef dived deeper into her soul. No longer was she as comfortable to speak to him. In bed, Abigail watched the movement of moonlight. From deep in her mind came the memory.

'Don't forget, Abigail, there are those that prey on someone like you. Some are lonely that just want to chat, but some departed souls only come back to cause malice. After all, we are all travellers through time, imparted from material things, keeping the gateway to the living open. Hate will make them to come. Don't hate, love. Being lonely is not hate, it's sadness, that's what brings us to you. Hate will only bring the wrong to your door. Once they are there it's hard to keep them out.'

Maybe it was the pleading that made it happen. The moonlight disappeared, and the coldness came in, despite of the heavy warmth of the duvet. The door opened, and Dyna walked in. Abigail, though frozen in place, couldn't contain her happiness.

'It's you, I really need you! It's absolutely fantastic that you are finally here, please help me.' Her answer was unexpected, cold with sharp edges.

'I told you to leave us, do it now or you shall regret it forever. Do not listen to him, he is a menace, a dangerous spirit.' Her floating figured body was going from one side to another. She was pacing like a dog trying to find out where the treat is hidden.

'You will travel, do not go! You will meet new people, do not engage! You will be offered to buy, do not buy!' Her demands were accompanied by a pointed finger. Then the cold came closer; her floating dress swished across the floor until she fully faced Abigail. Their noses were touching. Abigail felt her breath on her mouth.

'Should you abide by my words you'll live, should you not, you'll die. You are opened to the evil one. He will take you as his own, he will rip out your soul to replace it with his.' With the blink of an eye her face moved away. Floating in one place, finally with a kind mother-like voice, she spoke for the last time.

'I am leaving forever, locking the door behind me. It must remain shut, so no one can answer. I will miss you, my darling, please do as I say.' A couple of swooshes later the door clicked closed. There was still a sentence remining in the air whispered by numerous different voices: 'this way is shut.'

Abigail's gut was clenching with anger. Everyone had abandoned her; she was now completely alone. In the morning the mirror in her bathroom was steamed up again. Each morning there was more water inside the flat than outside. With a mad thrash she wiped it with the palm of her hand. When her face was revealed, the dark circles on her skin made her mad.

'I am strong, and I can do whatever the hell I like. I will have Dan as he is mine and mine only. I am not going to share him. I am NOT GIVING HIM UP!'

Chapter 3

The travel was awful. The other passengers kept giving the hen party evil looks because as soon as they boarded the bus, the alcohol was poured out. Natalie, giggling with the other hens, swigged from a smuggled bottle. Most of the passengers weren't English or just didn't approve of young girls being out about traveling under the influence.

The bus was comfy enough with its cheap blue and yellow striped fabric. Obviously, Abigail had to keep pretending that she was cool about the engagement. To be in, she took the bottle with unmarked clear liquid in and took a swig of it. By the time the bus gets to Belgium the mixture of alcohol, drugs and exhaustion should kick in. What a daft idea, going to a hen night on a bloody bus across Europe! The destination had been her suggestion, but she'd had a plane in mind, not a grubby bus. In a huff Abigail folded her arms, watching fields full of cows flickering by. She stretched her tense neck and it clicked into place.

Still, it would be worth it as if she managed to get some good snaps of Natalie covered in men, then that would be proof Abigail needed for Dan to find out what Natalie really was.

It was more exhausting than initially thought, especially as Abigail had never had her claustrophobia so severely tested as on this trip. In Folkstone, when the bus drove into the train of a Channel Tunnel, Abigail's lips tingled as the bus made its way through the belly of the earth.

'Abi, are you OK? You've gone terribly pale, hon.' Those were the only words Abigail remembered once she woke up in France. It was Natalie's voice again.

'Abi, please wake up. Are you okay? Should we call doctor? We can ask the driver to stop?'

Her lips were still tingling, but with a shaky voice Abigail managed to respond, 'Yeah, I'm fine.' The smell of her own vomit-scented breath made her gag.

'Seriously, Abi, you scared me, ever since we went into that tunnel you've said nothing and then you just collapsed. Apart from being white as a sheet, you're sweating buckets! You've got to speak to me. Are you OK?'

'Nat, of course I'm fine. Deep in thought, that's all. It's a long journey. You know I like to keep myself to myself on the road.' Despite the sickness developing in her stomach, Abigail tried to keep calm. Counting in her head helped distract her from the sickness but by the time they got to Belgium, she'd managed to vomit in each country they passed through.

After the third time, Natalie pulled a face that meant one thing: you poor thing. The other girls gave the same looks but Susan couldn't keep her mouth shut.

'You've been especially quiet since the tunnel, haven't you?' Susan looked out from behind the mirror she used for reapplying her lipstick.

'Strange, how you started to keep yourself to yourself since Dan decided to go after Nat rather than you.'

Karen, the peace keeper, but gossiper nonetheless, interjected.

'We all know you wanted him, but now you need to move on. Enjoy yourself! There are plenty more fish in the sea.'

Abigail's knuckles tightened around the full sick bag like she might strangle it. Her eyes bore into the girl's foreheads.

'Karen, Susan, believe me, that is exactly what I'm intending to do. But it would be much easier if you'd keep your large noses out of other people's affairs. Unless you'd like to assist me with the vomiting. The bag needs emptying!' Both cringed at the bag in disgust.

'No way am I touching that,' snorted Karen and together with Susan went into their own hushed conversation about something. Abigail stomped off to the bus toilet to empty it ensuring that the bag swung by their faces as she walked past.

A little further on the journey it was no longer possible to watch the world going by as the darkness set down her lengthy cloak. Most of the passengers hushed out any conversation, which suited Abigail. There was a whisper from Karen's direction, but nothing you could make out. A small glance back confirmed it was Karen, while Natalie was out for the count. Not long, and Abigail sank into deep, dream-filled sleep.

***

The mist was going down from the woods. Tall pines like arrows pointed to the gods above. The air was moist and chilled. Then the whisper came from within the forest. It flew past Abigail's cheek, making her shiver as it went down her spine.

Abigail stood before the trees alone with a large lake behind her. The long reeds hummed as the wind gently swayed them. Her feet were cold like the rest of her body but not from the wind. Some other presence could be felt. She wasn't alone, somebody was watching her. The mist now reached and swallowed her whole. No longer were the trees and the lake visible. The whisper intensified.

'I am watching you. I know what you want. I can get it for you, but you must give me what I want. If you do as you're told, I'll reward you by giving you the one your heart desires most!'

The mist gave way, but this time Abigail was facing the water. A small light emitting from the middle of the lake started to creep towards her. As it reached the edge it became obvious it was more than just a light. It was a picture lying on the surface. Curiosity got the better of Abigail, and she stepped towards it. The picture was of Dan, sporting one of his beautiful smiles.

'Sweet.' Abigail loved that cute, confident smile. Her arm extended to try to reach the apparition, to grab the image, to bathe in it, but as soon as the tip of her finger touched the cold harsh water, it all went dark as if someone had turned the lights off. Unable to move due to the thickness of the darkness, as if her finger had frozen to the lake's surface, unable to see or move, a flicker blinded her.

The mist vanished, the trees reappeared, and a dark hand grabbed hers from beneath the water surface. The grip of the black hand was fierce, whispers followed. By this time, they came from the woodland, sounding differently. There from the darkness was a figure walking towards Abigail: a woman, surely, as the figure wore a dress that fluttered in the wind. The flapping sound of her dress got louder the closer she got. Once her face was visible Abigail gasped. Dark hand released her. Turning towards the figure, Abigail swallowed the harsh nothingness in her throat.

It was her, the woman that started appearing in her dreams after the connection with Josef was sealed. Her sad expression changed to fury and hate the closer she got, eyes glowing fiercely red. Her bare feet made a crunching sound as they stopped right before Abigail's face. Evil grimaced with hollow, black eye sockets shining red where the whites would have been. The woman exhaled. Her breath chilled Abigail's forehead. As she cocked her head, her lips opened a little with a grimacing curl. What came out was nothing but a whisper, though her words were clear:

'You can't have him! You must stop your need, or he'll come for you. He can only take you on the one path, the path to hell! Once he has you in his power he'll never let you go until you are with him in hell. You must stop!'

By the time she finished talking, her black eyes were crying blood. Slowly it rolled down the pale face until it soaked her long brown hair. Spots of blood soiled her white dress. It was just then that Abigail realised the dress was a wedding gown. Though she wore no ring, this woman was a Bride. Then yelping in pain whilst clutching her chest, she fell to her knees.

There was so much blood! Abigail sprang up, trying to staunch the flow, but the sticky substance sprayed all over her, coating her hands. Her mouth opened to scream out loud, but nothing emerged, and nobody was there to help apart from dark hands extending from the woodland, taking a grip of the Bride's body. The floaty body was being pulled back into the forest leaving a trail of blood shining on the wet grass in the moonlight. Her whispered cries still pierced the ears. Then halfway to the woods the hands released their grip and the Bride collapsed onto the grass dotted with its summer blooms. The daisies and foxgloves turned red and then the ground swallowed her whole before the mist rolled in again. A tang of iron rose from Abigail's bloody hands, but there was nothing to wipe them on. The moonlight emitted stronger light, bouncing the shine off the thick substance Abigail was covered in.

'The lake, I have to wash this off …' Abigail turned towards the water, but even the lake was full of it. There was blood everywhere. The whisper returned as the reeds clattered together. Not the wind this time: From out of the reeds Josef made his appearance.

'You cannot wash that off, my dear. It's what you must do for love. You need to get your hands dirty, you need some blood on your hands. Only then you can have your man.' Though his voice was more pleasant compared to the Bride's, it still made Abigail step away. His husky, playful voice was frightening. His skinny frame came closer. His feet squelched with each step through the boggy ground in the reeds.

'Only then can I give you what you want. So, listen and listen carefully. You will be offered a ring. You must buy it! This is your only opportunity. If you fail, you will never have him.' He pointed his bony finger towards the lake. The breeze played with the surface, creating ripples Abigail could hear. Beyond that was silence. The reeds were moving soundlessly; not even a frog croaked. It was as if the place were under a spell. A fog bank just above the lake separated where a light shone out. From the deep came a picture of smiling Dan. It floated towards the edge and then flashed away.

'Wake up, numpty, you were crying in your sleep.' Natalie hurled herself onto the seat, causing it to bounce.

'Susan now has plenty to talk about, giggling about it already. Seriously, do you have to embarrass me like this? You're my best friend but sometimes I do wonder why I keep having you around. You're not what you used to be. Just try not to embarrass me anymore.'

Eyes wide, Abigail downed the iron taste in her mouth. 'Sorry' was her only response. Susan was in stitches. Abigail pushed her body deep into the seat hoping for it to swallow her whole. What a strange dream. If only she could have asked someone for an advice. It had felt so real.

**

The destination was ahead, but the unpleasant journey had sapped all Abigail's energy. The motorway sign for Brno beamed ahead. Abigail longed for a shower and a comfy bed to stretch onto. That image was soon replaced with doubt when it turned out Susan and Karen had teamed up to book a cheap hotel.

The girls argued that limited funds had left them no choice. As they stepped off the bus, finally in Brno, the centuries-old architecture and fresh, crispy morning air were revitalising. The bus station was right next to an eighteenth century train station, and its baroque structure was a welcoming sight. Natalie called up a taxi to take them to the hotel. They might as well have walked, seeing as it turned out just minutes from the bus drop-off.

Abigail felt her face drain as soon as they stopped by their hotel.

'Is this it? Seriously, this is where we're going to stay?'

Karen smirked as she handed some cash to the taxi driver.

'What did you expect, princess? A palace?' The old Skoda's suspension jolted as they offloaded their luggage in front of the shabby old door of the so-called hotel. The brown paint was peeling off the door from damp. The taxi took off, leaving them all standing outside.

'Come on girls, I'm sure it's better than it looks. Anyway, it's cheap!' Susan chirped and pulled at the antique handle.

'I bet if you open the door the whole lot will come down,' commented Abigail as she stuck her finger into the cracks in the wall. The facade was completely original, dating from the beginning of the previous century. It certainly was an antique. Susan walked in followed by Karen. Abigail was last in. She'd been right: inside was even worse. The main entrance had what was once upon a time a carpet but was now a flat mix of fibres trying desperately to cling to each other. They checked in with a greasy hair, dull-eyed receptionist lacking any type of form of greeting. The noise of a scratching nail file was the only thing pre-occupying her and her nicotine-stained fingers. Without a word she threw the keys at them after they signed a very yellow visitor book. Their rooms weren't much different in decor. Thankfully Abigail spotted that at least there was a mattress, though after inspection she nearly cut her hand on the springs sticking out.

The smell was only to be described as urine mixed with

old socks. She lobbed her suitcase down onto the floor, which disturbed some cockroaches going about their business. There wasn't even a bathroom, just the room with bed. To make things homier, the bathroom was a shared facility tucked away at the end of the claustrophobic corridor with its warped, mouldy and peeling wallpaper. The cherry on top was that her room was furthest away from the bathroom. To get clean she had to walk through this cockroach-infested passage with its mould and falling plaster. Most likely attending to hygiene here would simply lead to catching some terrible disease in this prehistoric corridor. By the time she got back to her room she would need a second shower. But her exhaustion got the better of her and she let her body fall onto the mattress. Ignoring the springs digging into her spine, she closed her eyes and tried to meditate to counteract wanting to strangle Susan for booking this place. Holding a tequila bottle bought somewhere in Germany, Natalie walked out of her room as Abigail lay there examining the ceiling as if trying to make out if the cracks on the ceiling spelt out some secret message.

'Go on, have a sip. That'll numb you to this rat hole we ended up in. Don't worry, we'll have a good time, promise. I've heard great things about this town.' She took a swig before holding out the bottle, but Abigail shook her head.

'I've only just overcome the travel sickness.' Though Abigail didn't particularly share her excitement, she had to hold the pretence.

'Natalie, I think I need to make my way to the bathroom. My mouth feels … ugh, like a prison full of musty body odour.'

Natalie giggled at the expression. 'Abi, you always come up with the most hilarious expressions.'

After some shuffling through her suitcase, Abigail found her toothbrush. 'You mean like "the food is falling into you like Germans into trenches"?' With a cheeky giggle, Natalie had a sip as Abigail finished looking for her toothpaste.

Abigail couldn't think of anything but a nice hot shower where she could close her eyes and let all the dirt wash away from her body. This relaxing image vanished once the door to the bathroom was opened. The so-called shared shower was like a fifties-bathroom nightmare. The tiles were green and orange with a simple chipped mirror hung on a huge nail above the sink. The sink sported one grey mush of soap, while mould lurked over the taps. Her fist flew at the sink when nothing but cold came out of the hot tap. Her knuckles stung with the impact. Defeated, she stepped into the cold shower cubicle, letting her body be flooded with cold water. The chilly water jolted a flashback from her memory: a dark hand touching her. She was facing the Bride again by the lake, and it felt so real. The wind, her breath mingled with the sound of trees rustling: the chills came up her spine. Her head shook as if she was trying to flick out an insect that had fallen into her hair, but it was hopeless. The image was there, unwilling to leave. It was Natalie's laughter that snapped her back.

'Go on Abigail, don't hog the bathroom, we all want to have a go.'

***

With a muddy taste in her mouth thanks to the yellowish tap water, Abigail made her way back to her room. Susan ran into the bathroom before Karen even had the chance to make it. As Karen was bickering by the closed door, Abigail lay down on the mattress, ignoring the cold metal spring pressing against the back. Suddenly nothing worked: arms, legs, everything paralysed! With her eyes pinned to the ceiling, Abigail recognised the signs: one of her episodes again. But usually it didn't happen in the middle of the day. Her pulse quickened as the door creaked open. Dyna walked in.

'Leave now, Abigail, forget Dan. Do it now or you'll die.' The slight relief that it was Dyna rather than Josef was short-lived. Dyna wasn't ready to answer any questions or to speak.

'Leave now, forget, leave now, forget …' She was like a broken record.

'Go on, Dyna, stop it already! I'm fed up now with the same answer. I heard you and it's not like I can leave, and anyway, why would I die? Lately you're so full of "don't do this, do that".' Dyna's brows moved to frame her eyes into a disapproving look. Her skittishness, her quick, repeated glances at the door, told Abigail she shouldn't have come.

'I have to go. I shall leave you now, as you belong to him. I cannot help, the pathway was shut, but you've re-opened it! I gave you advice you ignored. I'll take my leave but soon I shall see you in hell.' Just like that she was gone. The lights in the room flickered before completely going out. Then the floor started creaking: a new presence entered the room! As it shuffled its feet towards Abigail, quick swishes and scrapes on the floor accompanied each step. She panted; it was the Bride from her dreams. And she was inching towards the bed.

'Go to hell!' Abigail spat, trying to keep control of the situation. Her protests didn't help; her pulse throbbed in her temples. Lifeless, her body lay there, with her breath growing more ragged the closer the Bride got. A little movement distracted her a second. There was someone else in the room! From out of the shadows it made a move towards her. Abigail's eyes darted around the room, looking for more. How many had come?

'I'm here, and I can give you what you want. So near am I that I can feel your need. Yes, I can help, but you must return that favour. What do you wish the most?' This voice belonged to someone else, and it stopped the Bride in her approach. Abigail watch her spectral form floating, gaping at the second presence, maybe even as surprised as

Abigail when the man started speaking. Within seconds the Bride took off into the darkness with a scream. Abigail wanted to shout out for Natalie to come, but only a tiny squeak emerged from her dry throat. The owner of the voice emerged from the shadows and joined Abigail by the bedside. The deep-throated, ghostly, timbre frightened her.

'I know you have doubts. I know everything that is in your mind. I promised to help, so I am here to remind you of that promise. Tomorrow a gypsy will offer you something to buy. You *must* accept it.'

Goosebumps prickled up her arms while a chill froze Abigail's face: slowly, terrifyingly, the monster was stroking her limp arms. Each stroke made the little hairs rise anew. Josef's breath, as it rasped through his yellow teeth, left an eggy smell.

'You need to pay,' he continued, 'and not engage in anything more. If you do as I say, you will be forever happy in Dan's arms. If you don't, you lose everything, and I will let her have you.' His scrawny finger pointed towards the place where the Bride had vanished. Shortly after he finished speaking, his figure retreated into the darkness beyond the doorway and the lights came back on as the door creaked shut. The feeling returned into her arms. In the next room Natalie was roaring with laughter, shouting something through the wall. Surely this had been a dream, caused by tiredness from the long journey. The corner from which Josef had materialised was empty now but it looked as if the curtain had been moved. It must have been the curtain that scared her into thinking someone came to her in the middle of the day. She was imagining things because of the tiredness. Unwilling to brave that bathroom again, she rolled over and searched through her handbag on the bedside table for her happy pills. Knocking them back with some sleeping pills, Abigail hoped she could catch up with much needed sleep. Even the scuttering cockroaches couldn't bother her. It was only the knock on the door, followed by Natalie barging in and throwing water over her face, that woke her the next morning.

'Go on, sleepy head, wake up, we have all day ahead of us.' Reluctantly Abigail opened one eye to be greeted by the sight of Natalie's grin.

'By the way, yesterday I got a bruise on my leg because I walked into the bloody bed when the power cut happened. Susan still thinks that it is the most hilarious thing that happened here.'

'Hold on, what? A power cut?'

'Yes, you're telling me you didn't notice?'

'Um …' Abigail's teeth felt fuzzy as she ran the tongue over them. 'My lights were out by then.' Which was the truth. There was no need to share with Natalie that Abigail was communicating with ghosts in darkness. Last night's goose bumps returned, with the feeling of ants running all over her skin. Just the thought of Josef being behind the power cut! Next Susan barged in from the corridor.

'And then Karen couldn't find her way to the loo,' continued Natalie, 'so she followed through.' Both roared with laughter. That explained the guffawing last night after that strange dream.

'Are you finally happier today and ready to join the living? Ready to have some fun? Seriously, if Karen messes herself again, you'll have plenty to laugh about.' As if to underline the point, she chuckled.

'Seriously, I'm going to use that against her forever!' Susan interrupted Natalie with a smirk.

'By the way, me and Karen have lots of good places to see. We picked them from the guide book and the internet. Put your glad rags on, girl! We're going to have breakfast first, and after that we're going to kickstart this hen party.'

Abigail's positivity remained at a low as Susan stopped in front of their breakfast venue. The golden arches, symbol of international junk cuisine, beamed down at them.

'Susan, Karen, with all the guide books, internet and what not, you chose this? We travelled thousands of miles to have a breakfast at McDonald's? Great choice, both of you, you are truly culinary experts of Eastern European cuisine!'

Karen smirked, ignoring the comment as she stepped inside. Her expression was wiped blank when the cashier, eyes wide, informed her they didn't serve breakfast. Susan insisted on seeing the manager, equally puzzled, who confirmed the breakfast story. They tried asking where they could find one, but all they got was 'Go to your hotel.'

Hungry and bored, they tried to look for some place that served breakfast. The town walkways were surrounded by quirky baroque buildings. Each house sported a different character, each with different detail above the door. One house had a carved animal above the door whilst other had man busy at work. It was gorgeous. At the end they all agreed that unless they wanted to eat cockroach pancake they wouldn't be eating at their hotel. Finally, they made it through an alley to yet another town square and their hopes sparked up again. This time the square, one of many this city had, was missing the water fountain the previous one had. This was smaller, but the shops more modern. As pointed out by Susan, this city didn't have one dedicated town centre. The little alleys all ran higgledy piggledy like octopus tentacles. A flock of hungry pigeons fluttered down to them.

What made this town centre more appealing was the unique architecture. One building had carved pillars with male figures supporting the huge structure upon their shoulders. Each of these men wore a different expression. One thing they shared was the stance of exhaustion: they really looked as if holding the facade of the building was hard work. At the same time, they exuded pure strength, one looking onto the visitors in defiance, another bearing a look of pain.

Abigail admired the stonework, transfixed. Minutes later, when she looked up, the girls were nowhere to be seen. Frantically she dived into the nearest little street, taking an educated guess of where her friends might have gone. When something grasped her arm she nearly screamed, but as she whipped around to see who had grabbed her, she was met by a woman in rags. Still, her eyes, dark as coal, made Abigail shiver. She couldn't understand what the woman was saying.

'Sorry about my mother,' said a voice. Abigail's eyes darted towards the sound to see a young woman with long, black hair tied up into a ponytail. Her green and red skirt swept the cobblestones. 'She would like to read your palm.' The little gypsy woman clasping Abigail's palm eye her up quizzically. Her petite frame held a proud head with jet black hair tied into a bun with a floral scarf. The young woman who could speak English was a little taller. The resemblance was uncanny. The old gypsy took a deep breath and pointed at the lines on Abigail's skin as the daughter translated.

'Your future is there. Would you like to hear it?' Abigail scanned her surroundings for her friends as if she needed help with her decision. Her curiosity took hold.

'OK, what can you see?'

The old gypsy turned her gaze fully at her palm. She was a good actress: dramatically she went into a "trance", mumbling incoherently. Her daughter shook her and together they had a little argument. The old woman threw something into the daughter's hand and pointed at Abigail.

'I am so sorry about this, but she cannot read your palm. It is too sad! You are in danger! It usually doesn't go like this, so please accept this gift as an apology.' From her hand she passed a little silver cross that lay mixed in among all sorts of other trinkets. Something else caught Abigail's eye. It was gold. Between all that rubbish there was just one simple gold band. With experience of antiques hunting at boot sales in the UK, Abigail guessed it to be from the fourteenth century. Instead of taking the cross she lifted the gold band.

'Can I have this one?' The old gypsy started mumbling again and crossing her chest repeatedly. The daughter pushed her away.

'Please excuse my mother. She really isn't herself today. This ring was only found this morning in the nearby woodlands. You can have it, but I must charge you!' After agreeing a price of 500 koruna, Abigail passed the notes onto the gypsy. The old woman became really agitated, shouting at the young one, then grabbing the cross and pressing it to Abigail's forehead. Now screaming the same sentence, she held the cross there. The cross was burning her forehead but somehow, she couldn't move. It was Karen with Susan that swung her around.

'Where the hell have you been? We've been looking all over for you! Natalie's gone to check the other street for you, so she should be near. You should stay away from those gypsies. Didn't you read the guide book?' Abigail wanted to show them the ring, but the old gypsy grabbed her hand trying to prise off it out of her closed fist.

'Go away, leave me alone, help! I am being robbed! Police!' The old gypsy woman was chanting something in Czech. Her daughter tried to help to wrench free her mother's hand. Natalie came running and with a little shove the gypsy was thrown away from Abigail. The old gypsy got back on her feet. She stopped shouting but kneeled before Natalie. With dilated pupils she muttered something as she kissed Natalie's hands.

'What is she doing? Why is she kissing my hands, what is she saying?' Natalie's voice quavered, making her sound worried. It was the daughter that spoke:

'I am so sorry about my mother. I don't know what's with her, she isn't normally like this. She really lost it today!' Then she addressed Natalie directly.

'Apparently, I am meant to warn you to stay away from the evil one, the one that bought the ring. She can't have it, as once she has it she will cause menace. Take it away from her, run away, go back home. That's what my mother wants me to tell you.' Natalie didn't have the chance to ask more questions, as the police turned up. They took notes but as nothing was stolen and the young gypsy apologised so they didn't get involved any further.

A young man who had been watching this with the crowd of spectators turned out to be a great help in settling things down. His English was good enough for him to translate to the policeman what had been happening. When the police left, he turned towards a shocked Natalie. 'I am sorry this happened to you. How can I make it better so that you know that Moravian folk are a friendly bunch, not loonies?'

It was Abigail who spoke first. 'You can take us to the nearest place that serves fresh coffee and cake, so we can at least put some breakfast into our bellies!'

Natalie regained her confidence and locked her arm into his. 'Go on girls, there's a good little shop just around the corner, just follow me.' Natalie chatted non-stop all the way to the shop.

'That daft woman started to shout something and frightened the shit out of me.'

With his broken English he responded, 'I suppose you would like to know what she was shouting about.'

Karen, in desperate need of having a bloke, tried to flirt a little. 'The thing I want to know is what your name is, handsome.'

Abigail rolled her eyes. 'Seriously, Karen, are you truly that desperate?'

'Just ignore Abigail, she only joined us on this hen trip so she can pull. Don't expect anything else,' sneered Karen.

The man smiled back. 'Well, I am Petr, and I can happily translate for you what her daughter didn't.'

Karen went for pull-line number two and responded with a husky voice. 'Oh, do tell us, we are most intrigued.'

She was completely engrossed in his big brown eyes above his long but nicely shaped nose. It suited him as it fit his tall, wiry body. Karen sidled up to him to gesture that he was hers, so Natalie stepped away and let Karen take his arm.

'The lady is a known gypsy in town, though I've never seen her in this mood before. She really was acting strangely.'

He looked at Natalie. 'When she grabbed you, she said you're a dead woman walking! Someone has taken a fancy to your man. And apparently, the devil will succeed. The rest you were told by her daughter.' Petr then pointed at Abigail.

'When she grabbed your hand, she was asking you to give it back.'

'Most strange that is,' Susan piped up. 'Are you sure she just didn't want some money for the performance of scaring us? Abigail, what did you buy from her?'

Now wasn't the right time to advertise that Abigail managed to get herself the bargain of a century, so she brushed the question aside with a shrug. 'Oh, just a trinket, nothing of value. Ohhh ... this place looks like good place to eat.'

'That's the exact place I was taking you,' chirped Petr as he pulled the entrance door and a little bell sounded above. The smell of fresh coffee was inviting indeed. The little tables added to the cosy décor. Once they ordered they all got chatting to Petr about charm of this city. In a true Moravian style, Petr agreed to be their guide for the day if there was a pint of beer at the end of it.

Abigail only listened with one ear as her focus was on the gypsy. She was sure to hear the old gypsy repeating "Josef". She stroked the ring inside her pocket, thinking if this had been the thing she'd been supposed to buy. It had to be real, coincidences like this didn't happen often. Josef was real! The gypsy must have known about him as she spoke to Natalie about losing her man. Not one pang of regret that Abigail felt for Natalie was if the future was going to unfold as the gypsy foretold. Abigail was ready to do anything to have Dan. Josef was there to get her what she desired most: he said so himself the night before. To ensure she didn't lose the ring, she slipped it onto her finger. Its heavy circle fitted perfectly. As soon as it found its place on the ring finger, her thumb was stroking it with desire. With each stroke the ring fit more snugly as if it was moulding to her skin. Abigail didn't want to be parted from it.

***

Petr took the girls around the town and characterised the Moravian people as friendly folks resembling hobbits. They loved their land, which gave them the materials to make their own brew. Their beer was a national treasure. Basically, Moravians settle their own affairs over a good cold beer. To emphasise the fact, Petr took them to the church of Saint Jacob in Rasinova Street.

'Ladies, this church is my proof. Just look at this ancient building, the house of God. Does it look serious to you?'

Abigail felt uncomfortable to be in the proximity of a church. Somehow, she didn't enjoy its tall structure. To keep the conversation to a minimum, she blurted, 'of course it's serious, it's another boring church, which is something you can find nearly everywhere around the world.'

Petr smiled, led the girls to one side of the main entrance and pointed up to one of gothic windows. With dislike, Abigail stepped closer to the church despite the ring tightening around her finger like a serpent.

'I'm sure you've already noticed that this beautiful gothic building has no gargoyles? A gothic building must have these, right?'

Karen giggled pathetically while Natalie stared at the stonework, squinting her eyes towards top of the gothic window. Petr carried on as he felt he would soon lose his audience.

'To give you the full picture, I need to give you the whole story. The history goes the town needed a church. The town council sent a message to the many craftsmen around to ask who would take on the job. Two craftsmen wanted the money but in typical Moravian way, council would only pay for one church. Being council, they couldn't make their minds up as to who to choose. After a cold nice beer, they decided whoever finished building the church first would be the one to get paid. The loser would have to walk away with nothing.' Petr pointed to another church in the distance.

'Those church towers you see in the distance are the loser's church. That's why this church has no gargoyles, because the builder cut the work short by going less fancy, so he could finish on time.' Before Petr could carry on, Natalie interrupted and pointed back at the church beside them.

'Ha, you are wrong! Look there's a gargoyle!'

Petr smiled. 'Well spotted. That is my main point. Though the craftsman won, he did spend time on this single gargoyle after the payment had been made. In true Moravian style, it sends a message. Hence it is only above this window facing the losing church. Look closely, what do you see?'

Abigail's patience was running short. By now the ring was strangling her finger. 'Who cares what's there. Let's get a move on.'

Karen ignored the remark and burst out laughing. 'Look, it's a human backside! It's mooning us!' Petr kindly clarified for them that little piece of history.

'It's an angel holding his little hand on his buttocks, mooning the loser's church. Though, if you look closer it has even deeper meaning. From below you think it's an angel but when look directly at it, it's a man and a woman locked into a passionate, ehm, well, you know what I mean.'

Natalie roared with laughter, sending spatters of her spit everywhere. Abigail couldn't manage the pain anymore. Somehow, she didn't want to laugh, but run. Her feet kept pushing her further away from the church. Petr was savouring their surprise.

'What did I say about the Moravians? The town council did notice this little detail, but that was way after the architect was paid. They settled the affair in a local pub. Clearly, they were not going to pay him again to do additional work so what I am led to believe he had apologised to the priest. That was it. What would be the point of taking it down? He had won a bet after all! However, ladies, there is another side to the story. The historians believe this poor craftsman wasn't paid. He was a known joker so when he was asked at least to finish this window, he happily accepted. The result you can see here.'

'Awesome, this is the only church I've ever seen that has pornography on it!' Abigail grabbed their guide by his arm. 'Hey, let's get a move on.'

'Abigail, don't be such a grumpykins. Go on, don't you find this hilarious? Right, let's go inside!' It was the rash turn of her friend's neck that made Abigail freeze in her step. She could feel her eyebrows sinking with madness and rage.

'I said, we're going!'

After that, Petr somewhat curtailed the town history: with Abigail's mood, it was uncomfortable to stay in one place for long. Abigail scanned his expression, and it told her that it was the unspoken vibes between her and Natalie that worried him. Then he told them the story of a drunken bet that resulted in a large wheel being installed on one of the walls near the town hall.

'Now we know what the wheel is for, but what's the croc about?' Susan pointed above her head.

Petr crinkled his nose. 'Nobody really remembers, but apparently, the crocodile had been swimming in the local river and to get rid of him, the townsfolk fed him meat with stones, so he sank and died. The other theory is that he was a gift from a Turkish king but due to our cold winters he perished in the frost.' Petr looked to be deep in his thoughts for a little while as if contemplating as to what else to say.

'There are many variations on the crocodile story. You pick the one you like best! Now I'll show you one more interesting building, the old town hall. After that we're going to enjoy some of our best local beer.'

'Finally,' mumbled Abigail in bored fashion. The sun was beaming heat down, so it was about time they stopped to refresh. Large oak doors opened to a small pathway facing a building with five very lavish tall stonework pyramids.

'Why is the middle one broken?' Natalie's hand shot up with extended index finger.

'It's most likely not broken,' answered Susan. 'After the stories I heard today, I bet that there was some bet or beer involved.'

Petr agreed. 'You're right. Despite the money shortage, the town council decided on lavishly carved stone obelisks above the entrance. At the end they only budgeted for simple work and when the master craftsman was finishing the last one they told him they would only pay for some of his work, unable to afford the lot. A Moravian never leaves his work unfinished, and you can see the result. It's the craftsman's message to everyone that the local town council is bent.'

Petr took a glance in Abigail's direction. From the way he looked at her, trying not to stare, yet landing his eyes on her far too often, Abigail concluded she made him uneasy. She fidgeted with her nails, flicked her fingers, then spoke up. 'Right, are you going to take us somewhere to eat now? I'm sick of all the history.'

Susan smacked her lips. 'I must admit, I'm hungry too.'

Petr took them to a restaurant called Švejk Restaurant & Pension. Outside it didn't look too fancy but the smell of roasts and spice wafted out invitingly. Abigail's stomach rumbled as they took the stairs up. A waitress showed them to a neat table with red-and-blue checked tablecloth. Susan took a quizzical look at the food that other people were tucking into. Each plate seemed to be accompanied by a golden pint.

'It all looks delicious. Petr, what should I have, what would you recommend?' Petr ordered everyone a beer and downed his first two pints in seconds. Then as a king upon his throne sipped his third pint slowly, enjoying each last drop of the golden nectar. After a relaxing belch he commented:

'The third is the one you need to enjoy! The first two only kill the thirst.' He belched again but nobody bothered to give him a stare. Abigail noticed that Susan had gone all gooey again over him.

'Petr, this part of the Czech Republic is so relaxing, kind, human. I wish England weren't as stuck up as it is now. I wish people could just belch in public. The English are so reserved!'

Petr furrowed his brow. 'Well, being Moravian is like being a hobbit: you keep quiet about the dark stuff, about the history you're not proud of. There are plenty of sad stories I can tell you but as I am a Moravian I would rather pretend they never happened. There's too much misery around each day, so there's no need to remind us of misery and sadness of the past. We have to have a laugh in our lives.'

He took a swig from his last pint. 'OK, ladies, I have some work to attend to, so I must make a move. This place is really nothing much in décor, but they compensate with the wonderful food. As your company is a true pleasure, I would love to invite you to meet me and my friends tonight.' He sent a cheeky wink into Susan's direction.

Karen pulled out the town map to discuss where to meet while Susan kept batting her eyelashes at him. Petr concentrated on Karen's questions, but you could tell his mind was on Susan. By now they were exchanging guilty glances.

'Here we will meet up.' Petr pointed on a place at the map.

'It's a thirteenth century themed underground pub where they make the beer the old-fashioned way by using honey!'

The waitress came with plates laden with food, so Karen tidied her map to make space. Petr handed her a note with the address and crude drawing of where it was supposed to be just in case. Then he scribbled his mobile number down just before he left. Through the chatter each girl tucked into her food.

'I can't wait to meet Petr again with his friends!' peeped Susan. Winking at Abigail she said, 'Maybe there will be a man in there for you, Abi.'

Karen, though unwillingly, accepted that she has no chance with Petr. 'Ok, Susan, he is yours, but you do make sure you stick to him and not decide to go for his friends, as it's my turn now'.

'Of course, hun,' stroked Susan Karen's hand.

Abigail couldn't care less about men as she wanted just the one, though she felt a little excitement at the prospect of having a party. The only showstopper was the ring on her finger, as if it tried to focus her on what she was supposed to do. It kept burning on her hand throughout the day. She tried to ignore it but was glad that the day was running out quickly. The shopping seemed to drag on and on, so she was glad to be finally standing with her friends in front of the Stredoveka Krcma, or Medieval Tavern. As promised, Petr was already waiting for them with his friends.

'English girls are popular,' he said, grinning as he introduced them. Abigail couldn't remember them all:

some of those names were tongue twisters. But one guy grabbed her attention. He had one of those unpronounceable names, but she reckoned after a couple of pints she could get at least part of it right. Still, at the end it turned into vowels and consonants of unknown origins. Written down, his name was Zbynek, but out of Abigail's mouth it was an approximation, at best.

He had gorgeous jet-black hair with green eyes to match. Being from Eastern Europe he had an attractive large square jaw. He spoke little English but that didn't matter too much. Once all exchanged their names it was time to traipse down the dark, gloomy staircase into the underground. They were seated at a table with goatskin on solid wood benches. The whole place was lit up by candles. The glasses were made as they would have been in the thirteenth century to match the pub's décor.

The servers grinned and loaded one beer after another onto the table. The hen night had finally started: the girls were drinking with good company. Petr came onto Susan and they went in for one snog after another. Natalie, as always, was surrounded by three men trying to gain her attention and Karen was so drunk she fell asleep on the table.

When Zbynek leaned towards Abigail, she mistook his intentions and leaned in for a snog. When he came up for air, he only managed to say, 'OK, I was going to ask ...' before Abigail threw herself onto him again.

Not sure whether it was the sound of traffic that woke her or the migraine, Abigail was surprised to find herself in the hotel bed. She could only squint; the sunlight hurt. Her hand shot up to cover her eyes as she tried to delve deep into her memory to remember what had happened the previous night. She wasn't sure ... Had she slept with Zbynek along the way?

'I am never, ever drinking again!' she mumbled as her body tried its best to sit up in bed to help her wake up. On her way to the appalling bathroom, she overheard a conversation between Susan and Karen.

'Jeez, Susan, did you really sleep with him? You're such a floozy!' A cranky, drunken voice answered.

'Karen, I'd rather be sleeping with a man than being dragged out of a pub completely paralytic. Seriously, at one point we were thinking of calling an ambulance to check your pulse!'

***

The few days they had in the Czech Republic flew past very quickly. The stay in Brno come to an end, and Abigail was strangely happy about going back, though at the time the ride back clouded her mind. The only positive was that this time the journey felt shorter, thanks to a strong cocktail of sleeping pills and diazepam. Abigail wanted to be on her own, so the deep sleep facilitated that. She had had enough of listening to Natalie on how she couldn't wait to see Dan. Now she had the ring she had new hope that things would change.

***

Abigail made it to work on Monday only to find Natalie telling everyone about the hen night.

'Oh yeah, Susan and Abigail might have more stories to tell. Observations, I shall say. They can describe in detail exactly what the Czech men are like, size wise, you know what I mean!'

Everyone giggled, but clearly Susan wasn't much pleased with Natalie. 'All right, we did sleep with the locals! Here goes Abigail, go, pester her but leave me alone. I have so much work to catch up with!'

Despite the sleeping pill hangover, Abigail felt it was going to be a great day – Karen was also in a bad mood and Natalie kept going on and on about the hen night and her wedding plans. Thankfully everyone left her alone. Maybe it was the expression on her face that did it, but nobody followed Susan's suggestion of quizzing her on the hen trip. The vampire-like skin and bloodshot eyes Abigail had noticed on herself earlier probably weren't particularly inviting. It was Natalie that broke the silence just before lunch.

'Abigail, will you go with me for the dress rehearsal please? I need you there to help me pick the right dress.'

The ring started throbbing again on Abigail's finger. With her head still down to dissuade conversation, she didn't appreciate this lunch-time disruption. Natalie must have known she would decline or try to scarper, which is why she approached as a lioness would stalk prey. The last thing Abigail wanted was to be involved in the "wedding" conversations. She tried to get out of it anyway.

'Sure, Nat, when are you planning to go? You see I can't go. Boss has set a meeting with me.' The lie was immediately shot to bits.

'Silly Abigail, I mean go right now. Look, it's lunch time anyway. I know the boss has just gone out for lunch so it's extremely unlikely he'd ask you to meet with him when he is not here!' Bother! Abigail had not expected her to say to go now. The was no way she could manoeuvre out of this.

'Nat, I'm not sure I can go now.' She had to try it on by pointing at the pile of paperwork that lay on her desk for the exact purpose of getting herself out of uncomfortable lunch time offers.

'Abigail don't try to fob me off with this old excuse. I invented it! You must come, pleeeease! It would mean the world to me if you could come.' Natalie's puppy eyes followed as she stopped talking.

'Jeez, all right, I will go but promise you'll be quick? Just give me a couple of minutes to finish this off.' They left the office together ten minutes later. Sadly, it got more uncomfortable as now Dan had decided to join.

'Hello, two of my favourite girls.' Dan was in a good mood. A throaty "hello" was all Abigail managed. Natalie threw herself into his arms.

'Oh darling, I'm so excited,' Natalie purred into Dan's ear.

Meanwhile, Abigail despised their happiness behind them, her ring throbbing as if it was mimicking her mood. She hadn't expected to get to the shop at all but celebrated the fact she did despite of the couple's ridiculously embarrassing behaviour. They were like teenagers stopping every second to kiss each other. It was hard to ignore them. At least finally Abigail paid attention to her town's architecture. There wasn't much interest in looking around as she only moved in because it was small enough to keep things private but large enough to have all commodities on hand when needed. It was old fashioned with a nice market place surrounded by mostly Victorian buildings.

The bridal shop was one of those Georgians property with large windows. This allowed them to display vast dresses in the huge tall shop windows. The lady inside was already beckoning them in.

'Welcome, come to the back. I've prepared the three dresses your mother chose. I beg your pardon; I was meant to say your future mother-in-law.'

Natalie pulled a long face.

'I sent you my ideas for a dress. Were they included?'

'Yes, they were, exactly as you asked, but Mrs Johnston requested to see them yesterday and picked these three out of the bunch.' Dan placed a quick peck on Natalie's cheek and left the shop.

'It's bad luck if I see the dress.' That's exactly what Abigail was hoping for, some good bad luck. She was imagining all of it, the locusts, train accidents or possibly fatal car accidents. With these wicked reflections, the ring gave final pause and stopped throbbing. The thoughts kept flooding her mind as her thumb stroked the now-silent ring.

Natalie disappeared with the dressmaker into the back of the shop as Abigail sat down on a squidgy seat by the changing rooms. The whole shop smelled of moth balls mixed with perfume. The radio was playing in the background, but it was hard to make out what group was singing. A couple of people walked in to book some dress fittings but apart from that the whole shop was empty. Only the clattering of the shop keeper's heels overpowered the radio. The only time Abigail was disturbed was when Natalie walked out of the changing room dressed in her final dress choice. It was beautiful. Natalie made the dress look like a million dollars.

'Natalie, I'm not sure if I should say this, not having seen the other two, but seriously, this one's perfect. So beautiful!'

A smile crept over her face: the kind that made the eyes sparkle and turned the cheeks into little apples. Some people might call this kind of closed-mouth smile a sign of smugness. Either way, it was clear this was exactly what she'd wanted to hear. She booked delivery to her home on the day before the wedding. On their way back to the office, Abigail faced the Spanish inquisition about Natalie's dress. Each answer felt like a stab in the back. The ring was throbbing again, and Abigail's mind got more clouded. That was *her* dress, she was the one destined to wear it!

***

By the close of day Abigail's mental state was shattered. To distract her mind, she put on the stereo, and when her favourite song came on it opened the flood gates. Joni Mitchell's "Both Sides Now" blasted from the speakers to drown her cries in music. It was this song that she dreamed of listening to when cooking dinner for her husband. She would walk around with a glass of wine, doing random things such as chopping carrots until a hand would grab her from behind. A gentle kiss would land on her ear and that hand would turn her head towards his lips. A wonderful long, needy kiss would follow.

'Keep your eyes shut, honey, I want to kiss your face all over,' a husky voice would say. This song would come on again and this dream guy would just sway her hips with hers, until his hands would slide down her back, and lower. To the mellow sound of the saxophone, he'd caress her; pressure in all the right places.

His hands would slide up to her nipples, stroking all her favourite spots, while she stepped out of her knickers and pushed him onto the kitchen chair, gently sitting him down with her on top, feeling him inside. Exactly like that, up and down until they were all spent. Abigail dreamed this each time this song came on. How many guys would know this music? Answer: probably not a single bloke in existence, it being a depressing girlie song.

'And now I'll never get to test it on the man destined for me, now that Dan has been stolen from me!' Abigail sobbed to herself. This stupid fantasy featured Dan, obviously. It was only a wish that could never come true. First, Dan did not even know she had these thoughts about him. Second, even if he knew, he would never do anything about it with Natalie's claws in him. She wasn't planning to leave him either, so there was no chance that they would ever be an item.

The song finished but the tears kept coming. This music therapy works. Not many people knew listening to music helped Abigail to express herself. As she listened, all the emotions come up to the surface. That night it was around one o'clock that she finally fell asleep. And then it happened again.

As her eyelids closed before exhaustion set in, darkness grew in her room, swallowing all moonlight. With her eyes firmly shut, the chill penetrated her skin, even though the radiators were on. The traffic sounds from outside got replaced with a gentle breeze and the humming of pine trees swaying with it. She saw herself back at the strange place, and her feel felt cold as she stood barefoot on moist grass. Her finger with the ring burnt into her skin, glowing bright orange. Abigail wanted to see what she was holding as her fingers were clasping something. It was twigs she held but the orange glow the ring was emitting revealed she was covered in blood. It was everywhere, spilling from between the trees. And then Natalie walked towards her, with tears coming out of her hollow eye sockets.

'Abigail, Abigail, I'm so lost. Please help me, don't kill me, please, help me. I love you like a sister, give me this ring, give it to me!' Then another voice came in from the black night. Its sound was harder, sharper than Natalie's.

'Don't give this up or you will be giving up on him. Keep it safe with you.' Abigail's whole body shook awake. 'No, no-no-no-no!' That night it happened as if on a loop. Each time waking was uncomfortable as if someone was standing there at the end of the bed: just a figure, breathing quietly, completely still as if trying not to break eye contact, though no eyes were to be seen. It was just a silhouette. Each time she woke at the sight of the figure there, standing, watching. Each time she asked herself whether she was seeing things, she fell asleep again, then woke up, until finally she dropped into an exhausted sleep.

***

The days were dragging along, time playing with Abigail like a cat with its prey. At work the atmosphere was getting tougher but the only comfort she received was in the knowledge that she had the ring. Quietly she stroked it to calm herself though spite and hate was taking over.

Susan stopped speaking to her. Over and over the boss kept asking her to come into his office, asking what the trouble was. All Abigail wanted was to shout at him that of course she was feeling horrendous. Still, the twit asked repeatedly, like a broken record.

Abigail was used to going for lunch with Natalie talking endlessly about life, supporting each other, but now the lunches were dull as they mainly consisted of blabbing on about the wedding preparations. She kept boring everyone with her wedding magazines, bridal hair, etc, etc. Nobody was safe eating sandwiches on the office sofa. Natalie would ram a wedding magazine under their nose despite everyone trying to hide between the cushions.

'See this? What a wonderful idea! You can rent chair covers to match any wedding dress with a bow in colours of the groom's waistcoat. How delightful! Isn't it? Should I go for it?'

If Natalie was prepared to get Abigail's honest answer it would most likely to be something like –

'You can also use that lovely bow to tie around your neck and hang yourself on it to give us all a break!' Instead Abigail had to choose the words carefully.

'I'm not sure, Nat, you'd better speak to Dan. His mother might have some different ideas. Isn't she the one who's been helping you with the planning?' It was clear that mentioning her mother-in-law was a below the belt comment, given how they couldn't stand each other. That was exactly why Abigail did it.

'I hate that woman. She's changing everything I want at my wedding. She keeps manipulating Dan into agreeing. I tell you now that once we're married I'll only see her at a special occasion.'

Thankfully it winded her so much she set off and left Abigail alone. After that, she stopped mentioning the wedding, apart from sending an invite to check one of the venues she'd chosen. Great. Another

Saturday ruined. Abigail smacked the keyboard so hard the keys sprang loose.

***

When Abigail left the office, she bumped into Natalie in the car park chatting to Dan by his FAFC – the Fucking Absolutely Fabulous Car. If Dan were hers, she'd clean that bloody thing in nothing but a spritz of Chanel No 5, she thought to herself, smirking as she approached the car. Typically, Natalie was already complaining about it.

'Oh, it's so noisy,' she kept blabbing on. That was the whole bloody point of having an Aston Martin, to hear the power when you hit the accelerator. Natalie caught Abigail looking.

'Abigail, are you going to be able to come with us to check the hotel now? We have a meeting there to speak about the arrangements. His mother changed the time, so it's no longer Saturday.'

Dan wasn't convinced it was a good idea.

'Natalie, Abigail might have plans already. She might not want to spend the whole evening with the two of us.'

Not the two of them, but if it were only Dan, Abigail's answer would yes. She almost dared to speak the truth.

'No, no plans. Let me join you. I can come if you really need me there. I'm interested to see it.' She was going to do anything if I meant spending a bit of time near him. Breathe the same air, smell his aftershave, listen to his voice.

'Wonderful, Abigail, I'm so pleased you can come. I'll show you our honeymoon suite. I saw the photos of it in their brochure, but I bet it's a thousand times better in reality!' Dan placed his arms around both women's shoulders and gave them a light squeeze. His aftershave lingered, and the soft cotton of his shirt pressed against Abigail's skin through her thin blouse. No matter that the concrete of the car park felt cold, her whole body warmed at this touch.

'Go on, my two favourite girls. We have work to do and if you both behave I'll treat you to a meal at the hotel.

There's only one problem. With the car being a two-seater, I can only transport one of you.'

He produced the keys from his pocket and jingled them in their faces. Natalie rolled her eyes whilst Abigail beamed with excitement. 'So which one of you will be the lucky lady?'

An uncomfortable pause settled around them. Abigail didn't want to jump around and shout "me, me pick me", though it was obvious that Natalie wasn't interested at all.

'Dan, you're making out like it's an honour to sit in that metal box with the seats that dig into your spine! It's an old rust bucket.' Dan's smile disappeared. He looked at his toes.

'Silly mare, it's sporty, not uncomfortable!' blabbed Abigail. 'It's a classic!'

Dan picked his head back up. 'Ah, go on, I don't care, I'll never go anywhere in that car ever again. Once was enough.' Natalie shuffled towards the only other car parked there, a little red Mini. After some fumbling in her handbag she found her key. Winding down her car window, she shouted, 'See you there – if you ever get there in one piece!'

***

This is awesome, Abigail cheered to herself as she made herself comfortable on the passenger seat. Dan strapped himself in and turned on the engine. It was purring like a tamed lioness. No point looking for the radio as there wasn't one. If only Dan knew what was running through Abigail's head. All she could think of was how much this car turned her on. The brown leather upholstery carefully hand-stitched. The lovely polished wood hand-built for the dashboard. All of this was giving her a high. Glancing at Dan behind the wheel created the need to run her hand across his leg, slowly. She wanted to whisper in his ear, in a low, gruff voice, to drive, to concentrate on driving while she'd unzip him and take the whole package into her mouth and he'd grunt with pleasure. Until he'd drag her out of the car, throw her over the bonnet and rip her knickers off.

Natalie never was a good secret keeper so during their "girl talk" she revealed the fact that he hadn't been that well satisfied with her, who liked things perfect. She wouldn't do it anywhere apart from her bed nor did she like to experiment. Sod it, for Dan, if he wanted to do it with another girl Abigail was ready to share him. She'd have done anything he asked. He was seriously missing out!

By the time they turned up at the hotel her knickers were wet. Natalie was waiting, already tapping her foot in disgust. Abigail made Dan take the long way, so she could savour this fabulous car for a little longer.

The hotel was wonderful, sort of modern gothic with plenty of character, and two huge columns inviting visitors to enter. A man ran towards them once they disembarked the car with plenty of paperwork in his hands. He extended his arm in greeting balancing the paperwork in the other.

'Hello, my name's Stephen. Mrs Johnson asked me to meet you here today. Please follow me. I'll take you to the main room, where the magic happens!'

He stretched an arm towards the hotel entrance. Abigail was still distracted as the only magic would be to seek out all the places that could offer privacy. Was there a gazebo in the private gardens perhaps in which she could finish herself? Her "loins" as they called it in romance novels, were truly throbbing. Clearly Abigail wouldn't have made it in a romance novel. None of those flowery words could describe this feeling. She was just plain horny.

That bloody car and Dan, she should have declined going with him and gone for the Mini instead. The only sexy thing about a Mini was the gay bloke driving it! Dan noticed that she was looking at his crotch. To try to remedy her bad behaviour she threw her head in the other direction.

Natalie poked Abigail in the shoulder. Thankfully she hadn't noticed it. 'Go on guys, let's check this place out!' Her golden hair disappeared in the large wooden door hotel entrance with Stephen scuttering along. Abigail followed, still trying not to look at Dan. Inside, both were dragged to the room Natalie chose. As Abigail followed her, she even started considering shagging Stephen, who was clearly gay. The sex-deprived cannot be picky; beggars can't be choosers. If only he'd been prepared to bring mates.

Abigail was that desperate that one of the receptionists had her thinking of the practicalities of putting on a strap-on. Anything was a better distraction than the painful thought that the wedding was going ahead. The ring was emitting a low burn continuously, so she got used to it, but what made things difficult was trying to ignore that things were still going ahead. Thankfully Stephen rammed one of their brochures of different menu choices into her hands. It was like a cold shower. The wedding: it was happening. Dan was far further from her reach than ever. Her stomach turned.

The menus were extortionate but that didn't worry Natalie. Why would it? She wasn't the one paying. Dan's family was footing the bill, despite tradition. That was why Natalie's family kept quiet about it and left Dan's mother to sort things out.

By the sound of it, Dan's mother was a very skilful manipulator who'd managed to change things to her ideal wedding rather than Natalie's. That was why Natalie was so strung out. Though Natalie tried not to show it, the occasional lack of makeup, the unwashed hair were all signs. She wasn't Mrs Perfect anymore. The dark circles could no longer could be hidden underneath concealer.

The hotel staff took them around the rooms where the food would be served. It was a large rectangular area with enough space for dining tables and a large podium in the corner. A nice little bar was tucked in the other.

'This is perfect!' Natalie beamed. 'We'll have a band there, and please remember we want the bar open the whole time.'

Natalie was good at bossing other people around. The fact that she had a large pound sign attached to her forehead made Stephen her best friend. It was his job, as the hotel wedding manager, to keep any spending bride as happy as possible. He had to make sure whatever she wanted was agreed to. For Natalie it was easy to spend someone else's money.

Abigail really wished that she could go around spending someone's money, but there wasn't any husband to marry. She was getting sourer the closer the wedding got. Sour puss was most likely what she'd end up, a dried out old prune with a walking stick bashing everyone on the head should they want to show affection in public.

Yes, she would become one of those old ladies protesting kissing in public places, writing letters to the government to ban kissing on moral grounds and protection of public health.

As Natalie ran around showing sketches of her table seating arrangements, she dreamed of having her own wedding, right there. She despised the fact that it would never be her dream to live. Turning away from Natalie, she stole a peek at Dan. He was standing there looking serious, his top button undone.

She couldn't take it anymore! The ring throbbing, the hate bubbling inside, she went into the hallway to escape. Her hands clasped the marble fireplace as she tried to control her breathing. The oversized mirror with its antique cracked glass above her showed her reflection: enlarged nostrils, the clenched teeth, the scrunched eyebrows. Her reflection had her hypnotised. Only the clattering of a metal tray on the tiled floor tore her gaze away. It was a waitress who was now picking up pieces from the floor. Her hands were shaking. Stephen ran in to check on the noise. Natalie and Dan followed. 'What the hell were you doing?' Stephen snapped at the waitress as he helped her by grabbing bits and pieces and plonking them onto the tray. The waitress skittishly glanced at Abigail and whispered, loudly enough for Abigail to hear:

'It was the mirror, it was the mirror …' She was shaking so much Stephen shooed her away.

'Go on, I'll finish this up. Go and have a break, you're all over the place.' Crying, the waitress ran off. Stephen tidied up apologetically when he noted Natalie standing behind. Abigail saw her chance.

'Sorry guys, I forgot to say I have to get home. You carry on, I'll get a cab.' Dan looked disappointed.

'Are you sure? I'm treating you to dinner. The food is wonderful. Do stay.'

'No, I have to go. Really, don't worry.' And with that she dashed off.

Chapter 4

The worst had come – the wedding was only a week away. A whole seven days away, if you looked at it from the positive, or from the negative, just seven days closer to Natalie's wedding. Abigail hated the moments of seeing Dan in the office just working, keeping an eye on the task at hand, ignoring the whole world around him. Just sitting there concentrating, oblivious to everything else. Abigail found it hard to focus and was flicking her pen between her fingers, quietly tapping it on the desk. On occasion she saw the glance Dan gave her but thankfully Natalie hadn't noticed. She was going through a spreadsheet, her nose nearly stuck to the computer screen, frowning.

Ring ring! That was the only thing that unglued Natalie's nose from her screen. Abigail's ears pricked up.

'Yeah, the flowers?' Pause. 'OK great, I'll come take a look!' She jumped up and scratched in her handbag. 'Right, give me twenty minutes.' With a grin plastered to her face she skipped off to the door as Abigail pretended to look deeply into her papers, massaging her temples, trying to be more convincing. Shuffling and clattering sounds from across the office made her look up again later. It was Dan packing up to go for lunch. With Natalie still out, she saw an opportunity.

'Have anything planned for lunch, Dan?' He looked up from fishing his wallet out of his drawer.

'Not really. Want to join me in the park?' *Doh, of course I would, you dummy*. The words echoed in Abigail's head, although she chose her words wisely. 'Yeah, sounds alright. Looks like everyone else has taken off, so it would be nice, thanks.'

They walked to the park like in the old days. 'Hey, do you remember the time we got completely plastered the first Friday you started?'

He laughed. 'Ha! Do I remember? Of course! To this day I still can't recall how the hell you got me home, though.'

For Abigail this was what she wanted, it was what they'd had before he fell in love with Natalie. It was like old times, two friends having a laugh together. As she chewed her sandwich, Dan gave his brief overview of the failed attempt of picking the wedding waistcoat.

'Abi, seriously, I went bright purple when the lady said that she had to go fetch the larger size! Really, I've been on a diet, I've gone cycling each night since I proposed but it's not coming off!'

Abigail accidentally spat out some crumbs. 'Wasn't it raining, Dan? Yesterday, I mean. Did you go cycling in the rain?'

He raised his eyebrows and with cheeky smile he replied, 'Yes, and I got soaked. Turned up at my doorstep thinking I looked like a stray cat that needed to be towelled down and placed in front of the fire.'

Abigail giggled and their eyes locked. There was something between them, electricity. The ring started to throb on her finger. She wanted to kiss him, to tell him that she would be happy to towel him down. He shifted uncomfortably, then reached for the plastic carrier bag that held his drink. He pulled out the bottle and before taking a sip of the fizzy drink, as if reading her mind, he responded.

'Abigail, I really like you, but only as a friend. You're a good, beautiful person. I really know one day you'll meet someone who'll appreciate you for who you are. Who'll take care of you. I really do believe that, but I love Natalie. That's not going to change.' There was hope: a "like" always had a possibility of turning into love.

'I always wanted to ask, Dan ...' She swallowed. 'Did you ever think that if there were no Natalie, that we could be together?' Abigail's stomach lurched a bit; those words were so hard to say. It was even harder to hear the response.

'Abigail, I do love you, but it's more of a sister love. It's different with Natalie. She's my everything. I'll always think highly of you. You're smart, beautiful. You deserve a better man. And we can't ponder about if Natalie isn't here. She's here!' He had turned to his watch.

'It's time to go back, lunch break is soon over. Come on, I'll treat you to a mocha.'

With heavy heart Abigail accepted, but the drink tasted like the mud that clouded her mind. Clenching the coffee cup in her hand, the burning of the hot drink prickling her skin felt deep-rooted like the hatred she now felt towards Natalie. The ring vibrated on her finger as if trying to churn up all that loathing. On her way back to the office she tried to keep up the conversation but felt stupid and helpless. How could a ghost would do what he'd promised? How stupid was she for believing! She left the coffee on her desk and she made her way to the ladies' room. The ring had to come off. The door slammed behind her and the familiar Febreze toilet smell surrounded her. The ring was throbbing but soon it wouldn't be, it would be off. With the other hand she pulled to try to take it off, but it was fruitless. Each pull felt like it was being pushed the other way back onto her finger. After each attempt a chilly grip tugged at her heart: each time she brought her hand close to the ring for another attempt, it was repelled, like two magnets with reverse poles.

***

Natalie's wedding plans were in full swing. Flower this, bow that, try the dress, blah blah blah. Who cared if the flowers were mixed colours or different shades! Abigail did have to admit that the bridesmaid dresses weren't that bad. They were wine red, handmade to flatter any figure. Nothing though, could keep her positive. Each hour closer to the wedding made Abigail more irritated.

Nothing stopped it! Nobody intervened. Abigail felt stupid, if she had a true friend and shared his with them, they would most likely laugh: 'Oh Abigail, you really thought you can see ghosts? Seriously?'

That's what they would have said, which is why she felt totally and utterly useless. Anything that could distract her from the wedding church rehearsal was a good thing. The church they'd chosen was lovely. The old, characterful building had been standing there for centuries with its sandstone gothic detailing. Standing proud in the middle of a tiny town, surrounded by a lawn full of old gravestones. How many people had stood there over the centuries and sat upon these same pews? How many got married, christened their children and then were buried at the grounds of this beautiful building?

'Abigail, what do you think about the hymns we chose? I chose *Abide with Me,* but Dan thinks it's one of those funeral songs. Do you agree?'

Abigail agreed with Dan but wasn't up for too much of a discussion.

'Natalie, I don't know, I'm not sure. It's your wedding and you know best what suits you. I like the hymn but agree with Dan.'

How glad Abigail was that the priest interrupted.

'Sorry, ladies, but I have another couple coming right after you. We need to wrap this up as quickly as we can, please.'

Thankfully the whole thing was over and soon Abigail was grateful to close her front door behind her. The ring was now continuously throbbing. Each attempt to get rid of it ended same way as before. First it was the magnetic repulsion, ice in her heart and then the most enormous wave of fear washing all over her. A panicked feeling that if she took it off, Dan would be gone forever. Despite the pain she couldn't get it off at all. With each passing day the intensity increased.

The night before the wedding she woke up screaming. The ring felt as if it was on fire. The Bride was in her dreams, screeching and shouting. She chased her like she wanted to kill, all the while screaming in a language Abigail couldn't understand.

***

The day arrived: Dan would be lost forever, far from Abigail's reach. She was woken up by the warm rays of sunshine coming through her window. What was usually a cheerful way of waking having the opposite effect today. Abigail threw her pillow over her head to cut out the sunshine.

'Bring me hail, lightning, locusts, anything!' With a grumpy stomp she made it out of her bed. Like a waddling penguin she made her way to the kitchen but nothing in there appealed to her. At the end all she could muster was dry toast washed down with strong black coffee. The make-up had the same outcome – failure.

'Argggggh, nothing is going my way, nothing is right!' She threw the mascara tube into the sink. By now Natalie would be up with the hairdresser. The make-up artist would be there, plastering paints onto her to make her even more beautiful than she already was.

The predictions were correct because as she knocked at Natalie's parents' home the make-up artist ran out to her car for more blusher. The preparations were in full swing with people rushing about. Natalie's mum was making calls about the last touches whilst her dad was scuttering about, trying to find his coat.

Some flowers were already delivered and the freshly cut smell of them was everywhere. Natalie chose those wonderful baskets full of dark red roses to be placed at the entrance of her church, so the same smell would be there waiting for them too. Abigail knew as she was there when Natalie showed off the flower arrangements she chose.

Though Abigail could never seem to find good enough justification to spend on flowers, she appreciated the gesture none the less. They were there standing in large baskets reminding her that most likely she would never have a man to make such gesture nor her own wedding for which to choose flowers.

With a sigh, she made it past the flower filled hallway into the kitchen hoping to remain unnoticed until it was the time to leave. However, her choice of hiding place was doomed. The kitchen was dealing with influx of crowds in between being silently empty. There were people coming in and out that Abigail didn't recognize and after the fifth time she was asked to make yet another pot of tea she decided to seek out a better spot. Thankfully Natalie's home was large enough for one person to get comfortably lost. Accidentally she walked into Natalie's bedroom to find Natalie sitting there on a chair in just her white lacy bra and knickers.

'Abigail, come on quick, sit down, you'll have to sort out your make up. You can't look this miserable at my wedding!'

The hairdresser walked in to start Natalie's hair. That made the make-up lady redundant, so she had a go at Abigail. After what felt like centuries she was finally pleased and with a big grin of satisfaction on her face passed a mirror to Abigail to examine her masterpiece. Abigail's jaw dropped when she caught a glimpse of herself. She looked younger and refreshed.

'Abigail, you look gorgeous! I have plenty of single young men lined up. I asked Dan to invite some of his single friends. Isn't it great?'

Abigail returned her jaw to its normal position. *Oh, glorious, I've turned into the little desperate cast-off that would take anything with a heartbeat.* She wasn't ready to share her true feelings with Natalie yet, but her sarcasm had no end; she wanted to slap her even though it was her wedding day. Maybe in the past Natalie had been like her sister for whom she felt sisterly love but now it was just pure hate.

'Good, hopefully I'll meet someone worthwhile, but now I need the loo.'

For a moment after closing Natalie's door, Abigail rested her head on the wood. Holding her bag near, feeling the dread in her ribcage, she made it to the nearest bathroom. The lock clicked into place. No interruptions allowed. Even the bathroom had fresh roses in a vase that made it smell more like florist than a bathroom. Ha, at least they weren't that posh: their tap was dripping into the sink and some lime scale had collected around the drain. The tablet blister pack popped under the pressure of her fingers and soon she had two little pills in her palm. She threw them into her mouth, immediately regretting her choice. The bitterness spread along her tongue. Thankfully the cold tap was near, so holding her hair she leaned to drink directly from it. At the end the bitterness disappeared, leaving her only with a little sensitivity around her teeth at the splash of cold water. The tablets should help to numb her a little to the whole pile of horse manure that awaited when the wedding started. The diazepam worked well: just half an hour later she couldn't care less if she was going to marry Dan or the next king of England. It wouldn't have bothered her if someone poked her with a red-hot fire iron.

Three hours later the limo arrived to take everyone to church. Natalie looked so enchanting. She beamed with pleasure; she was full of happiness as she floated into the car. Abigail was already in the car thinking of nothing but the taste of the tablet as if it came back and spread all over her tongue again. Stupidly she'd left the blister pack in the bathroom and it was too late to ask for the limo to turn back. She had to brace herself for the worst, which still lay ahead.

The traffic flowed effortlessly. Lots of cars hooted as a nod to the happy occasion. The white ribbons on the car flapped madly in the breeze.

The church was as beautiful as Abigail remembered. Inside, the frescos depicted pain and suffering, the usual church art. Churches were like emotional blackmailers: if you don't turn up for Sunday, do look and check out these frescos, this is what waits for you, you atheist! She looked up and noticed the last glance Dan gave her. Then, all eyes were turned towards Natalie taking her last three steps towards Dan at the altar. She was met with smiles and happy mutterings, while some guests followed Natalie's mum who was dabbing her eyes with Kleenex.

Natalie drew out her steps, taking her time to extend the ceremony. She was the peacock that was envied by Abigail, the crow, that common and plentiful bird of uninteresting plumage. Natalie's make up suited her perfectly. Her dress was body hugging, classy but sexy, with miniature pearls everywhere.

Abigail had always known she'd be her bridesmaid one day; that was their promise to each other. What wasn't expected was being her bridesmaid while watching her marrying *her* man. HE IS MINE, Abigail wanted to shout out loud. She wanted the sound of those words to carry through the whole church, so people outside could hear. So that there was no mistaking who Dan belonged to!

Her body started to shake, cursing everyone underneath the breath as the ring burnt into her skin. Natalie took one more step towards Dan. Two more and she'd be beside him, her man, HER DAN!

Dan, the idiot, had that stupid expression of pure happiness, how sickening. Natalie took her second step. The shaking intensified, fuelled by hate so Abigail bowed her head towards the floor to avoid eye contact with anyone who might guess her thoughts. It was the breathing, the icy breath that made her pick her head up. There was something in between the music that played as

Natalie made her way to the altar. Abigail focused on the space between Dan and Natalie to try to figure out what it was. It was whispering, and the voice was growing louder as the shadow moved from the corner of the church and made its way to stand behind Natalie. The flowers in the basket were rotting the closer the shadow got, dropping their petals all over the floor like droplets of red blood. Then the shadow took a shape. Finally, it all was clear. The shadow was Josef, walking so close to her he was virtually stuck to her back, creating the image of a shadow. He poked his head out to see the groom, then his dark eyes locked onto Abigail. That moment time froze, and Josef spoke. His skeletal body clicked into place when his scull turned towards Abigail, his jaw opening.

'Are you ready to do this? Are you sure he is worth it? Do you really want him more than anything else in the world? Make your decision now! I am giving you this one chance, one chance only! You must decide before she takes her last step, because then you lose him forever. This is your last chance!'

Josef pointed his scrawny finger towards Dan. Abigail's eyes widened at the sight of his unkempt yellow nail. How he could appear just like this in broad daylight, with her being awake? How could he take that form? There wasn't time to ponder as all the way at the back of the church darkness grew with clouds of steam coming her way and a figure floating out of it.

It was the Bride appearing as if from nowhere. She was clutching her chest from which the blood was spilling out onto everything, slowly dripping onto the path to the altar. The ground was covered in it, red and sticky, and her whispering voice sent shivers down the spine.

'You will never have him! Turn him down before it's too late. Otherwise I must get you myself, to save the others before they are chosen to die!'

Stop stop stop … Abigail desperately tried to control her thoughts. Josef gave his last words on the matter.

'She has nearly taken the last step. If you really want him, you'll need to think hard. Give me the answer or I shall leave, never to come back again. You shall never have that chance to have him ever!'

The Bride floated closer, turning the whisper into a loud, angry shout.

'Do not listen! Do not agree, you weak, pathetic human, he, the one you desire the most, was never destined to you. He will NEVER belong to you!'

In her confusion, Abigail's deepest desires, locked away in her heart, took over. With her mind mired in hate she made the decision.

'I want him! I do want him! Stop this wedding, please! He is mine, MINE, MINE!'

Those words rushed from her thoughts before she could analyse consequences. Without a moment for her to grasp what had been done, she had made a pact with the devil. There was no time to understand the price of her happiness.

'You will have him.' Those were the last words Josef said before he started to laugh madly.

'You will have him, but first I have to take her with me! She is mine. You gave her to me!'

Time started again, and Natalie was already taking her last step towards the altar, unaware of anything. Other than Abigail, nobody had a clue of what was about to happen. Dan turned his gaze gently towards Natalie, now just half a step away. She raised her head to give Abigail a smile before turning towards Dan. Both mothers were radiant, with happy tears glistening in their eyes. Dan was admiring beauty of his bride. Abigail frantically looked around to see whether anyone else saw what was happening.

Josef's hand penetrated Natalie's chest cavity, gripping her beating heart. Abigail panicked. Could anyone see this, anyone? She whimpered as her emotions took over and her body started to shake. She grabbed the nearest hand:

Natalie's mothers. She just quickly glanced at Abigail with a smile. At the same moment Josef ripped her heart out and clutched it in the palm of his hand. It was still beating, sending blood gushing out everywhere. And he stood there, squeezing the heart until it finally stopped beating.

'I am giving you this opportunity of having the one you love most, but for that you must pay. I will be back when the time is right. For now, this belongs to me.'

As soon as he spoke he was gone. That whole performance was just for Abigail. Nobody else had seen it! Abigail tried to steady her hands, which were shaking violently now, as the ring glowed orange. Only then, as Natalie finished her last step, she collapsed. The hand holding onto Abigail's clenched, digging the nails into her skin. Natalie's mother's face drained of all blood. There were screams from some people but most just stood there in disbelief. Then the frantic running started. Someone shouted to call an ambulance whilst others attended to relatives falling to their knees in shock. The clattering of heels onto the stone church tiles sounded like bullets. The priest with his outstretched arms was mumbling some religious spiel whilst Dan sprang up for action. He bent over to examine Natalie. Clearly, he noted no pulse, because he started resuscitation. Natalie's mother, frozen in shock, could do nothing but squeeze Abigail's hand. As if on cue everyone stood up to take a better look or see if they could help or try to understand what had happened. Hushed whispers and quiet conversation echoed around the church, underpinned with wails and sobs. Natalie was just lying there on the cold stony floor in all her beauty, the innocent bride all in shiny white dress, unspoiled yet not moving. It was clear now that what Abigail saw was completely different from what everyone else saw.

To her eyes she was lying there in a pool of blood with a hole ripped in her chest. The whispering came back again; this time turning into a roar.

'You greedy witch, you greedy witch, you greedy ...' Abigail shook in fear, as she recognized the voice. It was Natalie's! 'I'll come for you, I'll take you to hell!'

As soon as it came it was gone. Abigail's heart raced as she thought of the Bride from her dreams. It dawned on her that she looked just like Natalie, of course! She was darker, though, and the hole in her chest was not empty, as Abigail could always see her heart beating slowly, seeping blood with each beat. Now the Bride from her dreams was right in front of her, the metallic breath hitting her face, freezing the tears midway down her face. The Bride's eyes were gone, so it was just hollow sockets looking at Abigail who could simply gawp.

It was all just a dream, must have been. Soon she would wake up for sure. Abigail stood still among all the commotion holding onto Natalie's mum like two statues in between tourist crowd. Ambulance staff turned up within minutes trying to get through all the onlookers, pushing their way through. One of them pulled out a defibrillator and tried to resuscitate Natalie. Other ambulance personnel tried to make space for the stretcher by pushing people gently away. One of them shunted the two aside. It was this push that woke Abigail up to realize that this was no dream. Her stomach churning, tears flowing, she realized what she had caused. Had anyone else seen it?

Questions sped through her head like flames on a fuse. Was the Bride telling the truth that Dan would never belong to her? Had she just killed her best friend for no reason at all? She pulled her hand free from Natalie's mother and ran towards the paramedic.

'Don't do that! Can't you see that there's a hole in her heart! It's blood, you need to stop the bleeding!'

She madly tried to staunch it, but people looked at her as if she had lost her mind. Abigail kept trying to stop the blood, but the doctors kept pushing her away.

'Miss, calm down please, there's no blood. It's the shock. You need to sit down,' shouted one. Abigail looked around and saw Dan's father. Running towards him she tried someone to see sense.

'Can you see, can you see her blood? It's all over my hands.' The guilt seeped through her whole body which gave way and she fell to the ground. She woke up sitting upon one of the many church pews with Dan's father holding onto her shoulder. The ambulance staff had stopped resuscitating Natalie; it was pointless.

They placed her body onto the stretcher with grave faces and wheeled her away. One paramedic stayed behind, holding onto Dan, who was sounding like a cub that had just lost its mother. The ambulance staff covered Natalie in blankets they brought with them, but the swathes of fabric and petticoats of her dress still peeked out in irony. Everyone stood aghast, many with hands clutching at their faces, their hearts, each other. Natalie was pronounced dead and taken away as the priest mumbled something about God.

Abigail finally understood what Josef had had in mind when he said that he was going to help. Her hopes that a caring ghost would just scare Natalie were all naïve dreams. Her hopes that ghost would show Natalie how she could be happier without Dan were wrong believes as the ghost has something entirely different in mind.

'How did I agree to this?'

Abigail fainted again only to wake up beside Dan's father. The old man's cheeks were wet, but the sound of Dan's crying overpowered all other sensation. His mother embraced him as others gathered near. He was in pieces, wailing like a tortured animal, a beast in pain. Others just sat there in silence trying to make out of what had just happened. Some took their leave.

***

Abigail clutched the cold porcelain bowl close to her as if cradling a baby. Her knees were hurting from the hard-tiled floor imprinting itself onto her skin. She had no memory of how she had ended up in these strange surroundings but the one memory that kept coming back was the last look Natalie gave her. It wasn't clear if the continuous vomiting was due to the guilt that penetrated her stomach, the shock or the amount of alcohol she had had. Most likely it was the toxic cocktail of all three. Despite the guilt, it occurred to her that Dan was single again. Somehow that gave some comfort. Each time the only positive thought made its way into her mind, her stomach made it known how sickening her thoughts were. As if it was her stomach repeating to her that she had turned into a killer.

As she squeezed her eyes shut and clutched her throbbing head, memories of the previous night started edging in to fill in the memory gaps. The stale taste of beer and the harshness of – what was that, tequila? – returned. She could remember staggering out of the church, wanting so badly to not think about what she'd seen, and deciding to get completely drunk.

She had walked into the first bar near her home to pull the first guy who showed interest. No longer was she worried about anything. What more was there to do? This was the Everest of all of mistakes so there was nothing more to worry about.

Seeming that there was nothing more to empty out of her beaten stomach she lifted her head and looked through the doorway to the crumpled sheets on the bed. She dropped her head back onto the arms, causing the toilet seat to clunk back in its place. Here she was in love with Dan, but instead of trying to be there for him, she got drunk and hopped in the sack with this … Who was he even? There it was, in the bed was a man with grey hair and rumpled skin, snoring away. A person that Abigail hoped to never meet again. Now, minus the beer goggles, staring at his snoring form, Abigail wondered how the hell she had decided to go with him to his place. The bedsheets were clean for sure, but he was completely opposite of what she found attractive. He was very chubby old guy at least twenty years her senior. He was probably a very nice guy, but he was so not her type! Quickly dressing up to make a quiet escape Abigail pondered whether Everest was really the mountainous culmination of her mistakes or whether she'd completely jumped over the mountain already.

She rushed out of the door before he woke up and started to ask stupid questions like – 'can we can meet again' or 'can I have your number?' Now, in the sober light of day it became clear how far she had fallen off the moral/ethical ladder all the way down to hell.

***

The only idea she had was to hide from the world in her little flat. She kept having flashbacks of Josef's hand holding Natalie's heart, and the sound of her screaming. Unsure of how the week had gone so quickly, as it felt like seconds, unsurprising knock at the door disrupted her. She clasped her hand to her hand as soon as she opened the door.

'Dan! I don't know what to say.' He had a wrinkled face from the number of tears that he shed, his skin was grey, his eyes were blotched and red. He looked like an eighty-year-old man. The grief had done that to him.

She pulled the fluffy pink nightgown tighter around herself, picking at bobbles of pilling and then patting at her hair to feel the state of it, smooth it down, something.

As he stood there with his shoulders slumped, she did a quick day count in her head. It had been a whole week already since she'd closed herself in her flat with nothing but pills and alcohol. The HR lady had been unusually sympathetic, not questioning when she called in sick. And now it hit her that she hasn't had a wash or been out of bed since that terrible one-night stand. This was the first human contact since.

'Abigail, I couldn't think where to go. Can I come in?' he croaked.

Completely lost for words Abigail gestured him in. 'I'm sorry about the mess. I haven't touched a thing for a while. Such a mess. Sorry.'

She hadn't spoken with Dan for a whole week so seeing him in such a state made her feel guilty. .

'I'm so sorry, Dan, I am so sorry about *everything*!' The tears streamed out of her as the floodgates of guilt opened. Her lips repeated the 'I am so sorry' sentence about a thousand times before Dan stopped her. He gently placed his palm over Abigail's lips making her to stop. She could only blink the tears away as they stood in the hallway.

'Abigail, please hush, nobody could have known what was going to happen. Please don't cry. You must come out to face the world. It is worth living; don't close yourself away, you're the only one that can help me now. I haven't been out of bed the whole week either. You are the only one that loved Natalie as much as I did so I need to be near you, so I can feel that she is here with us again.'

He wiped took the hand off and wiped her tears away with a sleeve of his shirt. This was the thing she needed, so close for a kiss, nearly perfect. That's when she took note of her flat. It was like a bombshell, used cutlery everywhere, takeaway trays with rotting food inside. That was the wakeup call she needed.

'Oh dear, I am such a bad hostess. Look at this place, it's awful. And I can't think of anything apart of taking more drugs, so I can sleep. I'm in bits. Just look at me! I'm so sorry.'

Dan took a deep sight and with a fatherly voice took his leave to the lounge picking up the mess.

'Abigail! Stop saying you're sorry, you didn't kill her! It was a heart attack! I just came over because I heard from people you haven't been to work for a whole week, you aren't answering calls or emails. Everyone at work thinks you topped yourself! Abigail, you must be strong and snap out of it. I know that you are hurt but trust me, I feel the same. We all are. We must be strong for our and Natalie's sake. She wouldn't want us to be sad. Please sort yourself out, come back to work, just do it one step at a time. First, take a bath. Seriously, you could enter the smelliest skunk competition and win right now.'

At the last sentence he turned around, hands full of rubbish, he winked. He was right, she did smell, the whole flat did. To Abigail it smelled of deceit, not dirt. Who cared; he was in her flat, worrying about her welfare. She knew that the guilt had to go, she must move on otherwise it would all have been in vain.

'And, if the prize for that skunk competition is money, I might think of entering before I hit the shower. A little short on this month's mortgage, you know.'

Dan walked to the kitchen to retrieve a bin bag he started to fill up with all the mess.

'Abigail, I'm not sure anymore if you should enter that one. You might make some skunks very sad. You know what, you'd better go and have that shower.' He waved his hand in the direction of the bathroom in between picking up the empty alcohol bottles.

'I'll try to tidy up this mess. And I'm hoping to find something resembling a cup, so I can make you a nice hot cup of tea. What do you think? Is it a deal? Just don't forget to brush your teeth! If you leave them at that state any longer, they will all fall out!'

The shower was lovely. She could hardly believe it: out of it a whole week on drugs and sleeping pills! Still, in that time, neither Josef nor the Bride had appeared, so maybe this was the future, the bright future with Dan by her side. Surely all those horrid events had been just a dream, her own imagination going overboard when she saw Natalie's beating heart being ripped out of her chest. All the emotion had messed up her head. She was just poorly and died of a heart attack. Dan said so, which meant it was true. He wouldn't lie.

The shower was like a spiritual cleansing, washing away her sins. Each little drop hitting the shower floor was that little bit of guilt escaping her body. She lathered her skin well and scrubbed away. She massaged her scalp as her hair finally got the treatment it deserved. The hot water nicely warmed her whole body and somehow from a zombie she turned her back to a human being. Slowly the bubble-gum scent of her favourite skin cream enrobed her from top to bottom. The dream had become reality. She had Dan in her flat, helping her out, giving her comfort. He was ready and single and she sure wasn't going to miss that chance again to have him to herself. She was sure to take that one more chance she was given. This one she wasn't going to mess up, this one she would succeed at.

Chapter 5

The day of Natalie's funeral came quickly. The wedding party, now turned funeral gathering, carried Natalie's coffin towards the freshly dug grave. Dan was one of the men carrying her; he was weeping, trying to keep it together was useless. The black suit contrasted with his red face. From behind him, mourners followed as the cloak of darkness swallowing all light into their black clothes.

They made their way through the gravel path which crunched underneath their feet, sounding like a dog chewing its bone. The small graveyard was full of old trees, providing some shade from the strong sun. The only happy thing was the insect hopping about. The gravestones were there like sore thumbs, sticking out of the ground to remind us of how short our lives truly are. They were open books presenting summaries on how people died and what could become of each one of you. A child, two years of age: died from consumption, a girl, no age: died at birth. A father, thirty-two years of age: died during the war and so on, there were so many. Now one more was joining them, Natalie, twenty-seven years old: died at her wedding.

Once they got to Natalie's final life destination, everyone positioned themselves around the dark freshly dug hole. The earth smelled fresh, as were the beautiful lilies that lay in a wreath upon her coffin. No matter if one would try to forget, death was all around, graves as far as the eye could see. Abigail had no escape, her mind running overboard she couldn't shake Natalie's deathly eyes turning upwards as the last bit of life left her body. The beauty that has left this world, leaving the body behind, the body that is the disposable shell for souls. Trying to glance away the guilt made her meet another reminder of her deceit. Dan was full of pure sadness, worry, love!

All those things he should have been giving to her, not Natalie! Abigail tried to control the flashbacks of Natalie's wedding day, of the second that Dan froze, realizing she wasn't moving. The wedding guests trying to stand up to see. Both mothers wailing uncontrollably. Questions being thrown at Dan's father as he was trying to resuscitate her. The panic of sheer confusion. Josef standing there as calm as water on a lake. The Bride, dark, bleeding, staring at her. A crow flew by screeching, resting itself upon the nearest grave stone as if she also was invited to say her final goodbyes. Briefly the crow's glistening plumage made Abigail think of shining blue/black colours than the blackness of the hole. The crow flew away as something else caught its eye. Abigail had to turn back. They were all there, the wedding guests. Dan's parents eyes hadn't moved away from the coffin. She stood there with Natalie's head by her feet, looking at the destruction she created. Nearby her parents whimpered quietly. It was painful seeing Natalie's dad trying to read what he'd written as his final goodbye.

Everyone was touched by his speech full of love for his daughter, though it made everyone cry that little bit more when he finished. Well, not everyone. Abigail felt nothing but jealousy. She had no father to do such a thing. Even now Natalie had more than she ever could. She had beaten her again in showing her incompetence from beyond the grave.

Abigail pretended to swat a fly bothering her but, she was swatting the awful thoughts away. Nobody noticed that small hand movement. Her cheeks went pinkish with guilt. Quizzingly she circled around the mourners to check whether anyone noticed.

Her gut was screaming by now, ripping her insides out. Abigail had to control the desire to scream out that she had killed her. Her throat begging her to cry out, and at the same time it seemed she'd throw up.

When Dan gave way to his emotions it made things worse. How could she do this to the one she loved most?

The crow made its appearance. This time it rested on a small broken bench nearby. This bench was a silent observer, a witness to where some poor relative had sat crying for hours. The crow began to tap its beak onto the metal frame as if trying to mock her. Each tap made her skin crawl that little bit more. Then a quick gust of wind sent the leaves in the trees batting together. A chill spread over her neck with the sting of frost, and then came the words:

'Don't worry, I promised him to you and you will have him.' Abigail whipped around. Could the others hear this voice? Could Dan?

'Don't forget we are acquainted now.' Nobody could sneer like Josef.

'We are so alike! Our greed is greater than anything else. If we want something we go to hell to get it.'

His words we so near; still she felt his breath on her cheek: icy, but blazing at the same time, like the aftereffect of a stinging slap.

'You have her now, leave me alone! This is just a dream, none of this is real.' No matter how hard Abigail wished it in her head, Josef wasn't going to let it lie.

'No!' The shout rang in her ears, making her whole body twitch. Josef was standing right next to her, his rotten breath offending all her senses.

'I am real!' Mocking her he made a wind blow between the mourners. He was jumping from behind people, imitating their eye-dabbing and wiping his nose with his lip curled tight. And he kept waving to draw her attention. As if she could ignore him.

Now Josef sat down next to the crow as if bored with all the running about. When the crow stared at him, he left the bird to have the bench and draped himself on one of the graves with an expression of lust and enjoyment. He just lay there, grinning, his hands folded underneath his head.

The only time he sat up was when the first lump of ground hit the wooden coffin. He laughed out loud when they threw the flowers in one by one. He was sitting there with his wild hair and sneering grin full of jagged teeth, mouthing,

'Are you happy?' and, 'Smile. I gave you what you wanted.'

Abigail couldn't hold her pose anymore, and by trying to avoid his gaze, she angled her head only to meet Susan's cold stare. Begging with her eyes, Abigail tried to communicate with Susan.

'Can you she sees him?' With no feedback from Susan, Abigail gave up on the idea. To escape the freezing stare, she turned her head towards her left. That's when she noticed her boss for the first time. He'd turned up with his wife. There was no escape for her guilt. Her gaze returned to Josef, the scrawny man with his beady eyes. His horrid face was full of lines, making his skin appear to be falling away from his skull. It made his eyes look larger, rounder, darker. The teeth were yellow and stained; the hair hung limply in rats' tails. He looked like homeless man at before death, though he was the exact opposite – too alive and energetic. Abigail decided to move to escape his gaze. She sided up to Susan and asked, shivering as she drew breath, 'Can you see him?'

Susan gave her a puzzled look while dabbing her nose with a tissue. 'What do you mean, Abigail?' she whispered. 'You mean our boss?'

Abigail pointed towards where Josef stood looking bored.

'No, beyond the boss is a man sitting at that grave by that large tree, by that broken bench, can't you see him?'

Susan scowled and waved finger in Abigail's face.

'Abigail, I really don't know what you're on about. I see a maple tree with a grave underneath, and the bench, but that's it. Abigail, seriously, are you going mental? Are you aware why we're here? Go away!'

Susan was so angry she punched the air in desperation as she stomped off. By now the men were almost done burying Natalie's body and only the top of her coffin was showing. Most people took their leave for the wake. Abigail's last bit of hope of someone else noting Josef faded. He was still there with a blade of grass in his teeth, relaxing, stretching himself out on the grave. That had not stopped him grinning but at least he'd quit talking. Abigail stood there transfixed by his face. Only then she noticed someone touching her arm.

'Come on, Abigail, you have to leave her now. I know how much she meant to you but we all have to accept she's gone.' It was Dan. His eyes were bright red, run out of tears, and completely spent.

***

The wake was at Natalie's home and despite their large driveway, people had to find a space on their street to park their cars. Dan's was parked right by the front door. He must have stayed overnight.

Abigail made it to the kitchen, away from lounge where everyone else was. Her hopes to find a bottle of something strong were immediately crushed as she heard Natalie's mother's voice. The only escape was the good old toilet beneath the staircase. A quick dash later, she bumped into a red, blotchy Dan. She gasped in surprise, and they looked at each other in silence a moment. Her heart strings were having a hard time of it, and she couldn't hold it. She embraced him.

'Natalie wouldn't want to see us upset.' He gently returned an encouraging squeeze. The little room smelled of lavender-scented hand wash.

'We have to go on, because our lives haven't ended.'

All Abigail wanted was to throw up. So ashamed she was, she avoided his stare. It appeared the constrained space of the room made him at ease. It did the opposite for

Abigail. Her stomach lurched the way it had been threatening to do all day, and she stuck her head over the bowl just in time. When she finished he wet a towel and wiped her face for her.

'Gosh, look, there is a pretty face underneath all that.'

This joke was like a first snowdrop flowering from out of the fierce cold of snow.

'Thank you. I don't know what else to say. I'll try to be there for you if you want me to. Just call me.'

Dan gave his first genuine smile since Natalie's death.

'I will, Abi, promise.'

***

After that smile he seemed friendlier and even sought Abigail's company, and she enjoyed being showered with his attention. She had to make sure it continued, which is why her choice of clothes started to resemble Natalie's. Even the make-up matched her style. The effort worked wonders as their meetings were no longer limited to work lunch breaks. The texts kept flowing in daily. Abigail started to feel human again. Daily routine mirror checks were the proof as it was a completely different woman who was looking back. This one had perfectly combed hair with carefully applied make-up to match the outfit of the day. Dan at her side was like a golden prize she won, she had to match it! The message shining from her phone was the prime happy moment for her:

'Abigail, mum would like to invite to you have Sunday roast with us. Will you come?'

Abigail couldn't contain the happiness. She kissed the mirror with glee. She had been waiting so many years it was impossible to believe the day had finally come. She was ready to meet his family properly.

Obviously, there were some bad days, though. Those happened when Dan pulled out his 'Wow, Natalie used to say that,' but then his face would fall. And then he'd cry on Abigail's shoulder about how he missed her. Each time it felt like a knife going through her chest. It was the guilt as she tried so hard to be like Natalie, so he could fall in love with her, but that just brought with it the guilt of how she had got him.

The days helped with hiding the guilt. Sometimes Abigail managed to forget it entirely. The longer they were together the better she got at denying what she had done. The only problem on the horizon was Josef. He kept appearing when least expected. As their relationship grew, so did the frequency of Josef's visits.

Once he appeared when Abigail was doing her weekly shopping. With the sensation that someone was watching she turned her head away from the aisle of tinned food. There he was, right at the end, hands across his chest, leaning on the shelves like a stroppy teenager. When she did a double take, he was no longer there.

Josef was like a bad memory appearing everywhere. He appeared in the office, just passing by in a corridor. He was at the GP's surgery, looming around patients, or he was in the corner of the room when Abigail discussed work with her boss.

Abigail sank her hands into the warm dish water, wondering when Josef would give up and leave. The heat of the water relaxed her as her hands disappeared under the bubbles as she washed up the dinner dishes. Dan was the head chef so washing up was her job. Now she could hear him pottering about her lounge DVD collection to find a movie to watch. There were more dishes than her drainer could take. It was such a tiny kitchen she had to move the saucepan to the other side of the room to let it dry on the cooker.

As she turned around with the slippery saucepan in her hand she was met by a grim-faced Josef. He was standing there, right before her, his face so close that his deathly breath brushed her cheek. In her fright she jerked her hands and the saucepan clattered to the floor. Immediately the apparition was gone. The ringing carried everywhere, sending Dan her my side.

'Everything OK, Abi?'

'Of course.' She tried to control the shaking. 'I just have butter fingers, you know. I'll be fine.'

Dan wasn't buying it.

'No, you're not OK. I've been noticing recently, you keep dropping things and have the shakes afterwards. You've got to see a doctor. If you won't go, I'll drag you there myself.'

He picked up the pan, gently inspecting it. He placed it onto the cooker and grabbed Abigail's wet hands. Then just like the saucepan, he inspected her hands for any cuts.

'You keep having these "butter fingers" daily. Now you dropped the saucepan, yesterday you dropped food onto the floor, the day before the toothbrush as you stared at the mirror. Your behaviour is not normal. I care for you, so please go and see your doctor.'

***

Dan gave her no choice; she had to go. One of her pet hates was being in the waiting room with all the elderly folks coughing their lungs out.

There was nothing to do but sit in between all the sick to see the precious commodity called a GP. In front of Abigail sat a guy she vaguely recognized. The elderly lady had a hacking cough like a seal pup. The smell was overpowering, an odour of rotten fish and Sulphur. Trying not to face the lady, she took her attention back to the figure ahead. The smell worsened, sending beads of sweat to her forehead. That person wasn't from work: it wasn't a friend. As her realization became clear so did the person's intentions. Josef slowly turned his head towards her without moving his body. It was just the head that turned, the body stayed in the same position. Abigail, fixed to her chair, felt the sweat drop into her lap.

'I am here.' That was all Josef said.

To see his head turning a full 180 degrees was disturbing enough, but to hear him speak, despite having so many people around, even more. It felt as if he was inside her head. The red alarm with her name on the screen didn't make her move either. The receptionist had to come to tap her on her shoulder to point out that her appointment is due. She still felt shaken inside the GP's surgery, and it didn't help when he placed his palm over her hand.

'What's troubling you, Abigail, how can I help?'

The man was always pleasant. There was cheekiness behind his expression. Somehow, she knew that in real life he was different.

On this uncomfortable plastic chair, she thought she resembled a troubled, naughty girl. Josef was there with too. He followed her into the room and sat on the examination bed behind the GP. He lay down on this bed with his arms crossed at the chest. His head turned towards Abigail and he mouthed, "I am Natalie". His awful grin made her shiver.

'Abigail, are you alright? How can I help you?'

This time the GP turned up the volume of his voice.

'I'm fine, well, not really, I need … I don't know.' Abigail blurted. 'I need something, I need pills.'

With raised eyebrows the GP questioned.

'For what exactly? I'm going to come clean, Abigail. I spoke to your boyfriend, who is very worried about you. I must say I can see why, because since you walked in, your attention has been somewhere else. I was going to do a questionnaire but instead I'm going to refer you to a psychiatrist right away, considering your history. I'm also sending you to do some MRI scans just in case there's something in your brain that is stopping you having full control of your hands, as Dan told me you keep dropping things?'

Abigail had completely ignored everything he said apart from the word 'boyfriend'. Had Dan called himself that when he spoke to the GP? Finally, it was here, Dan was calling himself her boyfriend! Nothing could make her miserable. Abigail smiled.

'I'm glad you're smiling and taking in my advice. I'll organize the letter and you can pick it up tomorrow afternoon. You'll need to pick up both letters. I still want you to have the MRI.'

In a drunken-in-love moment she babbled something sounding like "thank you" as she left the room. That Dan was her boyfriend was the only thought in her head.

***

It was the perfect evening, ending in a perfect night of passion. Abigail enjoyed watching Dan sleeping. He was just that more gorgeous, so innocent. They lay in a deep loving embrace, intertwined, but then a jolt of electricity ran through her. It was that familiar smell that woke her, the rotten flesh. Initially it was hard to make out the shapes in the room but there was one new shape, right beside Dan. It stood there in the darkness, just breathing, his dark beady eyes were shining, his scrawny hands rose over Dan's head.

'Do you want me to crush his head now? Because I will do that unless you do what I ask.'

Abigail swallowed air. Blinking hard she tried to erase that image before her. Unmoved, Josef continued.

'You will go and find me nine unhappy brides! You will gather them for me by passing them a token, a wildflower, which will connect them to me.'

Josef smacked his lips, savouring his words. Leaning his head towards sleeping Dan, he continued. 'Then show them what I have done for you and how happy you are now. Tell them that they can have what you do if they will believe. I then will help them as I helped you. Tell them how it feels to hold the man you love close.'

It took a while to digest his words. 'What the hell are

you talking about?' she whispered, trying to take control. 'Get the hell out of here!'

The ground shook, and the duvet was thrown to the other side of the room. The light came on and off, flicking, and things were being thrown all over the place. Picture glass on the walls burst into millions of small particles dropping to the ground like snow. Dan was lying there, not sleeping but not alive either. With flashes of light, the room changed, bathed in a cold yellow light; green linoleum tiles were under her feet, and she screamed at the sight of Dan's body. He was lying on a pathology slab, his severed head in a bowl resting on a trolley of stainless steel. Josef was screaming his lungs out. His temper only calmed as he needed to talk. His screeching voice said:

'If you fail, that is what becomes of him.'

Then the light died, and Abigail felt herself drop back into bed. Her heart was pounding. She desperately wanted to cling onto Dan, who was now simply lying asleep beside her, his body restored. But she couldn't risk waking him, so all she could do was hover her hands over him, trying to feel the reassuring warmth from his body. From a blue glow in the corner of the room, Josef pointed at Dan's sleeping form.

'I'm giving you some time to think, but soon I will be back. I'll make sure not to leave you alone. You won't forget what you promised me!'

Then he was gone. The duvet was still in the corner of the room, the lights all out. The things that had been floating all over the place, picture frames, a clock, toiletries, a hairbrush, all sorts of cushions and trinkets, all collapsed onto the floor with a crash as he left. Some ornaments broke in the fall. There were dents in the wall and glass scattered on the carpet. Only now Abigail noted the trickling blood on her sheets. In the bathroom, she discovered a cut on her forehead.

Thankfully Dan slept through. Quietly she tidied everything, bandaged the cut and went back to bed. The next morning, she made up a lie that she had fallen from the bed. He was worried, which was nice as what they had together had turned to love. It must have, otherwise he wouldn't be so considerate. There were times that Abigail felt jealousy at Natalie, particularly when she found Dan in bathroom crying over her photo. Her patience was running thin; she really had to control herself not to shout out, get over it and move on. She had to take a leaf from his book and be caring no matter the circumstance. With the wretched ring melded into her skin, she had to act soon.

The gypsy had known it and she should have listened then, but if she had done so she would never have had him. The relationship took priority, with Josef being hard to ignore. She could no longer control the fear he caused. His demands said as ground his teeth.

'Give me what I want, and I'll go away. Otherwise I take what I gave you. I'll take him with me to hell!'

She could no longer take it. The all clear from the GP from medical perspective was another stake at Josef being real.

If there was a doctor she could just let it all out with, 'Hey, I have this ghost that follows me in my dreams, who now rules my life. He makes me jump, he scares me but as he killed for me I am bound to return the favour. He now wants a payment of nine unhappy brides.'

She wasn't sure how anyone would take that. Despite the fear there still was the hope, the doubt. Could Josef really do anything beyond terrifying her? All he asked her for was to find some unhappy crazies that didn't want to get married. How the hell was she going to find such women? No, despite the night of terror, the scan being clear, it was all in her head. So far nobody had realized that she was having visions, she had managed to ignore him for so long and nobody else ever saw him either. She made her up her mind on the subject – he wasn't real. It was all just her imagination.

***

Josef clearly disagreed with her decision and his rage grew so he appeared frequently, anywhere, any time. Once in the office Josef appeared as she was pouring hot water into a cup, making her jump and subsequently scald herself. Her natural reaction of pointing at him hadn't gone unnoticed. Dan had had enough, and demanded she book that psychiatrist appointment as a matter of urgency. It was torture as Dan couldn't see Josef sitting with him on the sofa, gesturing and running a finger across his throat, pointing at Dan.

'That is what will happen to him if you keep being ignorant to my needs. I am losing patience and I usually have plenty.' The sofa cushion fell to the ground as Dan shook Abigail.

'Abigail, are you actually listening to me? All you're doing is fiddling with that ring of yours, looking right past me! I'm trying to help you. Please listen.'

Ignoring Josef, Abigail gave Dan her full attention.

'Sorry, love, I was thinking, only because this thing is hurting my finger today. I must have swelled up during the night.' Pointing at the ring, desperately trying to show Dan she was listening. Truthfully, she didn't want to see a psychiatrist as she'd have to admit that something had to be done about her situation. Dan took pity and let out a sigh of a relief as he sat next to her.

'I worry about you, Abigail, I really do.' He took hold of her hand.

'Wow, Abi, where did you get this ring anyway? It looks very old. Did you inherit it?' Abigail brushed off his question as quickly as she could.

'No, just something I bought abroad. Let me make us a cup of tea.'

***

It had been a particularly hard day, but Abigail had managed to get through it. The pain kept radiating from her finger into the spine. The girls at work had one of those Natalie remembrance days so wouldn't stop talking about what she had been like. Dan kept going on about the psychologist, so it was tough to settle down her nerves when she made it home. The evening went in the blink of an eye and she was ready for bed, hoping that taking the prescription sleeping pills would help her forget the day.

'Do not take with alcohol' was the warning written on the tablets, which Abigail ignored. She was aware of the side effect of drowsiness when taken together as she used this to help her to sleep like a baby. In bed Dan kissed her goodnight as they cuddled up but before she closed her eyes darkness came towards her. Then, from this darkness Josef stepped out.

'Hello, sleepy head. You haven't listened well, you haven't delivered. It can cost you greatly. Ah, look at the man of your dreams laying so nicely next to you. His lashes so long, his mouth slightly open, a shame he must die. Well, it will be sad to see him dead, but you've left me no choice!'

The scream filled the room with ice. Abigail wasn't ready to back down to give Dan up, he was hers and she will fight for him.

'No, I've had enough of you. Go away.'

She jumped out of bed thinking of nothing but how much she wanted Josef dead, out of her life, out of her dreams.

'Go away!' She kept screaming all the way to the kitchen, showing the shadow further away from the bedroom. As she turned to check Josef's whereabouts, he was just there, facing her his breath so near. His words came through his yellow teeth.

'I am here to stay. I am here to make you to keep your promise. You will not get away from me. I've given you all your happiness. I am the one that you have to listen to.'

Abigail's fury had no end. 'I am not here to listen to you; you are nobody but an idea in my mind. You are just a fault in my head, wiring gone wrong. I won't listen! I'll make you go away.'

Josef's expression changed from anger to interest. 'Oh, my dear love. You who gifted me your most precious commodity, your soul; you who belong to me. Do show me, my dear, exactly on how might you get rid of me? I am most interested to know.'

Abigail had been breathing hard, trying to gain control. Another dream to haunt her, another dream that felt real.

'Hang on, this is a dream, I'm in control, not you!' she spat. 'I am not in my kitchen now: this is a dream. I am lying in my own bed, in a deep sleep!' She looked around. The pans and knives were still on the worktop where she finished had left them after chopping vegetables.

'I am not here, I am in my bed. If I am not here neither are you. You are not here!' She grabbed the knife off the chopping board. 'You are in MY dream, I control your fate, so if I make you die, you will go away forever, because I killed you, you will no longer come!' Josef had a smug smile on his face.

'So, my dear, you think that if you prod me with that, it will be the end?'

'Yes, I know how!' She sprang up towards him with speed screaming, 'I know how. I hate you. Die!'

She grabbed hold of his shirt and placed the knife to his throat.

'Now it's time to die, you bastard! I've been waiting for so long for this.'

Ready to cut, something didn't feel right. There was a force tugging at her back. The shirt was slipping through her fingers.

'Let me go, he has to die, let me go!'

She spat these words like poison arrows towards Josef. Then with a thump, a haze descended as pain spread across her skull. Though she thought she was still sleeping, the situation was quite the opposite – she was in her kitchen. Before passing out she loosened her grip on the knife handle as she recognized the shirt she was holding. It was the same that Dan had worn to bed that night. It was Dan, unable to speak, with a line where the blade was pressed against his throat. The hushing calming voice from behind her was her neighbour who came running into the house, thinking they were being attacked.

'You've been sleepwalking, Abigail,' Dan said.

'Talking to yourself, shouting to yourself.' Rubbing his neck, he reached for her. 'And when I got here, trying to shake you awake, you grabbed the knife and tried to cut my throat!'

Abigail felt dizzy and put a hand to where her head hurt. The torch in the neighbour's hand had some of her hair on the edge of where he'd hit her head.

'Sorry,' he mumbled.

If the neighbour hadn't turned up, Abigail would have succeeded. Dan was holding his throat where a small cut bled. He staunched the flow with his fingers.

'Abigail, please, now are you going see the specialist? Don't you understand, you must see someone!'

His pleas were interrupted by the neighbour. 'Come on mate, I got to take you to hospital. Someone needs to look at that.' He pointed at Dan's throat only to turn his gaze back at Abigail.

'I am taking you too. You need to explain what the hell happened here. They'll be interested as to why you tried to slit his throat! I had no choice but to hit you over with the torch as you weren't going to stop.'

At the hospital Dan pushed not to press charges and made their neighbour be a little less descriptive with the detail. Puzzled, the doctor on call treated them for minor injuries. Still puzzled, he handed over a letter to Abigail.

'Here you go, this is the referral. You are lucky to have such an understanding boyfriend, as I would have you sectioned right now. If you don't attend tomorrow to see the specialist, I will issue an order.'

***

So, Abigail ended up sitting in a psychiatrist's waiting room again. She tried to read the Readers Digests on the table in a room full of expensive furnishings with sofa upholstered in floral fabric. The coffee table was wood rather than chipboard. Even the coffee came from beans rather than some coffee substitute.

Being in this shrink's waiting room would have been a better experience if the nosy receptionist could have stopped giving her the eye. Nobody could deny that being a receptionist of a shrink would give you good grounds for a nice dinner conversation. She was one of those that put her large snout into people's files to look at their personal affairs. Hence the receptionist was now guessing whether Abigail was making up the schizophrenia or whether she truly had post-traumatic stress disorder.

Josef's laugh was still fresh in her memory when she was passed onto the referral note.

'My dear, you are also losing your mind. I believe sooner or later you will GIVE ME WHAT I WANT!' Josef spat when he stopped laughing on her way back to the car.

'Abigail, the doctor is ready for you.'

You can sweet talk as you like but I know you're a witch, thought Abigail as she picked up her handbag. Inside the consultation room was more pleasant than the waiting room. It was clear this was not a typical NHS consultation room.

The sofa was twice as nice as the one in the waiting room, the table was some sort of export from the Indian subcontinent and candles with different scents were all over the room. A large fireplace occupied the main position on one wall and a large carved lion desk was on the other side where the psychotherapist sat.

'Hello, seat yourself, Abigail, and have some water.'

Dr Passan pointed at the water jug at the coffee table.

'Look, I need to explain myself. I had a bad dream that felt real. In it I was being attacked so naturally I tried to defend myself. The reality was that I was holding a knife to my boyfriend's throat. He fought for his life when our neighbours barged in and managed to get me off him. I had been in what seemed like a deep sleep or a trance at the time and it was only when the neighbour hit me on my head that I woke up. Only then I saw that I had cut him. His throat was marked where the knife had gone. I still can't figure out how I got to the kitchen to get the knife out or why I had that awful dream.'

Sparingly she shared details as she didn't want to reveal being able to see Josef. Nor was she planning to say that he was there with them at the hospital right then, smiling and hopping about from behind doctors and nurses, making her jump as they tried to take care of her. His voice repeating endlessly: 'Give me what I want, and I'll go away.' She wasn't ready to admit that she would start looking online for unhappy brides.

Dr Passan managed to drag her back to present.

'So, Abigail, the doctor on call informed me you kept saying there was a man in your dream that made you do this. Do you know why this man is appearing? What is the reason he chose you and why he keeps coming back into your dreams?'

Abigail look askance.

'I really don't know why me. But he is real, you know. He follows me everywhere. Sometimes he makes me jump. He isn't just in my dreams!' she blurted out.

Dr Passan stopped shuffling his papers on his desk.

'I believe you need to start to think about it. When was it you spoke to him first? When was it that he appeared real to you, as you say? Standing there, in a room, just talking to you?'

Dr Passan had a good point. Most likely as he would have done his job he would know her whole history and her "invisible friends".

'I don't know, Doctor, but it started happening after my friend Natalie died.'

Dr Passan put the papers aside.

'Ah, your best friend whose boyfriend you have now? Am I correct? I must be honest with you Abigail, but could it be guilt? It does sometimes happen that guilt has this effect. Do you think you feel guilty because you have Dan, Natalie's fiancé, right?'

Abigail wanted to run out of the room.

'Anyway, Abigail, I'm not trying to make you feel guilty, but it seems we need to find out when the man appeared, what he wants and then find the solution that he goes away. From your notes I can see that there was a period where you had no visions of "others" so that's a good sign. If you have managed it before, then there isn't a problem to repeat it again. However, to do that we need to delve into why suddenly they appeared again. Has this vision asked for something from you or is this man there only to frighten you or pass a message, you think?'

Abigail couldn't explain why Josef chose her, nor why he wanted unhappy brides.

'Dr Passan, if this man, who is in my head, and whom I call Josef, decided to pick me for whatever reason, call it guilt, should I do what he asks?'

Dr Passan pondered the question. 'As long as it does not kill anyone or if it's moral, ethical and completely legal, why not? If that is the task you have been given it might be reason that you need to do that. What has he asked you to do, Abigail?'

Unsure, Abigail spilled the beans. 'He has asked me to meet up with brides. He has asked of me to meet with other women who will marry soon but are not happy about it. He wants me to meet unhappy brides. Do you think he wants me to meet them to cheer them up? He has asked me to pass them a token of wildflowers. He says if I do that they will be marked to be happy, to be free.'

Dr Passan contemplated it a moment.

'It might be, Abigail, that you are telling this to yourself as deep in your mind you want to marry this boyfriend of yours. It might mean you set yourself this task. Probably deep inside you want to cheer yourself up that you no longer need to feel guilty in being with a man whose fiancée was your best friend, now dead. Go and speak to these women and see whether it will help. See whether this man will go away. However, don't forget we need to have regular consultations as what you have done could have had a severe outcome! There will be repercussions if you miss an appointment.'

Abigail went silent though she still had many questions. Why must they be unhappy? Why nine and not ten? Dr Passan wrote down some notes.

'Abigail, it's close to the end of our consultation, but you do this training and try to ignore these voices in your head. Listen to them but try not to answer. You will come back in a week and tell me whether meeting someone helped. See you next week.'

Abigail took the training sheets from his hand ready to walk out but he interrupted: 'Don't forget to pick up your prescription. Ensure that you keep taking the prescribed medicines. They will help.'

Then he released the grip on the papers and waved her away. The receptionist was ready with the prescription and smug smile as if to say that Abigail was a fake. Only outside on the pavement could she feel free. A small glimmer of hope was still there.

Chapter 6

Dr Passan's pills worked; those little white beads that jiggled in the palm, mixed with the bigger white buttons finally helped her to catch up on sleep. Instead of violent dreams Abigail now faced the same more placid dream each night, a film-like flow of repetitive patterns. The dream felt real but instead of featuring Abigail, her persona was that of a twenty-something woman with nice glossy brown hair hiding her face while large blue eyes shone from behind and a smile gleamed in the perfect oval. The brunette giggled at a quip from another much younger girl. This one was dressed in ancient clothes with a white cap and corset-style dress all the way down to the feet. Chickens clucked around merrily, providing entertainment as each tried to beat the others to the corn.

'You need to make them jump for it, Anna, they are so funny!'

The one whose name had been pronounced turned her face fully towards the younger girl.

'No, Nela, you make them jump the way you hold their food in your hands. Inviting them to peck from the hand is unwise. They will hurt you.'

Now Abigail saw through Anna's eyes. In the dream she *was* Anna: The Bride! The woman in blood-stained white who had been haunting Abigail's dreams for months: the one who had come to Natalie's wedding saying that Dan wasn't destined for her, this was Anna.

Though the same person as the frightening Bride, this Anna was no nightmare. Here she was presenting herself to Abigail as what she was when she was alive – unthreatening and beautiful. The dream continued as the younger girl looked up and pointed to the distance.

'Anna, look, I wonder who that is with Father. Why is

he speaking to him? Oh look, he is holding his foot.'

A light breeze made Anna brush off strands of hair obstructing her view. The seeds in her hand escaped to the pleasure of the chickens who raised the volume of their clucks. Mesmerised, Anna's pupils targeted the man, for he was interesting indeed. He had in tow magnificent beasts, their coats glistening in the sun. The horses neighed and gave each other the occasional snort. One had such light brown coat that he seemed made from pure gold.

'Oh lord, Anna, look at those beautiful horses!'

The sound of hooves brought the attention of the villagers who took delight at inspecting these beautiful creatures. Anna only gave brief attention to the horses as she couldn't keep her eyes away from the handsome, slightly older man sitting beside their father in a cart pulled by their two mules.

Nela dropped the from her hands and ran to their small cottage gate to get a better view. She ignored her little bare feet, vulnerable to splinters from the old wooden gate posts. She held herself up against it, straining her neck. Some of the other women noticed the man as Anna had. Clearly, he was in pain, but trying hard to pretend it didn't matter.

His face was beauty itself though pain distorted his features. He had short brown hair with gorgeous blue eyes, and his clothes were cut from fine cloth and beautifully stitched. His mannerisms were very grand, but his hands were those of a manual worker. The ties meant to keep his shirt in place had come undone, and the women stared at the rippling muscles of his chest and arms. It was obviously the result of handling these strong horses. His chiselled chin just added perfection to the features that were already reminiscent of a Greek god. What made Anna wake up from her dazed stare was the little poke in her side.

'Anna, you are in love!' giggled Nela.

'Shush, Nela! Go feed the chickens or I'll tell Mother I

had to help you again. You need to start doing things on your own otherwise no man will marry you! Nobody wants a woman who doesn't want to work!'

As if inconvenienced by the delay, some of the horses snorted with displeasure, tapping their hooves on the dusty road.

Nela's forehead changed from clean icy lake surface to that of a ploughed field. Anna was glad her warnings went into that thick skull of her sister's. The girl needed to understand her place in the world.

With one hand, Nela let go of the wooden gate. Pointing a finger, she responded. 'Well, Anna, I don't believe it. You are beautiful and work so hard yet you're past your best when it comes to marrying. Nobody will have you despite you being the perfect bride! It's true, you cannot deny it, and I heard Mother telling Father so yesterday. That means it must be true.'

Nela stopped as the cart got closer. She jumped off the gate and pulled at the cold metal handle to let herself out into the road. Completely unaware of the wounds she had inflicted upon Anna, Nela ran towards the cart, leaving dusty footprints behind.

'Daddy, I fed the chickens. Do tell, who is that man next to you?'

By the time the cart arrived at the gate of their cottage all the women onlookers, dropping whatever they were doing, had positioned themselves around the cart to get a better view. Their nosiness was there in plain sight. The men were more reserved, pretending to work whilst they secretly exchanged questioning glances. Like they were getting ready to sort this man, should any danger come out of him.

Anna had a good look and most of the village folk, old and young, were suddenly crowding their cottage gate by the parked cart.

Their cottage was grander than the rest in the village but was nothing compared to Mr Novak's farm house just couple of houses away. The old man was standing by his large homestead with its glass baubles hanging on sticks to scare birds from the luscious vegetables and fruit in the front garden.

The bleating, quacking and mooing of the well-stocked farm formed a soundtrack that made the horses skittish. Anna took a glance and the stranger smiled. The sight of her pleased him, but as the dream allowed her to share Anna's feelings, Abigail could tell Anna felt the opposite. The most beautiful girl of the village approached the cart. By now all the young men were watching. Her beautiful golden hair was neatly kept in a plait and the green eyes and round face gave her the childish look men seem to like.

'Hello, I welcome you to this village I can see that you are in good hands, but should you need any milk, our cows are the best around here. I shall bring you some myself to strengthen your bones if you wish.'

The man in the cart had his eyes on her as if impressed by her beauty.

'Thank you. I couldn't ask anything more of such beauty other than a hand to kiss in introduction. My humble name I shall give you: Martin. And what is yours?'

He reached her hand and planted a kiss on it. His voice was deep and inviting. Anna couldn't take any more of this. Yet again a younger woman had taken a man worth looking at.

Anna muttered, turned and rushed off past the chickens, the pig shed and a small potato patch to escape into the fields behind their home.

***

As the brown-haired girl departed, she hadn't noticed that Martin was looking at her direction. He was saddened by her departure, the way he looked longingly after her, but when he took a step in her direction, he was reminded of why he had been on the cart rather than walking in the first place. He winced in pain as he put weight on the leg and took the help the villagers offered.

As they asked him about himself he told his story. He was a horseman by a trade, constantly travelling to far-off countries buying and selling horses. A month was the longest he had ever stayed in one place.

Martin's horses were his life and he had seen many of these little villages on his way, but also large towns and cities, allowing him to meet all sorts of diverse people.

He told the villagers he had not planned to stay over, but a confounded foal had run to hide behind its mother who didn't want to part with her offspring. The mare indicated her displeasure by giving Martin a solid kick into his thigh and trampled his foot, possibly breaking some bones.

A man who had seen this happening took pity and stopped his cart to help, aiding Martin in calming the rest of the horses who got agitated by the mare's response and offering to take him to his home, so his wife could attend to his injuries. And this was how Martin came to arrive at the home of Anna and Nela: the man with the cart was the girls' father. He gently nodded to the man by the large farm house who took it upon himself to find some place to put the horses in for the time being. His farm hand helped to usher the beautiful beasts onto their spare pasture land whilst martin hobbled inside the cottage. Inside, the house was well kept. A young girl smiled at Martin from a corner of the room.

'Sit here,' the man of the house ordered.

'Nela, call your mother to attend to this man's foot and find Anna. Where has she gone?'

The young girl just shrugged her little shoulders. 'I don't know where Anna is, but I am going to fetch Mother now.'

Soon a woman entered the room. It was clear from her weathered face that she was used to hard work out in the fields. She took a cold cloth and drew it over the bruising.

'Thank you for all your kindness,' Martin said. 'I shall go tonight to sleep underneath the stars, so I am no longer a burden to you.'

'No, you are now our guest and you shall stay! That's the Moravian way. We don't have more beds for you, but we offer you to stay in the cow shed, above in the straw, which is comfortable enough if I place some blankets on top. We will take care of you until you have fully healed.'

It was apparent that you wouldn't argue with this woman, clearly the keeper of this household, so Martin accepted the only alternative to stay.

The night was warm and even in the dark Martin had a good view of the village and the cottage. The cottage had a nice cosy feel with the chimney poking out of the thatched roof. The back of the cottage faced the barn directly over a small courtyard, with a little interconnecting stable on the left housing the pigs and chickens. Maybe it was one of those where the roof spaces were joined together so more hay could be stored to feed and nest the animals over the long winters. Though his view on the right was broad with mature trees and land, what pleased him more was the good view of Anna's window.

He knew when she returned, not from seeing her, but from hearing the family scolding her over her rude departure. She hadn't said much, and now she was standing in the window, combing her hair in a night dress of sheer cotton. Martin could see the shape of her luscious breasts, which were a temptation to him. He had found himself drawn to this woman. He wanted to know her touch upon him.

The next morning Anna was up with the first ray of sunlight. Calmly but efficiently she started her day by attending to the animals. Martin supposed she hadn't been told of his sleeping arrangement, because he was able to watch her closely as she started singing to the three cows she was milking.

Anna's hair was up, but some strands were falling into her beautiful face which Martin now wanted to be near enough to kiss. He wanted to brush the hair aside to press his lips to her. Anna worked briskly and soon was walking back into the house, gathering freshly laid eggs on her way.

Through the window he watched her cooking breakfast with a smile on her face. He held his breath; the smile was so enticing. Anna's lips were full and ripe.

He wasn't a man to settle down to one place; he loved travelling. No other father would give his daughter to a horseman knowingly as it was clear acceptance of never seeing their daughter again. Who would take care of them in their old age? No, a daughter was a precious commodity, not an item to throw away into the wind.

Martin sat up at the sound of another voice. 'Morning, Anna, how did you sleep? I'm too tired to gather the eggs but it looks like you've done my work already. What's for breakfast? Have you seen the visitor? Isn't he handsome? The whole village thinks so. Have you talked to him?' The young girl was still in her night dress, her little feet swinging as she sat on her chair waiting to be served.

He then caught a slight glimpse of the woman who attended his wounds yesterday. Her deep loud voice confirmed it.

'Stop it now, silly little girl; leave Anna out of it. You well know that Mr Novak is interested in marrying your sister and has put forward rich dowry. Your father is in discussion with him about it so don't plant silly things into your sister's head!'

Anna looked up from cooking eggs. 'Mother have some breakfast.' She placed the plate before her mother.

Their father must have also walked in, but Martin was unable to see him from his vantage point. He realised it was the father because only manly voice boomed over at Anna. :

'Anna dear, take our visitor this breakfast. He's in the cow shed.'

Soon enough Anna emerged from the house, nearly tripping over one of the chickens on her way to the cow shed. She stomped her feet across the courtyard with a frown.

Martin was already waiting for her with a smile on savouring the fact she didn't know he was there.

'Thank you, my future wife, for this precious gift. I bet it tastes like heaven itself because it was made by an angel.'

Her cheeks went red, but she smiled, so Martin guessed she liked what he had said. She placed the plate full of food on a bale of hay stack nearby, turned on her heel and was quickly gone. Martin groaned, wishing to run after her but unable to. His leg was worse, and swollen.

After that morning, it took two more days before he was able to put weight on his foot. The family looked after him well but what he enjoyed the most was the view of Anna, getting ready for bed each night. The dreams he had about this girl. These dreams were like teasing fantasies he wished to be real. It was Anna who, each time, made the possibility fizzle out.

Though always polite, she kept rushing off. Not in a shy manner: much worse, it was the manner of a someone disinterested in his advances. Yet on the fourth morning things shifted. As he expected Anna to bring his food, he got a surprise as it was her giggling sister, Nela, who brought the tray.

'What is so funny that makes you break into giggles? Is it my wild hair?' Martin teased her whilst pretending to comb it.

'Not really, you aren't mad. Your hair is quite nice. Anna likes it too, I can tell, after all, I am her little sister. She doesn't take well to men. She is headstrong which is why she is still with us, why she hasn't married yet. My father is trying desperately to get some dowry for her. The old man, Mr Novak, is interested and is already buying Father out. If you want to have a chance you must get in before he does. I know Anna doesn't like him, you see.'

Though Nela was an innocent little girl, she had a good overview of an adult's life. He wrinkled his nose with displeasure.

'So, Nela, if you think your sister likes me, why hasn't she brought me the breakfast today like she always does? Why have I seen her walking away towards the back of the house? What business does she have in those wild woodlands beyond?'

Martin pointed towards the right side of the cowshed, which had view of large tall pointy pine trees.

'It is a nice warm sunny day and the lake is perfect for washing hair. That's probably where she is, having a bath and washing her hair. It's bath day, you silly!'

Nela had said it so casually, like it did not matter, that a young woman was at present in a lake, naked. Nela picked up his empty plate and with a giggle made her way back to the house. Just before she reached the kitchen Martin heard the mother call out to her to feed the rabbits.

Martin couldn't pretend or wait anymore. He had to get to that lake, to see her. He had to try to see her with nothing but her smooth skin. Yet he didn't know how he could creep up to the lake without her noticing.

Slowly, with the aid of a crutch, made his way to Mr Novak's in providing him with some payment for his trouble of looking after his horses and made an excuse for why he needed to take one for a ride. The horse's hide needed that extra wash anyway due to his oily skin. It did still hurt slightly to settle upon the saddle which creaked with his favourite sound as that was the sign to move on, be in control and travel far and beyond. His hair flew through the chilled morning air as he galloped towards the lake. It was easy to ignore the pain as his mind was preoccupied with what he would see once he got there.

The hooves clipped nicely across the stony way but there was a metallic sound indicating one hoof might be slightly loose. Another sound, Anna's singing, made him slow his horse to a trot. Some weeping willows hid the view, but he could see the small opening between the reeds leading to the open water of the lake. There, in the shallow water stood Anna with half of her body submerged, bent over, rubbing some herbs into her wet hair. The calm water of the lake only rippled against her hips as she reached with her palm to wet her hand. Her naked body was heavenly. Beads of water pearled on her skin and he was ready to jump off the horse to run his fingers over all of her.

Anna's spine straightened at the sound of horses snorting. Slowly she turned only to meet his stare. With the water dripping from her elbows she drew her arms to cover her sides. After the initial freeze she sprang up for action, making splashing waves in her haste to hide in the reeds. Martin jumped off the horse for want of another glimpse. He nearly tripped over her clothes that lay there on big grey stone. Martin found this amusing as if he didn't know that Anna was between the reeds someone might think that it was the reeds speaking.

'Go away at once! Give me my clothes now! I will have to tell my father. He'll be furious! And he'd send you packing. No more breakfast for you!'

Martin bent over to gather her clothes and slowly turned towards Anna's hiding spot. He hobbled that little closer to where she stood.

'Well that would be most unfortunate, as I would greatly miss your breakfast. You are nothing but an artist in the kitchen.' With these words he took another wobbly step towards the dense reeds until he glimpsed more of her body. He savoured each moment.

'Here, take your clothes, but you'll have to come closer if you want them.' The reeds bashed against each other and water sprayed towards Martin as she speared her arm forwards to try to reach. At each attempt her arm got closer Martin took a tiny step back so he would entice Anna towards the edge of the reeds.

'You must give me my clothes now, I beg you.' Taking another small step back, Martin wiped the water off his face with his sleeve.

'I'll give them to you, but you will pay me with a kiss! You wouldn't want to walk home in nothing but your skin ...'

Anna was so close he could see her face. With her arms she was holding as many reeds as possible to cover her body. Her eyes flashed with fury. Her next move was unexpected but well received. She let go of her curtain of reeds and marched towards Martin as if fully clothed. She came so close he could feel the soft skin of her breasts brushing his chest.

'Give me those,' she hissed, ripping the bundle from his grasp.

That was what he had been waiting for, and he could no longer control his need. Resting his arm on her, he edged his body up to hers. She met his eyes, gasped and melted at his touch, bringing her face to his. Their lips met and the kiss that followed was sweet and full of need.

Yet, the kiss over, Anna pushed Martin away so hard he lost his footing and tripped over the boulder and right into the water. Before he managed to get up, she had wiggled her wet body into her clothes, the fabric now clinging to her every curve.

'Now you are wet and look like a dead fish!' she laughed.

'Well, I need to warm up or I'll die from this water. I need another kiss to help me come to.'

Martin stood there up to his knees in water hoping for Anna to respond.

'You shan't be so lucky twice. You took the kiss, remember? You weren't given it.'

'But ... you melted!'

'Ha.' She tossed her head back. 'An act in a moment of desperation.'

Anna took hold of the horse where it was munching on the fresh long grass under a willow and jumped on its back.

'As payment, I'm taking your horse. My kisses aren't free! It looks like it will be you hobbling to the village with nothing but wet clothes, wincing in pain!' With that she dug in her heels and galloped away. Her voice carried with the parting words: 'That's your punishment for taking what was not for you to take!'

Martin's shivered. His muscles tightened from such rapid temperature change so slowly he hobbled out of the lake. He knew well that should her parents find out what he had done, he would be thrown out. But it was as if he were possessed. Now that he had kissed her, the want in him had grown stronger. The memory of her wet form against his chest quickened his pulse. He was ready for more, but a gentleman must wait, control his need.

***

Since that lakeside meeting, Anna seemed drawn to Martin. Though her lack of warmth, smiles or blushing told him she was still angry about the stolen kiss, now she stayed in the barn until he finished his meals. Whereas before she had always set down the tray and left immediately, now she waited silently as he ate.

Sooner than he expected his leg recovered. It could have been the food, but he suspected it was her proximity that healed him. He started to help with odd jobs like stacking wood. He never, however forgot his trade and ensured his horses were taken care of. Missing his animals, he felt reluctance in asking Mr Novak about extending the lease. Novak, however, replied it was a pleasure to have such magnificent animals on his land; he enjoyed taking care of them. During their conversation, Martin felt himself shifting his weight from the one foot to the other, and it wasn't just from the injury. Yes, he could tell Novak was a good man, but according to the village, this old man was destined to have Anna. Martin felt his jaw strain as they talked. Anna, with this man, over him? The pressure built up in his chest.

And then, the lake became the place where Martin and Anna met without anyone watching. Sometimes he tried to steal a glimpse of her as she stepped out of the water. Another time he noticed she was secretly watching him bathing. It was the day he took his horses for a wash. To keep his clothes dry he left them at the same place Anna had the first time they kissed. That stone was like an altar carrying so many wonderful memories for him. After setting down his clothes on the stone he ventured into the lake.

***

Martin was right, she was there watching him. By now she knew his body well. He was wild like his horses, and she found out that she enjoyed resting her eyes on his broad chest and shoulders. As he scrubbed slowly at the horses' flanks, the muscles in his arms flexed and rippled. She could see the outline of everything that was given to him by God.

Muscles knotted down the sides of his spine and his buttocks were firm. She had to look away. She was longing for his touch. She wanted more than a kiss. She wanted all of him, but how could she invite him in? How would her pride allow it, after the fury she had shown? But the urges kept coming from within her body, pounding at her head.

Finally came the day when Anna's parents left for market and she decided to go to the shed with the idea of staying there till the morning sun woke her. Usually the market journey took her parents two days, so as soon as the cart left the village she got ready. Once the first hoot of an owl sounded near, Anna blew out the candle and walked barefoot to the cow shed. Already he was waiting, shirtless, as the night was warm.

'I only came to say goodnight.'

Martin stepped towards her. 'I shall thank you for this pleasure but wonder if you could attend to my wound.'

Anna was puzzled. 'But you are fully healed.'

Martin took a step closer to her, being now so near that she felt the heat radiating from his body.

'I am not talking about my leg, Anna. What wound I mean is this one, my heart, because it is longing for your touch. Will you attend to it?'

Martin took her hand and placed it on his chest. His heartbeat tapped gently on her palm, increasing in frequency as she kept her hand rested there. His lips drew near, and he inhaled deeply. She could tell that her scent was sending his pulse into overdrive. Finally, happily, she allowed herself to melt completely at his touch. His ragged breath echoed her own.

They kissed again as they let their hands wander over each other's bodies. Though their eyes were closed, through the weeks of stolen glances they were familiar with each line and curve and had each other's form mapped out perfectly.

Slowly Martin undid the buttons at Anna's chest, allowing her night dress to fall open. With a sweep of his fingers it slipped off her shoulders, letting the fabric flutter down until the garment lay in a puddle at her ankles. At the same time, she freed him of his trousers and all that was left was their naked bodies ready to be joined in passionate love. She felt him inside, though it was her first time, it felt right and full of wonder. It was what she was longing for; to feel him against her body, to feel his glorious body upon hers.

***

Since that night Martin couldn't think of anything more than wishing that she might spend another night with him. They existed only in the bliss of their shared love, while her parents and the village were oblivious to their secret. It was a pleasure waking up each day, to see Anna walking to him, to watch him eat breakfast.

He agreed it wouldn't hurt to stay a while longer. The horses could wait, they were happy at Mr Novak's and he didn't seem to complain for he was in love with their beauty. Anna's father appreciated the help, as some things couldn't be done by a woman's hand. Martin wasn't shy of work and started renovation on their pig sty.

Their need for each other grew in intensity, though they kept their meetings hidden. Martin couldn't be happier for he never really felt the need to stay somewhere yet, he finally felt what love was like. In his mind it was as these wondrous days had no end, as these times with he would go on forever. She admitted the same to him and even suggested that they tell her father, who was clearly warming up to Martin.

'You should ask him whether he would take you in as his son-in-law,' Anna said on one of their country walks.

They had taken the dusty path though the grassy meadow, now full in bloom with wild daisies, hollyhocks and foxgloves. The only other sound accompanying them was the chirpy birdsong of a lark. Martin clasped one of the daisies between his fingers and pulled.

'You are one of those flowers, Anna, full of life, movement, beauty and vigour. You are as pure as a flower, the nectar within is the gold heart that you carry. You are more beautiful than anything else in the whole world.'

He tucked it into her hair as he planted a kiss on each rosy cheek.

'I shall go and speak to your father. I will ask him whether he would consider giving me your hand in marriage. I don't want to spend the rest of my life without you.'

Her beaming face was the answer he needed: the words brightened her as if someone had thrown a log onto a meeker flame.

***

Her father's reaction was unexpected. The man's disapproval and animosity towards Martin threw them.

'You are not taking my daughter away from me. Taking her away, travelling through the back of beyond, sleeping rough? Did that horse kick your senses out of you? I am not giving my daughter to any wanderer, a vagabond who doesn't see what life should be. We have been offered many gold coins, half of a farm, three cows, four pigs and ten geese by Mr Novak. What are you offering? Can you beat his offer?'

Martin stared into the distance. What could he give these people, after all?

'I could beat the offer, yes. I love your daughter. I can go away and sell all my horses. I shall come back with more gold than Mr Novak could ever have. Then I will have enough to buy a whole farm. My stock is highly valued the world over. Kings and queens are after my horses and I can get a hundred gold coins for any foal born to my golden horse.'

Martin was referring to a thoroughbred mare with bulging belly. He was not being entirely truthful: this was first time he had managed to get his hands on such a magnificent beast, and it would be his first opportunity to sell offspring from this beauty, but for now he needed to buy time. He knew the Turkish horse markets were the place for this foal, and he knew a jackpot awaited if he made it there in good health.

'I shall leave at once, but you must promise to wait for me to return. I put my honour before you: when I return, you will not find a richer man than me.'

The father paused. With a smack of his lips he made his decision, though it was the pleading eyes of his daughter that made him be lenient.

'Very well, then. Let us see what you can do.' Anna's crying, begging eyes had clearly gotten the better of the man. 'I shall give you a year, no more. Should you not return, I will have Mr Novak as my son-in-law.' To show he meant business, he banged the table with his fist, making the jug upon it jump.

With those words ringing in his head, Martin left the village with all his horses. But before he departed, he held Anna one last time, showering her with kisses.

'I will return, my beauty. I'll be back. Wait for me to come with the song of summer birds; I shall come with the summer breeze. Wait here upon this place where we are now. I will return.'

In parting, he gave her a posy of wildflowers picked specially for her. He jumped on his horse and with a sad expression he set upon his journey.

***

Though devastated, Anna was full of hope, for her lover had promised to return. Through the winter, which came early that year, she continued waiting. All the while, Mr Novak kept Anna in his sights, never missing an opportunity to impress her father. When the church bells sounded around Christmas, Novak brought a turkey, then some fish for Christmas, later some pork to take them through hard winter months and when spring came, a lamb for the pot.

With the arrival of the spring blossoms, Anna felt as if a fairy had cast a spell, speeding up time. Impatient, Anna's father started up serious discussions with Novak. Anna came upon the place of where she and Martin had said their final goodbyes. She picked a handful of spring flowers and prayed that he would return soon. Time was running out.

With each day Martin didn't turn up, she shed more tears. She wept long days, pleading with her father to wait a little longer. At first, he was agreeable but when summer came his patience left him. Without Anna's permission, he began arrangements for her wedding with Novak.

'You shan't tell me what to do, I am your father!' he roared. 'You will do as you are told. The wedding is in three weeks. That is set in stone, so even if the horseman arrives, you will have no choice but to marry Mr Novak! Your horseman is too late to stop the wedding now.'

These were the last words her father spoke to her about the wedding. As the day loomed over her, Anna visited the place of their goodbyes every evening. She spent her time crying on the wildflowers.

The day before the wedding she plaited a wildflower tiara and placed it on her head. It was a crown of deception, sadness and despair. Her mouth tasted of salt from all the tears, but her father's decision was firm. Anna looked like a rained-on rose petal, all soaked in tears, the briny drops decorating her long white bridal dress.

Her father organised two pigs for a feast after the church blessings. Anna watched the cooks setting the pigs up on their roasting pegs. She would rather have been one of those unfortunate creatures than having to marry one she didn't love. A horse-drawn cart arrived with barrels of beer. Those horses were a sore reminder of her love. How he loved to have one beer after a good day's work in the sun. 'Anna, this is like liquid gold,' he would chirp. Somehow everything had reminded her of how happy she used to be when Martin was around.

***

What she hadn't known was that, as she left the footpath for the last time, in the distance, a figure appeared. Martin had returned from his travels, now a rich man. His bet had paid off: a Turkish buyer supplying the Royal stables had got into a bidding war for the foal with another wealthy buyer.

He was sure he could have Anna back. No peasant farmer could decline sums such as given to him for that foal. He had sold all his stock apart from the one loyal stallion he chose to be his ride back to his love. He travelled for months, never giving up on the final prize.

Now he was back at the place he remembered so well. It was in full bloom just as it was when he said his goodbyes. He was unaware, though, of the flattened patch of wildflowers soaked by Anna's tears.

He pressed on and as the dusk settled, he reached his destination. Anna's house was already in darkness. Thirsty from his travels, he decided he might as well move on to the next town for some of that lovely beer and surprise Anna the next day.

The neighbouring village was decorated in multicoloured bunting as if they were celebrating his arrival. He walked past and soon he was at the inn that served that fabulous local stuff.

'Good evening,' he announced to some already well fed, drunken men sitting on the pub benches.

One man had a strange expression, darting his eyes towards him as soon as he entered. His face was scared, his eyes shifty, uninviting. Martin sat by the friendliest drunk and ordered a pint for all of them. He was celebrating, he had made it.

In his head he was planning the wedding and children he would raise. He downed the first and second beer to quench his thirst. It was only the third pint he started to enjoy.

'You are celebrating, I can see. As we do not know you, we assume you are one of the happy family members here for the wedding. It's going to be a grand one, though that poor girl. She looks like she is going to her funeral rather than her wedding,' babbled one of the drunks, happy to receive a free beer.

'Oh yes,' interjected the barman, 'you mean the weepy Anna whose eyes were once beautiful blue but are red with tears now. She will come to her senses. She wouldn't find a richer man than Novak. With him she'll have a happy life.'

Martin wanted to hit the speaker. That was his future wife he was talking about. The sweet loyal Anna. No, Martin couldn't accept it. It wasn't the truth. He was shocked as if struck by lightning. He tried to regain his calm by sitting up straight. Bewildered, he tried to still his breath to calm his thoughts. His mind was like fire doused in alcohol. His hand shot up to order more liquor. Drink would loosen their tongues, and he needed to know what was happening. The men with their drunken breath fighting for his attention gave away the whole story of the last year. With each new sentence his heart broke that little bit further making him drink more to try to dampen the anger rising in his chest.

How could Anna be made to do such thing? How could her father be so heartless? The alcohol left his thoughts disconnected.

'I can tell that after asking all these questions the men are spent and ready to seek their beds. They are truly drunk, sir. I also know the story of the unhappy bride, but I am not a stupid man. I can guess that you are the one who truly owns Anna's heart. You are the horseman, are you not?'

Martin tried to concentrate on this man. It was the same man he had taken a dislike to as he entered the pub. This man now made his move towards him when the others found it hard to hold their heads above their shoulders.

'Yes, I am the broken-hearted horseman. I am the man who gave up everything to have her. It seems pointless now. I sold my stock. I have nothing, I am nothing.'

Martin's last words tasted like a poisonous frog. It made him hide his face in his hands and weep openly. The man beside him winced.

'Oh dear, what a pickle you are in. I can see you are a man of fortune. Who else would entertain strangers with liquor? And as a man of fortune you can change the future. You just need to know how. I completely understand as I faced the same. I lost the one I love too. I, however, can help you, I can give you what you want.'

Martin was very drunk but also very interested. If he could change the future, then there was still hope.

'Is there a way of changing the future?'

'I can do that for you, sir, all I ask is for twenty pieces of gold. I will make it go away. I will talk some sense into this Mr Novak. I can give you what I want, I can make it go away.'

Martin thought it was a lot of money but in his drunken haze couldn't care less. He couldn't imagine living without Anna. He was ready to pay the devil his life, so he could be with her for one last time.

'If you can get Anna to marry me then yes, I shall pay you whatever you ask.'

These were his final words.

'Tomorrow you must be in the woods. That is the way to reach the old church in which the blessings are to be given. Those woods are where your future will change. And that is where you will hand me the twenty pieces of gold.'

The man walked away, and Martin fell asleep on the table, his drunken head too heavy for anything else.

***

The next morning Martin woke with a jolt. His head ached. Had he dreamed it all? He looked around. He had not moved, as he was still in the pub. His whole body was ached, sending tingling into his limbs as he moved them. The landlady was shaking him awake.

'Sir you need to leave, it's the morning now. We have many barrels to deliver to the wedding. Please do get up.'

Martin's head was pounding. He felt for his money pouch. It was all there.

'Do you know the man I spoke to last night? Do you know where he has gone?'

The landlady looked displeased when he mentioned the man.

'You mean that evil little man. I have never heard a good thing about him. He has been in prison many times. He also escaped more than one jail, and some think he is the devil himself. I hope you know he's a murderer. Stay away.' She leaned closer and lowered her voice. 'He murdered his lover's entire family, you know!'

This horrified Martin and the words from the night before came back to him. The man whose help he asked, the twenty pieces of gold. He stumbled out of the pub as fast as he could. Thankfully his stallion was ready and waiting. Martin jumped onto its back and galloped towards Anna's village, towards the woods through which the wedding party was making their way.

***

In the wedding procession, Anna was weeping, trying to concentrate on walking although her eyes were welled up with tears. She had managed to convince her mother to leave the wildflower crown in her hair, for luck, she'd said. Some of the flowers she clutched between her fingers. It was as though if she let the flowers fall, she would fall herself.

Her father walked by her side with her mother and sister behind. Her groom was beside her. He looked pleased. He had waited many years for this moment. To a man as devoid of looks as he was, the achievement of snaring such a wife must have felt better than meeting God himself.

The rest of the family were walking behind. The children were hopping about picking mushrooms as they found them in the thicket.

Suddenly Anna felt the tug of her groom's hand. The whole procession stopped dead, causing her to lurch. With a clatter of wings birds rushed off, up out of the trees, and it was silent. Through her blurry vision she made out a shape ahead. Only when her eyes sharpened she understood. Ahead of her was a man, ugly with yellow teeth and devil's eyes, carrying some form of metal stick in each hand. These sticks he pointed towards them.

What followed was something no one could have predicted. This man, evil himself, fired something out of these sticks. The crash made everyone freeze. Baffled, Anna gasped and whipped around. She clasped her hands to her mouth at the sight of Novak, her groom, no longer standing but lying in front of her, clutching his chest. Blood was seeping from him.

Then the ugly man held the second object towards Anna and fired. This time her father threw off his mantle of shock and ran at him. He was too slow for this madman pulled out a dagger and stabbed him in the chest in one fluid movement. He fell immediately. The children scarpered off, screaming, and the rest of the party started to scatter in all directions.

This man seemed to enjoy the mayhem. He laughed and danced over the dead body of her father. Anna was in pain and just like Novak she felt the gush of blood spilling out of her. Her legs were full of lead, pulling her knees towards the ground. Kneeling with her senses overloaded with pain, she bowed her head. It was the familiar sound that made her gather all the energy she had left to lift her head. It was Martin running towards the ugly man.

'Stop now!' The words didn't stop the monster: indeed, he pulled out a knife and began a stabbing rampage. Mr

Novak's own father was lying on the moss with his throat cut, Anna's mother gasped for air as she was stabbed in the chest. Anna's aunt lay beside her, trying to staunch the bleeding.

'Stop this or I shall take revenge!' At the sound of Martin's words, the madman stopped. He turned his body into Martin's direction.

'I tell you one thing, keep your twenty pieces of gold. This is well worth doing for free. As payment I am taking her. Let her come with the devil!'

By now Anna's heart was exploding within her and the pure red blood was turning the white dress burgundy. She moaned in pain, reaching out to touch Martin's face one more time again only to fall onto the mossy ground.

She lay there in the leaves still clutching the wildflowers between her fingers.

Martin let out a roar of fury. He catapulted himself onto the man and they fought like two beasts, each aiming to kill.

Martin wrenched the dagger from the murderer's hands and plunged it into his stomach. Still his rage burnt high, he stabbed the man again and again, finally in his evil heart. When the murderer lay motionless, Martin looked back to where Anna now lay. He ran towards her.

'Darling, please, I cannot live without you, I cannot be without you. I've been travelling the world thinking of nothing else but a future with you. Please darling, forgive me for not coming earlier. Please forgive me.'

His tears fell onto her face, washing away some of the dirt. He shook her limp body. 'Darling, please wake up.'

Anna opened her eyes for the last time. She dropped her hands from the wound but found just enough strength to reach for his face.

'Darling, I will always love you. I will see you in heaven when the time is right.' With that her arms fell by the side of her lifeless body.

***

Anna's declaration of love was the last thing she ever said. Martin's breath was ragged as he bent over her. Though her eyes were open they were just glassy emptiness. Martin wept and screamed in fury and despair, clutched wildly at the sky and retrieved the knife from where he had dropped it on the ground moments ago. Now he unleashed all his fury on the body of the murderer, stabbing relentlessly at the face, over and over until it was nothing but a pulp, and plunging the knife into the dead man's innards as if possessed. In the end, his rage all spent, he dropped to his knees beside Anna, where he sat panting and weeping until finally he whispered his love to Anna's lifeless body once more. And then he plunged the knife into his own heart.

***

Nela stepped out from behind the tree where she had hidden. She had never seen so much blood. Terror pinned her feet to the ground. A massacre! In front of her lay nine lifeless bodies.

When Nela finally ran off and raised the alarm, nobody wanted to go there to see the carnage. At the end it was the monks from the local monastery who came to bury the dead. Nela never returned, never set a foot in those woods ever again. Even upon her death bed she asked to be buried in the next village, not wanting her body to be carried through those same woods to the old church.

The foreboding the place held was worse because of how the burial took place. Unable to get any sense out of the shocked Nela, the monks couldn't establish who was family and who not. So, mistakenly the murderer was buried aside those he had killed.

One of the monks sat down to write of this madness in his journal for all to know what happened that day. The words that follow have been taken from this record.

'As I washed my hands of all the blood, what I saw was despair: the work of the devil himself. From this day we shall pray for those maddened by love that they do not put their love before God himself. We have buried these unfortunate souls along the road for everyone to see that love should never be put before God. He will punish such thoughts.

'We have erected nine large crosses for the family to come and weep for these unfortunate souls. The family refuse to visit the woods, scene of this ungodly crime, for fear that the undead souls will possess them. The poor child, the Bride, was placed in her grave with her wedding dress, though her wedding band could not be found. Surely it was lost or stolen. Instead we buried her with the flowers which she clutched in her hand, and which crowned her hair.

'Her groom was placed beside her and her father on the other. Her poor sister cannot leave the house, so gripped is she by dread. The horseman is also laid there. We were led to believe that he was the one who truly owned the Bride's heart. He is the one who took his own life and must suffer an eternity in hell. Yet we included him in the burial site with the rest as an example for everyone to see.

'The others were killed by means of this infernal new weaponry called a firearm, while one man, a wedding guest, we presume was so disfigured it was horrific. This poor man was ripped to pieces as if ravaged by an animal. His face was beyond recognition as only the bloodied skull remained. His eyes were nothing but sockets as if crows have plucked them out. His bowels were opened and lay all around for wild animals to take as offerings. We gave this poor man some dignity and placed him with the others, side by side with a cross for each.'

The monk placed his writing instrument down and gave a great sigh. It was difficult to write it down. He wished to erase these horrendous details from his memory. He hoped that by writing it down he could forget what he had seen. That he would never have to relive the tale by telling it; he could simply point the inquisitive to the manuscript.

***

That dream was still in Abigail's head the morning she woke up. It was like a movie she was unable to get out of her head. It was difficult to understand why she was meant to learn this or whether it had a meaning at all.

The thirst prompted her to get out of bed. Chills were going up her feet as she stood there filling up her kettle. Once the tap was off she turned to place the kettle onto the heater pad only to jolt a second later, sending splashes of water onto the cold tiled floor. Josef was right there, just standing, hanging about in a bored fashion.

'She has told you her story, ahh how unfortunate. That has nothing to do with what we have between us. I know you want to keep Dan. Then give me what I want! My patience is depleted and this is your last warning.' Each word turned his voice higher until it was only a high-pitched shout piercing her ears. Automatic response to cover her ears made her to drop the kettle.

The kettle shattered, shards shooting everywhere. Covering her the ears hadn't been enough to block out the vicious sound. As she scarpered through the kitchen some shards cut her skin until blood seeped through. The water from the kettle made the floor slippery and each step wounded her further. Abigail was like a mouse dropped into a bucket of water, desperately trying to get out by clawing at the slippery wall. Even out of the kitchen Josef's beast-like growls echoed. In the lounge her eyes darted for the best place to hide as her instinct took over. The only safe place was the embrace with Dan she fell into the moment he walked in, his phone to his ear. He held her tight whilst holding onto the phone.

'Yeah, she just had another episode. She's cut all over her hands, arms, feet and face. She's bleeding. Please come soon.'

The last sound she heard was the siren.

***

Head pounding, Abigail woke up to unfamiliar surroundings. Beeping of machines, constant chitter chatter of people with the odd alarm helped her to realise that she was in a hospital. Dan was also there, texting someone. The shuffling of the duvet made him look up.

'Morning, darling. How are you feeling?'

'Fine, love. I can't explain what happened. I'm sorry for everything.'

Dan took a brief pause from eye contact to face the floor.

'I know, love. You had another episode. I found you lying on the floor with broken pieces of the kettle all over. You were thrashing about like you were trying to get away from something. The wild look on your face was scary. Seriously, love, you have to do something about this!'

'Where am I?'

Unable to look in her face, Dan answered to the floor. 'You are in a mental ward, darling. Look, I had to deal with lots of stuff, you know. Natalie's death wasn't easy, and it caused me a lot of pain. You were there for me in the worst time of my life. I always had a soft spot for you, so it was natural, more like an instinct that we ended up together. I do love you. I do need you, but you have to start thinking about your condition.' He shifted his weight in the chair, so it creaked.

'It all got started after Natalie died, so we all agree you need to deal with that issue in your head.' With desperation, he threw his hands apart as if he was trying to indicate the size of the problem. Only then he was able to look Abigail in the eye. 'Don't you see? She's the reason. Her death is something you haven't sorted in your head yet. Natalie loved you like a sister, so she wouldn't want you upset. For her sake you need to get some psychiatric care.'

With his words hanging like a bad smell it was Abigail's turn to hide from his piercing look. How much she wanted to tell him how wrong he was about what he just said. Should he have known half of the stuff that was floating in her head, he would have turned around and left forever. One absolute to be sure about was the fact that Natalie would want her to be happy especially if she knew what was done. More likely she would have gouged Abigail's eyes out.

'Coffee? Tea?' The hospital tea lady barged in to get the order.

'Um, I'll have a tea please,' said Dan.

Abigail turned up her nose to the offer. 'I really don't know how people can drink that hospital fake coffee stuff. Thank you. I'll give it a miss.'

With the tea lady gone Abigail could carry on the conversation in privacy.

'I know what you're saying and I'm promising you I'll get better. You'll see it in a couple of days, everything will be normal again.'

She was cornered. Something had to be done. It was clear all the doctors were very reluctant to discharge her despite her being the perfect patient, swallowing all the pills like a baby bird. There were many therapy sessions to attend to where she had to pretend that all was normal, and Josef was invisible.

The more she pretended to not see him, the less frequently he appeared. Sometimes a stolen glance would confirm he was there, completely silent in the corner, with hands crossed across his chest like a bored teenager. Soon Abigail was able to ignore him completely and he just became the part of the furniture. Maybe she could gain some form of control over him after all.

***

The return home was heaven. The smell of real coffee and wood polish, with the scent of flowers and cut grass trailing through the window was heaven compared to that of body odour and disinfectant. She sank into the sofa. What a relief after those squeaky fake leather chairs and brick-hard hospital bed. Everything was going in the right direction now. She had fought off her demons and Dan hadn't run away. Not many men would understand a mental illness or be as patient as he had. He was truly a gem, busying himself in the kitchen making a nice hot steamy chocolate. The jingling of the spoon against the mug cheered her.

Handing her the mug, he said, 'Love, as we're celebrating, let's get takeaways. We'll just watch a movie and veg out.' The mug warmed her palms as she cradled it to her chest.

'What a good idea, yum! I'm really craving Indian food. The hospital mush tasted of old socks.' Dan delved into the takeaway menu he pulled out of his jeans back pocket. Then with a cheeky look he put it down and leaned in for a kiss.

'No worries, love. First go to the bathroom. There's a surprise waiting for you.'

He wasn't kidding. The bath was filled up with hot water and bubbles nearly spilling out. There were scented candles all around with a glass of wine and a book on the edge.

'Oh honey, you know me so well. I'm very lucky to have you.' It was a great surprise. Dan got everything perfectly ready.

'You're going to get even luckier. Just have a bath, relax! Take a read. I'll call you when the food's ready.'

A couple of minutes later Abigail's body submerged underneath the bubbles. The steam rose in a misty curtain, bringing the scent of jasmine and musk with it. The wine was the perfect ending to a good day.

Sipping it as she lay there reading really drummed in the normality of the life lying ahead. She had made it. She was living with the man of her dreams, twenty-four hours a day, seven days a week.

The memory of their first meeting was still fresh. He was gorgeous, tugging nervously at his suit button. His jet-black hair shone in the light. Natalie had immediately clocked the suit was Armani and the shoes were made to order. All Abigail saw was his immaculate chest underneath his crisp white shirt. The cheekily undone top button was a very inviting sight. His little habits were sexy as well as sweet. Sometimes he did this cute thing of pulling at his eyebrow when concentrating. It was so cute, that when Abigail approached him to ask couple of questions his eyebrows were sticking out like straw from a scarecrow.

His filing was based on putting papers into different piles on top of his desk. Some piles had torn papers piled up to the tip over point. Dan would stumble around for ages trying to find a specific piece of paper. Once he recognised the sheet he was after, he would try to retrieve it but the whole pile would collapse into one mess which he would spread all over the floor in frustration. Eventually he would get his bearings and get himself organised again. It was an entertainment watching him in this mood.

'I'm ready, hon, you can come get your food now. You have been in there already for thirty minutes. You'll get all crinkled up.'

It was a good prompt as the water lost its heat. The towel resting on the radiator warmed her up further. A little poke around made Abigail realise that she had forgotten to bring in her pyjamas so the silky red dressing gown hanging on the door had to do for now. Many men had taken it off, some slowly, some in a rush, but no one was as good as Dan.

As soon as the bathroom door opened the musk and jasmine mixed with the fragrance of curry. Her pace quickened at the same time her belly rumbled. It was odd to see the kitchen door shut as due to the cupboard-like size the kitchen felt suffocating. Dan never closed the door, so Abigail pulled at the cold handle.

'Is everything all right, love?'

From behind the door was a sight that Abigail thought she would never see.

'Marry me, Abigail.'

Dan was there on one knee with an open box in his hand. Inside was a huge rock. Red rose petals were scattered all around the kitchen. Some were also on the small kitchen table where a candle-lit dinner awaited. Her whole body shook with happiness. She covered her face with her palms trying to catch the streaming tears of joy.

The one moment had finally come, the one man she wanted more than anything else in the world was there, ready to take ask her to be his wife. Was all the hard stuff worth it? The hell it was! Abigail was ready to do anything to have this man all over again. Dropping her arms away from her face she launched them around his shoulders.

'Oh Dan, darling, of course I will marry you, yes-yes-yes.' The tears now ran down his neck as she pulled him close to her.

'Now that's wrapped up! Sit down and eat, love, you must be hungry.' He grinned, peeling her away from him.

She gave him the kiss of his life. What followed was amazing. The kisses got more heated and then they made love for what felt a century. Abigail was the happiest woman alive. Not even the cold curry after could dampen her spirit.

***

Outside, standing in the chill that felt to him like a caress, Josef smirked and rubbed his palms together. She was playing right into his hands, this Abigail. He tossed his head back as he laughed. The woman had no idea, but Josef was satisfied. Completely unaware of her fate, she had just moved closer to the edge of a cliff where all her happiness would fall into the abyss below.

Chapter 7

Abigail leafed through the bridal magazines spread out on her coffee table. She licked her fingers as she turned the page, a habit she picked up off her gran. All the women wore beautiful wedding gowns with sparkling accessories. Each page was a new mirror she could reflect herself in. A skin-tight dress wouldn't be the best for her figure, so she settled to mark the pages with the floaty dresses. Their own wedding day was drawing near, sending jolts of excitement to her now perfect life. Dan's parents were a godsend, his mum especially, as she took over the task of the flower arrangements and organising the make-up artist. Abigail wanted to have subtle make up rather than the over-the-top painted face of a tribal warrior.

She wanted a wedding completely different from Natalie's. That was the main reason she decided against a church ceremony. It would be very uncomfortable to stand in church before a priest, considering the lead-up to the whole thing.

The final venue was a historic little country house with a river running past it. The old mill had been converted into a wedding venue and popular with locals. Dan's mother joined her in looking around the place; after all, they were going to pay major part of the wedding, so Abigail had no choice once she showed interest.

When Abigail remembered that visit, she flicked the magazine shut. 'Here by this pond you can have some photos taken,' cooed the owner's wife. 'We usually have some swans swimming in it, so the pics will be amazing.' Her arm was extended towards the ducks waddling about, diving in to reach the green at the bottom of the lake.

'On the day we can provide main drinks with snacks on the deck overlooking the river. Once all guests have a glass in hand, we can set off fireworks from the other side of the river. You just need to tell me how lavish your firework requirements are. It's a splendid show.'

It was too much information to take in, but both were right. Abigail wanted it all, to have the drink on the deck with fireworks, to the photos by the pond with the swans in the background. Even the tacky rose arch walk was enticing. Throughout this Dan's mother was sticking her nose up to all the suggestions but not saying a word.

As there were leaving, the woman wrapped up. 'No need to worry about rain either, we supply all the gazebos your heart desires with no extra charge! It's all in the package. Do have a look at those brochures and let us know your demands. We are here to make your day special.'

Abigail felt nothing but special although all of that was very enticing indeed, it really boiled down to one key thing and that was the fact that she was marrying Dan.

On the way to the car they passed more waddling ducks. The atmosphere inside the car was like soup in a bubbling pot. The monster in the shape of Josef had now been replaced by Dan's mother.

'Abigail, darling, I have to speak my mind.' She looked serious, her breathing rapid. Her words were shooting arrows piercing the thick atmosphere, directed at Abigail's face.

'Abigail, I love my son. I love him more than anything in the world and should you have kids you'll understand one day. I've always wanted certain things for my son. I wanted him to respect his past, his grandparents and the place where they came from. We are, after all, Catholic. I do know that you have really enjoyed seeing this place, but it just won't do.'

She took a deep breath as if steadying herself for the final blow.

'I know it's tempting to get married here, but I must speak my mind. I don't want you to marry Dan here. You can plan the party for here, the fireworks whatever, but you won't marry in these grounds. If you want my blessing you will marry my Dan in a church!'

The fabric seats squelched as her body turned to face Abigail directly. The daggers coming out of her eyes worked with the poison escaping her mouth.

'Natalie agreed to it.' A deliberate pause to ensure the poison took hold. 'I don't see why you can't either. You and Natalie were alike, so I hope you understand my wishes. What I do know, which might make it harder, is that you do not want to get married in the same church. Fine, I agree it wouldn't be appropriate. I have chosen a lovely church, though the location might not be the best: St Marks, in the middle of town. That's where you'll marry.'

The nasty woman sent one last dart sent in Abigail's direction before her chubbiness settled back in her seat and she faced the front. She spoke the final sentence triumphantly.

Flabbergasted, Abigail could only gulp and swallow the invisible large chunk that appeared in her throat. She was aware of Dan's mother claiming to be a Catholic despite their father being Anglican.

The journey back went silently but each knew of the storm that was happening inside. Thankfully Dan's mother decided to fill the space with empty chatter about the florist picking a funny shade of yellows, which were 'not gold at all' in her opinion. Desperate to tell Dan what happening, Abigail chose to listen with the occasional nod. Surely Dan would take her side in not marrying in a church!

The uneasiness of knowing how Natalie truly died hung over Abigail like a cloak. After all, she was a sinner, too wicked for church. Trying to distract herself as instructed by the therapist she counted the number of trees they drove past.

'It was a pleasure spending this day with you,' Abigail said as they approached their destination.

'I really like the spot we saw today, the whole set-up. I'm going to book them so nobody else gets that slot. And I'll speak to Dan about the church for you, but I'm not sure what he'll say. Still, I promise we will think about it.'

No matter what move Abigail made, Dan's mum was well prepared to blast another bomb in her direction. 'You don't have to, Abigail, I've done it for you. I've spoken to Daniel already and he agrees. At least it's more practical, with the roof and all!' Her joke fell flat.

With a clunk of the car door all Abigail could muster was, 'Well, I need to speak to Dan about it anyway.' Unchanged, savouring the moment, Dan's mum chirped after her whilst the engine rumbled back to life.

'You might be wasting your breath, dear. The wedding is going to be there; the decision isn't yours to make. The place is booked. I spoke to the vicar. Tomorrow, be there at 5.00 p.m. sharp. We are doing a rehearsal. Speak to Dan if you wish but this will not change. Abigail, the only thing I'm asking you is to do this. I'm paying, after all, as you are as poor as a church mouse. If I'm stuck with the bill, I'm making the decisions. I'm not moving on this one. You have no choice. OK, I will see you there at 5.00 p.m. sharp. Thank you, Abigail, I knew you'd be sensible about this. You're as good as Natalie. Well, cheerio, see you tomorrow. Have a nice evening.'

With a blast of smoke and diesel fumes the car was on its way. Abigail desperately tried not to look in the woman's direction. With grinding teeth, squeezing her fists, she fumbled in her handbag pretending to find the key.

Back home, in another attempt to distract herself from the painful memory, she picked up magazine she hadn't leafed through yet. With her head full of Dan's mother's plans, the pleasure of flipping through the magazines had disappeared. Even now the ringing chirp of Dan's mother's voice returned to her memory as if she was in the next room. It still bugged her to know that the woman had manipulated Dan into it. Hadn't anyone considered it was *her* wedding? The church was so inconvenient, not just because of hypocrisy but also because it was right beside the main road, known for its traffic with hordes of people walking in all directions. Getting out of it was impossible. That smug smile had been the icing on the cake.

Worst of all was the wait for Dan to come home. A whole two hours later, after she had left a trail in the carpet from pacing, Dan finally made an appearance.

'Where have you been, Daniel?' He hated to be called that, which was why she did it, to prove a point. She got the reaction she'd expected as he took off his shoes and threw them onto the floor like they were on fire. One of the rubber soles made a black line on the wall he chose to stare at as he answered.

'You know nobody calls me Daniel, apart from my mother. I hate being called that. What's your problem?' he snapped. That was unexpected.

'My problem? Well, Daniel, the problem is *your* mother! That woman has gone and booked some church I've never heard of. Some place in the middle of the bloody town. What will be awful is to wait for all the guests to arrive when they're stuck in the bloody traffic, because *your mother* decided that she's Catholic. Well, what are you going to do about it?' Ignoring the mark on the wall, trying to get past towards the bedroom, Dan just gently pushed her shoulder aside.

'*Abigail*, fuck off!'

That was the first time she heard him swear, the first time he slammed the door on her, the first time they argued. But that was the point. It didn't make her feel good, neither was she good at calming her mind because she was cornered. Eventually, with little time behind, it was time to make up. If she should marry in a church then why not, it didn't matter, if she could have him. Some hot tea sloshed onto the carpet as she tried to open the door where Dan hid.

'Dan, darling, I am so sorry. I snapped. I shouldn't have. It's the wedding, it's driving me around the bend. There is so much to plan.' His shoulders were shaking. Sniffing sulkily, he took the warm mug.

'No, you shouldn't have! What you don't understand is that I spent all yesterday getting nagged by my mother. She isn't a woman you can ignore. I knew you wouldn't like it, but we have no choice.'

Putting the mug down on the bedside table he bowed to inspect his feet. Like a lost unwanted kitten, a small sorrowful sound left his throat.

'Darling, I'm so sorry I made you cry,' she said. 'Have a sip, darling, it's your favourite.' Dan dismissed it, leaving it where it was.

'That's not what I'm upset about. Abigail, the reason I was late is because I went to see her. I went to Natalie's grave. I told her everything, I told her about my mum, about you, about everyone.'

This was a huge blow. 'I do want to marry you, I do love you, but I will always love her. I hope you understand this, because if you don't, we can't marry.'

It was another kick in the teeth. Not just that his mother was a blood-sucking parasite. He was a pathetic loser unable to forget the past. Natalie was the past! Nothing more, just history, a nightmare passed. With a performance of her life, Abigail pulled out her best acting skills of self-control.

'Darling, of course, I completely understand. Are you going to be OK to meet up tomorrow by the church? We have a practice run; I don't want to be late. I know you have a fitting just before. Shall I just drive and pick you up on the way? Think about it, hon, and have that tea before it gets cold.'

A quick retreat was needed as the hot tea looked to her like great ammunition to pour all over him. Now she sat there going through all the magazines she hadn't managed to nose through yet. She made another one fly onto the table with such force it nearly broke the glass. Eventually, she had to be realistic. Church wasn't going to change. The door squeaked open. Dan appeared with an empty cup in his hand.

'Is everything all right?'

Though she wasn't as happy as she wanted to, the glossy magazine cover of a smiling bride made her take it in her stride.

'Yes, let's plan how we're going to make it to that church on time. Traffic is going to be a nightmare and we both know that turning up late is out of the question. Unless we want to face the wrath of your mum upon us.'

***

The morning after was something out of a Hollywood movie. They ate breakfast and had a whole steamy session on the kitchen counter afterwards. As Abigail tried to get the jam off her backside in the shower, Dan walked in, smothered her in soap, planted kisses all over and what followed was another session of amazing sex.

In the steam when he left Abigail run her finger across the steamed-up glass, practising her new signature – Abigail Johnson. Maybe they should argue more often if that was how they made up. Delighted, Abigail was still smiling like a Cheshire cat in the office.

Everyone could tell she had had a good morning.

'You look like a kid that got a massive lollipop!' was a comment Jeanette threw at her.

'It was a big lollipop and yeah, I sucked on it hard!'

Jeanette cringed but she shouldn't have made that comment without expecting a retort. Nobody was going to ruin her day today.

The day had gone so fast! Abigail was nearly late for the church pre-run! Her fingers were flying over the keyboard, typing furiously to finish the email she had to do before the end of business. Her typing was usually faster but the new pills that helped to get rid of Josef slowed her down. Usually an email would be knocked out in seconds but now it was a lot longer. The Enter button nearly fell out of its place when she hit it. Cocking her arm to note the time she shouted at herself:

'You're late!' Thankfully she could buy some time when picking Dan up along the road. Her phone chimed with a message.

'Make sure you're on time! The priest has another set of newlyweds after you!' Nothing surprised Abigail anymore when it involved Dan's mother. The internet browser took some time to load but Abigail had that little nagging thought she should check her route again before leaving. As she put in the address a picture with directions popped up on the screen. The church was a modern building with a very strange huge statue of Jesus on top. Jesus was taller than the church with hands outstretched, head bowed towards the poor mortals below. It certainly wasn't her taste at all.

It no longer mattered if Dan was beside her during the ceremony. A last quick check of the watch made her heart skip a beat. Even the dive into her handbag to fish out her keys was taking longer than it should. In between all the useless stuff one carries around finally the keys jingled to reveal where they were hidden. As she dashed out of the office she accidentally banged the door. In typical nosy fashion the receptionist tut-tutted about no need to slam the doors.

It didn't matter what the receptionist thought now. Time was ticking away and if she didn't get there soon she'd lose the opportunity to have a nice church meeting prior to the wedding.

The red and white barrier at the office park took its time again, slowly squeaking to open. Every minute counted and now she had to rush through traffic to get Dan, so they could make their way to the church.

She stepped on the accelerator, driving one-handed driving with the mobile on her lap, checking for the best route. One thing was sure, she had to dodge the traffic. Cutting in between cars, trying to figure out new shortcuts on her phone ... She knew it was dangerous. But she was determined to be on time. Not even the angry cyclist she nearly knocked over got her to slow down. With one hand on the handlebars, the cyclist used his other fist to shove the wing mirror inwards.

'You shouldn't be on the road anyway!' she spat at him. With one hand rummaging through her handbag, she watched the guy give her the finger. And then she slammed on the brakes, just in time to avoid the car ahead of her. No! She was stuck in it: the traffic.

The phone kept ringing and the clock ticked faster. Without indicating, she swerved the car left to cut in front of the cars on the roundabout. They all responded like the cyclist but that didn't work at all. 'Whatever!' she shouted, skipping ahead of the traffic, cutting off the old dear who was the primary cause of the block. The BMW behind her took a severe dislike to being cut off and started tailgating her.

'All I need, buddy, is to jump on my brakes and your nice Beemer will be buggered, mate!' Her stress levels entered a new dimension. The phone rang. With the road mostly clear ahead, she tried once more to retrieve it. Where the hell was the thing? The ringing stopped, and she swore. Then another call.

'You bastard!' she shouted. 'I'll get you!' And with that she tipped the bag upside down. Shaking it out onto the passenger seat finally released the phone, but it slipped onto the floor.

'Dammit!' Reaching for it, she strained at the seat belt. She leaned over, stretched, and finally the phone was in her hand. Only a few hundred meters more to where Dan would be waiting anxiously.

Getting herself upright again, her eyes were assaulted by high beams from the BMW. Squinting, trying to regain her sight, she took her eyes off the steering wheel. Her head instinctively went to her right towards the seat, where her palm was clasping the furiously ringing phone.

Still squinting, she felt her nose overwhelmed by the stench of rotten meat. Then a cry: 'Boo!' and she gasped.

Josef was sitting in the passenger seat, on top of the handbag contents. He was real, fully clothed, his face full of hate, his breath a deathly rot. The shock made her pull her body as far away as possible. As her body moved so did the arm controlling the steering wheel, taking the car over the curb onto the pavement. With metal screeching, the car lurched over the curb and flung Abigail's body towards the windscreen.

Within seconds she recognized another face that was coming towards her with alarming speed. Dan! Their eyes met as his head whacked the windscreen, changing the glass from clear to cloudy. The thump and pop of Dan's head was followed by the whole body bouncing off the car onto the pavement behind the now stationary car. Her knuckles white, Abigail, hyperventilating now, braved a look into the mirror. It reflected motionless Dan with a seeping wound on his forehead. Her screams bounced around the car. Each spidery hairline of the windscreen extended until it shattered into millions of tiny pieces, showering the whole dashboard with glassy beads. People ran to the scene from all directions.

A policeman was talking but all sound drowned away; everything deathly silent. The phone lighting up on the seat between all the glass was a sore reminder of where she should have been by now. Nothing made sense.

'She was driving like a lunatic! This guy was just waving from the pavement and she just swerved directly onto him!'

It was the BMW man shouting at the police, red-faced. Eventually the ambulance sirens went silent as the vehicle pulled up. Slowly the green-suited men surrounded Dan. The belly of the ambulance opened and swallowed the whole stretcher with Dan on it. The door clunked shut as the siren began to howl. Abigail was led out of her car by a policeman who took her to the second ambulance. Everything silent in her ears, all she could hear was the laughter. Nothing could drown that deep, roaring laughter. Josef was very pleased with the whole commotion, jumping in between Dan's limp body, to helping to shut the ambulance door, making his way towards the BMW man and turning his attention to Abigail. Arching his head backwards with the weight of the laughter, his yellow teeth glistened in the sunlight, his dark eyes aimed at Abigail. Just before she passed out, she remembered one final sentence he had said:

'What I give you I can also take away.'

***

Anna's dress floated above the water, her outstretched arms waving as her lips moved. 'I told you to stay away. I asked you not to listen to him. I gave you so many signs to leave it! To go away, yet you would not listen. I showed you the truth, but you didn't pay any attention to it, to the fact of whom you were dealing with.'

Abigail didn't need to check what was behind her. The swooshing sound of moving pine trees, the scent of earth and mulch, and the clammy breeze were all a clear indication of where she just stood. The only difference was this time the lake had no ripples. The bottom of the white wedding dress was floating on the surface and sucking all the water up the skirt. Mixed with the blood, the water turned red and sticky. When the dress turned from white to red, Anna's whisper turned to a throaty scream.

'I told you to leave. I told you to go away. You have failed everyone and now? Now you belong to him! I cannot do this anymore. I must take you to hell before you to do what he wants. The only way to stop this is if you come with me willingly.' Her body floated closer and stretched out her arms, reaching for Abigail.

'You must do as you're told; you must give yourself to save the others. You must come with me. You've been possessed by him; cannot be rid of him. He owns you. Surely you feel this deep within your heart? He will never leave you, you belong to him. Come with me NOW!'

The wind changed direction, tugging at her locks like a dog with a rag. It whipped the flowers from her hair, sending them into the air in a circle above her head. Not just her dress was bloody red, her eyes glowed red too. Her chest opened and through the opening her beating heart was spattered blood. The wind turned into a howl.

He voice was harder to hear now, but Abigail's own was audible: 'I cannot! I cannot leave, I will not, Dan is mine! Mine. I won't give him away! Never, now I finally have him I'm not giving him up!'

The Bride retreated her arms back to her sides. The slim fingers clenching up into a ball, hair a mess, her face clammed up. Eyebrows lowered, red eyes glowing, her face slowly turned into wickedness itself. The familiar smell of rotten flesh arrived with the wind. Josef stood beside Abigail, smiling his pointy-toothed smile at Anna.

'That's my girl, Abigail, that's my girl. Should you give me what I want I will go away. You can keep Dan, you can be forever happy. Should you fail, I will leave her to you.'

Josef pointed in the direction of the lake where the Bride stood still.

'I will leave that pathetic being to take you away should you fail, *do you understand*?'

Frightened, Abigail faced by the choice was unable to respond.

'Are you listening, you pathetic soul?'

With a gulp of air Abigail woke up. Nobody was shouting in her empty room. The curtains were drawn, shutting out the moonlight. The bedside table had the mobile phone on it. Some light crept through shutters on a small door window. The harshly over washed bedsheets, the door with a window and non-descriptive curtains were all obvious signs of a hospital ward. If that didn't give it away the nurses' chatter coming in from the corridor was the confirmation.

It must have been a dream! Hopeful, Abigail grabbed the phone to dial the last missed-call number. The dial tone rang through her head.

'Pick up, darling, I really need to hear you now, pick up.' After the eighth ring the phone was answered. The voice wasn't Dan's.

'Who are you? Where is Dan?'

'Sorry, madam, my name is Officer Alexander. I am holding onto Mr Johnson's possessions until they are picked up by his family. Sorry, miss, but Daniel is in the hospital after suffering severe injuries in a car crash. I am unable to say any more, but I will require your details as I have to log the name of everyone who calls this number.'

Slamming the phone down back onto the bedside table made the bed shake. Duvet tossed aside there was only one thought running through her head, she must see Dan. Slowly slapping her bare feet on the lino she made her way to the door. The cold door handle squeaked, and the light came flooding in from the hallway, hurting her eyes. The nurses turned to Abigail. One broke from the crowd to come to her.

'You shouldn't be out, love. Come, I'll take you back to bed. You had some pills that make you dizzy.'

She tried to usher her back into the room, but Abigail had none of it.

'Where is Dan? Where is he? Please take me to see him.' Maybe it was the pleading face or the sorrow that made the nurse change her mind. She walked off only to come back in couple of minutes with a wheelchair.

'Sit down. I can take you to him, but you can't walk by yourself, you must be reasonable. I must warn you, though, he's in a critical condition in an intensive care unit. We won't be able to go inside his room, but you can see him through the glass.'

All the hospital corridors looked the same. The whitewash peeling off the unkempt walls, the smell of bleach in every corner and worn chairs scattered everywhere. Each ward was guarded by a lock only allowing in those that had the key. Everyone else had to buzz in to explain their business. When they made their way to the lift one wheel started to play up. Unhappy to move, the nurse had to budge it into the lift. Inside she made a clucking sound with her tongue.

'There's something you need to know. Your fiancé's heart has stopped a few times. They're not sure he'll make it, but he seems to be young enough to get through this.'

The nurse gently pressed her hand on Abigail's shoulder and only retrieved it when the lift pinged the door open. Taking the lead on the wheelchair she pushed it all the way to the ICU entrance guarded by buzzer with a security camera. The nurse put her pass through the machine and the door opened to let them enter. Inside the ICU was a main corridor between five rooms with large glass windows. The other side was the main nurses' room from where they could observe all patients. The nursing station had all sorts of equipment: monitors as well as computers. Each room had one wall that looked like an aircraft control tower with large number of beeping monitors and IV stands. Abigail jumped up from the wheelchair leaving the nurse behind talking to someone as she noticed the room that had Dan in. She pressed her face against the glass, causing it to steam up with her breath.

Inside was Dan lying silently with a ventilator covering most of his face. His hair wasn't visible as it was covered in a large bandage. Wiping the glass with the sleeve, Abigail noted the alien in Dan's room.

'I knew you would come eventually,' mouthed Josef from Dan's bedside. He sat there in a chair provided for visitors, twiddling his thumbs until he had Abigail's full attention.

'I can take away what I gave you. Give me what I want, and I will go away. Don't and ... I will show you.'

With a grin he skipped across the room towards the machinery that was keeping Dan alive. Josef stopped by the cardiograph.

'Oh dear, the choices are overwhelming, what shall I do first? I do prefer the heart, the pumping, the feeling of muscle tightening,' said Josef as he pressed STOP on the ventilator. Breezing past the hemodialyzer, he stopped it only to pause at the electronic heart monitor. Twitching his eyebrows, his scrawny finger pressed the red button. The red light above the entrance was going mad. Unmoved, Josef pinched tightly the tube on the drip delivering the infusion to Dan's veins. Then he placed his hand onto Dan's chest.

'Do you remember what you saw the last time I touched someone's chest? Do you remember Natalie? I will take what is mine!'

The alarms were making a dreadful noise. All staff dropped whatever they were doing and rushed into Dan's room. With puzzled faces they started to resuscitate him. One nurse rushed about the machines pressing things rapidly. Beside them was Josef laughing, letting go of the infusion. Desperate, Abigail tried to warn the staff. Tight-fisted she hammered at the glass.

'Can't you see him? He's killing him! Help him, take that man away, the one by Dan's bed. He's trying to kill Dan!'

Dan stabilised, the staff turned their attention at Abigail.

The medic wasn't impressed. 'What is she doing here?' One of the nurses ran towards Abigail with a tranquilizer needle in her hand. Soon she was pushed into the wheelchair and taken back to her ward. With heavy eyelids Abigail made out the last sentence coming out of Josef's lips.

'Give me what I want, or I take him instead.'

***

Mentally exhausted, an apathetic Abigail sat through numerous psychiatric sessions, taking all the pills yet knowing nothing could help apart from doing what Josef wanted. Each time she managed to talk the nurse taking her to Dan, Josef would be there sitting by the bedside. Abigail nearly lost everything. It was her own private torture as nobody else could see Josef. He was a strong opponent with powers beyond her own. Initially each visit to Dan's bedside resulted in bleeding knuckles as she tried to get to Dan through the glass. Each injection given made her more apathetic until she was unable to beat at the glass, shout or even think. Under strong opiates and Josef's continuous presence, Abigail made the final decision. She had to do what he asked otherwise she would be leaving this place without Dan.

Alone in her room in the dark of night, she decided how to proceed. It should be easy to find the women Josef needed. Thankfully in the world of social media where individuals shared their deepest thoughts, there were bound to be those she needed. All she had to do is to pass them a posy, nothing criminal at all. She wasn't going to murder them or do anything sinister, all she was going to do was give them flowers. When questioning Josef why, his response was always the same.

'I will try to help them. Just pass on the little wildflower posy and ask no more.'

The corridor spanning the ward was always busy with people going off in different directions. That was the beauty of being in a mental ward. The nurses were too busy to bother with the patients that had not caused too much fuss. The patients on this ward were all dosed up to their eyeballs, just as she was.

To do this, she had to be sharp, so some cold water splashed up in her face should do the trick. Quietly she tiptoed into the bathroom making sure none of the other patients woke. Refreshed, she drew the privacy curtains around her bed and took out her laptop from the bedside cupboard. When they moved her from the private room she had before, Dan's mother visited and brought some stuff with her. Slightly irritated, she had dropped a large bag onto Natalie's bed and with a snippy comment of 'now I have to visit my son' she turned on her heel, dashing out of the ward. It didn't bother Abigail that clearly, she wasn't the flavour of the month in Dan's family circle, if she had some change of clothes, she could pick herself back up again to be ready to take care of Dan. Among some clothes, magazines and spare underwear was also her laptop, which was exciting indeed. Initially she was going to use it to watch some movies she had saved on there, but today it served a different purpose. The quiet sound of the Microsoft welcome lit up the screen. A dongle connected the ward to the world-wide web. Her ears pricked each time footsteps got too close to the door or another patient made a little groan in their sleep. Pulling a duvet over her laptop helped to drown the light from the screen.

Abigail had to be careful as the nurse that took her to see Dan when she first woke up was now watching her like a hawk. She was suspicious. Now Abigail could recognize the nurses walk as she stomped but due to her little limp the left foot was quieter than the right.

'Margaret, before you see the young lady, have you filled in the report for Mrs Small?'

It was her, the bloody hawk nurse. Abigail closed the laptop underneath the duvet and lay still.

'I'll do that later, Lindsay. Just need to give my patients their meds.'

Margaret walked into the room without knocking, as if she owned the place. Quietly, with speed, the laptop was shoved underneath the pillow where it would be well hidden. The nurse made her way through a small opening between the privacy curtains.

'Abigail, wake up, it's your final medicines for tonight.'

Abigail pretended to take her time to sit up as if she had just woken up, pointing her finger at the pills. 'I feel lots better. I don't think that I'll need these anymore!'

The nurse pushed the cup of water closer to Abigail. 'I don't think you can make that decision, dear. That's for the doctors to decide. For now, you swallow these. Here's water.'

The nurse watched Abigail's every move with her beady eyes. When Abigail swallowed, she opened her mouth to prove she had swallowed them.

'Well done. You're getting better in taking these. They should help you with forgetting your visions, so you can catch up on your sleep.'

Another groan sounded from the room. Her tone a whisper, Abigail leaned towards the nurse.

'I no longer see him. That makes me so happy. It must have been the shock of seeing Dan so injured. It was most likely post-traumatic stress disorder. Thankfully that would mean I get to go home soon, so I can start planning my wedding. Once Dan recovers we can carry on with our lives as normal.'

The nurse's expression changed to something gloomier. 'You don't have to fool me, dear. I've been in this job far too long to know a lie when I see one. You're hiding something, I know it deep in my heart. I don't think that you'll be leaving us yet.'

Abigail's jaw tightened. 'Get out and leave me alone. I'm better and ready to go home. The doctor is not going to listen to some nurse who never had the brains to qualify for MD.'

***

The nurse left the room wordlessly. It was common in these parts of the hospital to be sworn at, to be humiliated, or be attacked. She was used to it, but some patients were different, scarier. This girl frightened her.

'I can't put my finger on it, Lindsay, but that girl is trouble,' she mumbled to a colleague one she closed the ward door.

'I really believe she sees someone, I really do. To top it further, that fiancé of hers, his heart giving up, on and off, the machines not working and all that, you know, it's all strange. I was there the first time it happened, when she hammered on the glass screaming that some man was in the room, ready to kill her fiancé. I had a look myself and couldn't see anyone apart from the poor injured boy surrounded by medical equipment. Nobody was there. It was soon after when she got upset that the machines went mad like she was possessing them. I know the ICU staff very well. You know how they check their equipment. So how could the heart monitor fail at the same time as the drip and the ventilator? And it all happened within seconds with her screaming. I know you think I'm a fool, but you know me better than anyone else. You know what I believe in. There are things that we humans aren't aware of. There is always more.'

Meanwhile, another nurse joined the nursing station with more gossip. 'You know, I spoke to Jenny, who works in ICU. She's also spooked. The machines are checked all the time, but someone keeps turning them off and on as if by magic. Jenny is being bollocked by the head nurse daily now. There are things we don't know but the sooner that girl goes the better, I say.' All the staff now moved their heads directly to the ward door as if they sensed that someone was watching them.

***

In the bed Abigail retrieved her laptop from underneath her pillow. Still a little annoyed with the nurse, she found it harder to concentrate. The sleeping pill made her drowsy too. Abigail cursed the large, nosy woman with cropped hair that was most likely gossiping with the other nurses. There was no time to spare as the pills would soon make her too tired to concentrate. Her fingers spread over the keyboard kickstarted the Google search. "Unhappy bride" and "dissatisfied bride" and many others were added to the search bar.

At the end, Abigail homed in on the Twitter forum called "unhappy brides". Even Flickr had some chat lines on the same subject. Trailing though endless drivel of spoiled girls complaining about this and that or whatever else was not perfect, Abigail found what she was looking for, an anonymous post with location as London.

'I'm going to be married but deep in my heart I long for someone else. Are there more of you out there? Should I tell him I no longer want to go through with this?'

Lots of people checked this chat but no one had answered

'Hello, I'm in the same situation. It's such a personal thing. Do you think we could meet for a chat? I suggest the lobby of the Savoy in two weeks' time. Any more unhappy ladies? Join us.' Tap tap tap and send.

The opiates were kicking in hard so there wasn't time for anything else. Laptop stored way back in the bedside table, she fell into a deep sleep.

***

'Wake up. We have good news for you. Daniel is over the worst now! He has opened his eyes!' The nurse was holding Abigail's shoulder, shaking her a little.

'I need to see him; please can I see him?' The words came out instinctively.

'Of course, I'll bring in the wheelchair.' The nurse walked off to fetch it.

'I have decided to reward you for finally acknowledging my need,' came the whisper from the bedside table.

A slow turn of the head revealed Josef sitting on the visitor's chair.

'You have to leave me alone or I'll never be able to meet these women. They'll keep me here unless I'll stop seeing you.' Sitting in the bed, facing him, she spoke sharply but quietly, choosing the words carefully to avoid aggravating him. To her surprise his reply came in the calmest of voices.

'I might give you some breathing space. For now, I mean. Not for long, otherwise you might forget our little arrangement. I shall give you a month of peace, no more than that. You go see for yourself how well Dan is doing. Yet again I gave him back to you. Though this is the last time I will do so.'

His whisper was now louder, the sharpness of his words was like a blade.

'But remember what I gave you I can take away as well. I can take him away anytime I please, so you do as you're told!'

As his last words were spoken the nurse appeared in the doorway.

'Here you go. Sit in this chair, nice and slow so you won't injure yourself. I'll take you to Dan, he's been asking for you, you know. He's missing you too.'

By the time Abigail sat up on the chair, Josef was gone. The way to the intensive care unit felt like millions of miles away. People kept coming and going, in and out of the lift on each floor adding on an agitated excitement each time the lift stopped. Finally, the last door opened, and Abigail was wheeled into Dan's room.

'Hello, darling, how are you feeling? I miss you so much and the drugs they give me are so strong. I'm like a zombie most of the time.'

Dan managed to turn his head towards her. He still had scars across his face where the windscreen had cut him. The longest scar was the one across his forehead. Thankfully it was healing nicely.

'Honey, I am glad you are taking the medicines. You nearly killed me. I can't live with you if you won't fix this problem of yours. If you won't see the specialist I'll have to call off the wedding. I really mean it. I love you, but I can't live like this. I can't live in fear of not knowing when you are going to have another episode. I get frightened about this as each time I'll have to think – is this the last time? One day I'll die because of you.'

His words hurt but it was clear that he was frightened. The nurse was standing by the glass pretending not to watch but Abigail knew that she was being nosy. 'Dan, I promise you that the last thing you need doing is to be worried. There is loads of things rattling in my head, but they are sorted. I promise you, I am fixed.'

He reached for her hand and they embraced. Abigail clasped his hand tight, not wanting to let go. Laying her head on his chest in between the sobs she promised things would change.

'I no longer see him, darling. I no longer have these visions. The medication has helped. I needed to be closed off with the right treatment. When we are discharged, we can move on with our lives. I promise you that. I know what your mum says that it's my mental state, but it was the phone, my hand got caught, that's why I crashed. Please don't leave me. I gave up everything for you.'

The last words were true. What couldn't be said was that she gave up her best friend, because she wanted him. Shuffling herself to face him, to prove the strength, she kissed him on his lips.

'Dan, darling, I truly promise you this is the last time we'll need to speak about this. We'll not talk anymore now. You need to catch up on your sleep to get better. Rest my darling, it will all seem quite different tomorrow.'

Decisions taken, adamant she was going to be soon discharged, she let the nurse to wheel her back. Suddenly the chair stopped.

'Now, young girl, as I have you for myself, you need to be honest with me. Are you truthful about not seeing that man? I need to know, because I can give positive feedback on the daily report. What you said to your fiancé was really touching.'

Maintaining eye contact Abigail confirmed.

'Of course, I no longer see him. The pills are working. I think I was just trying to blame someone else for the accident.'

With a little 'hmm' the nurse continued to push the wheelchair towards the lift. When the door opened, she spoke.

'OK, I choose to believe you. You wouldn't lie to your fiancé. That would be appalling so I'll write that you no longer have your visions and with luck you should be discharged soon. Still, all that depends on the final decision by the psychiatrist.'

It didn't take long for the lift to get to the right floor and soon Abigail was back on the ward. Opening the privacy curtains let some of the sunlight in. It was the turning point that was needed. Josef was gone, the staff were finally working with her rather against her and it seems that discharge was only couple of days ahead. Bathing in the small amount of light that came in provided some time for thought. A plan was building inside her, slotting tightly together like Lego pieces.

The view from the window was quite good. There was a road running by with tall sycamore trees on each side. Taxis, buses and cars were coming and going. People were rushing all over to do their business. Rows of Victorian terraced houses opposite the hospital lent some character to the area. Abigail could easily imagine living in one of these houses with Dan and their three children with a little pet running about.

The hospital entrance had to be near as lots of people and nursing staff rushed by on the ground. To the right, the other side of the building had to be the entrance to the car park as that was where all the cars were going. A brief flash of light made her blink. When seconds later her eyes opened, a bird hit the window making a mark where it hit. A huge bang made the other patients jump. When trying to see if the bird survived, her blood churned. During the bustling scene was the Bride, Anna, clutching her heart, just like in the dream.

'Wake up, wake up, pill time!'

The nurse was above Abigail rattling the pill-dispensing pot. 'You must have dozed off after all that excitement. Here, take these. They are the new replacements that will help you not to be drowsy anymore as these you can take at home. This will help you manage but won't make you lethargic.'

Abigail did as she was told because time was ticking, especially if the dreams were back. Once the room was nurse-free, she retrieved her laptop. The computer was on Twitter. "Unhappy bride meeting" was now the subject flashing on the screen.

So many women had answered. Some with jokes like 'Let's drink to our unhappiness.' Or, 'Will someone help me to kill my fiancé, LOL?' The questions were just coming in floods. 'Where are we meeting? Where is this hotel? Can anyone give me the directions?' Abigail was flabbergasted to see that there were so many of them around that would knowingly marry but be unhappy for the rest of their life.

That was why the divorce rates were on the up and divorce negotiator adverts were on the rise as these leeches cashed in on people's misfortunes.

There were lots of women sharing their tips on how to get out of their wedding. This was huge progress as all she needed to do is just point Josef in their direction. It took a whole hour to scroll through the messages, but it was fruitful. There were three mobile phone numbers scribbled on her notepad with two home addresses. It really was shocking that people were so careless about their personal details.

Abigail didn't need to organize such a big meeting so once she got what she wanted, her Twitter post would be left to fizzle out by itself. After all, meeting with everyone at once would have been too obvious. She had to reserve time with them individually. Checking her list put some rose back into her cheeks. This was the answer to all her problems. The minor details of being caught if anything came out of this were nothing compared to not having Dan. Her biro circled around the first one, Kirty Patel. She had the most memorable number. Pretending that her mobile was broken she made her way to the hospital landline in the corridor near her ward. Thankfully the nurses trusted her enough to not imagine her a threat. Using the landline was insurance against Kirty's mobile having no record of hers.

After a slightly strange conversation with a young girl with an Indian accent, the plan was set into motion. With numbers and addresses memorized, she rested her head on the pillow.

That night back on the ward was the first ever that Abigail fell asleep with the satisfaction of a job well done. Finally, she slept dreamlessly and uninterrupted.

Chapter 8

Finally, Abigail was able to take a deep breath into her lungs that had felt so constricted by the hospital setting. Her nose was no longer being offended by bleach and body fluids but was gently tickled by the budding blooms. The discharge paperwork was the flag of freedom. In a way the hospital stay was useful because she had finally decided. It gave her time to build relationship with the women she needed to find. Especially Kirty Patel whom she was about to meet. Despite her newfound freedom, Abigail was nervous. What would she do if Kirty asked too many questions? The shopping street was full of people, rushing in and out of shops. Her sweating hand was holding the posy inside her coat pocket, fidgeting with its tip. Thankfully the large shop windows offered some distraction, so soon she was at her destination. It was a hotel chosen by Kirty standing tall between two large superstores. Standing there made Abigail swallow a stone. Her dry mouth was pleading for something wet. By now her ears were ringing with anxiety.

With no plan of going back, she took unsteady steps to enter the hotel. The reception was trying too hard to be expensive looking, but it was not that different from any other hotel with a modernistic look and cheap patterned carpet matching the curtains. Sashaying past the front desk she tried to look like she was supposed to be headed directly to the dining room. Once inside she clocked a small table stashed away in the corner. About two minutes later a well-presented waiter took her order. A latte should do the trick in trying to calm her nerves, she thought.

Kirty would be the first because she was carrying her heart on her sleeve for everyone to see. Being strongly grounded in spiritualism and symbolism (as Abigail had come to learn during their correspondence), Kirty wasn't going to find Abigail's suggestion unappealing.

She took the small posy out of her pocket. Her hand needed airing anyway, having become hot and clammy around the flowers. Twirling it through her finger she pondered its significance. It was a small mix of wildflowers consisting of daisies, monkshood, foxgloves and sweat pea. Josef had insisted on what type they had to be and that they had to be tightly fastened with a thin white ribbon. The posy didn't even smell nice like a bunch of roses would. Even worse, as the posy had to be dried, it lacked colour and odour. Abigail shook her head and put the posy back into her pocket as the waiter was approaching with a steamy glass of latte. Abigail wasn't doing anything bad so if she could have Dan with everything returning to normality, she was ready to meet some strangers. Brushing away a leaf fallen from the posy, she took hold of the hot glass. Slowly, eyes closed, she took in fresh coffee fragrance. Ready, she sipped the coffee, waiting for Kirty.

No more than five minutes passed before Kirty walked in. This tall slender Indian girl was beautiful. Her sleek coal hair shone. Her large oval face with huge brown eyes scanned the whole place until they both locked onto each other. Kirty's bushy eyebrows rose as if asking 'Is this you?' Abigail returned a smile in confirmation as Kirty made her way to the table only pausing briefly to speak to the waiter. With a clippety clop of her high heels, Kirty arrived by the table.

'Hello, Kirty, would you like some coffee? My treat.'

With just a trace of foreign accent, Kirty spoke softly. 'It's fine, really, I just ordered a chai so I'm OK, thanks.'

'Kirty, I wanted to meet because I believe that if people support each other, if we are more like a community, we can make a difference. When you told me what has happened to you I felt for you so much! I was so upset on your behalf. I wanted to help.'

They paused as the waiter came in again to place chai in front of Kirty.

'Oh, you're so right. I just wish people would look more into the pickle I'm in. No matter that we live here, our parents still abide by the old rules of arranged marriage. It's awful! The man they want me to marry is twice my age! Why did they agree? He's given them a large sum of money. It's a legalized slave exchange, not a wedding!'

Kirty tried to hold back her tears, sipping on the chai to regain her posture.

'Kirty, how old are you?'

She didn't want to say, but finally she caved in. 'I'm seventeen.'

She whispered it like she was ashamed.

'Oooh, so young and fresh, I love her. Their culture is so wonderful. It's a shame she isn't younger, I do like young fresh meat.' The words came in a chilled whisper from behind Abigail's right shoulder at the same time her empathy worked on her brain to stop this conversation. When she turned her head, Josef was not to be seen. There was just the wall with its geometric wallpaper and modernistic paintings. Only once she turned back to Kirty did she spot Josef who was slowly stroking that long sleek hair of Kirty's.

'Don't chicken out, my dear. I can smell her hair and I like what I see. I want this one. Ignore your guilt, carry on, or I shall take Dan instead? Who do you prefer for me to take, her or Dan?' Fiddling the tip of Kirty's hair, his pleading eyes blinked with an answer.

'Kirty, I am a strong believer that there is more to life than this. I believe in more, are you following me?'

Kirty tilted her head right to listen.

'Well, I'm Hindu, so I do believe. I do think there is more, but why are you telling me this?'

Abigail's guilt-ridden intestines swishing around like a tumble dryer made the conversation more uncomfortable the longer it took. She produced the posy from her pocket. Then she poured out the key sentence she had been dreading.

'Well, Kirty, I speak to ghosts. I spoke to one who has asked me to seek you, to find you as you as I can get you out of this marriage. All you need to do is have this posy with you during the wedding. The ghost has told me this.'

Kirty took the posy, instinctively putting it under her nose before inspecting it. Brow furrowed, her eyes closed to show long, black lashes.

'I really hope you are right, I really do.' Shifting her body to reach the handbag Kirty placed the posy inside it.

'The wedding is next week so if this mad idea worked out I'd owe you big time. I'm desperate enough to believe in anything. Still, I might be young, but I'm not that stupid. This conversation is over. I don't trust you. This is weird, ghosts don't exist. I thought you were coming to help me, to give me real legal advice perhaps. Instead you spoke mumbo jumbo. Sorry, but I just can't swallow it. What do you want, money? Read my palm?' Leaving the chai in the cup, Kirty stood up from her chair so hastily she bumped the table and spilled some. Wide-eyed, Abigail tried to took control of the situation.

'Go on, Kirty, of course I don't want anything from you, only your belief. I want you to know I mean well. I know it sounds crazy, but it worked for me, so I feel I need to spread this magic if I can make more people as happy as I am.' Grabbing hold her handbag strap, she pleaded. Kirty pulled back.

'I might do what you say, but don't contact me again.'

This time the heels didn't clip-clop but sounded like machine-gun fire instead. The second Kirty disappeared, Abigail took a run for the toilets and threw up. Josef was clapping her on.

'Well done, my dear, the first is always hard. I already feel the connection with that unfortunate soul. She is young, I like that. I must say I do love your first choice.

Do find more of those. Keep them coming. I'll give you freedom now, as I should follow Kirty. I need to fully absorb myself into her, enter her room and watch her sleeping. I cannot wait, so goodbye for now. Make sure there is another when I am back!' He spat out the last sentence, leaving her shivering with her arms on the cold porcelain of the toilet bowl.

***

There was no further contact with Kirty, which suited her well. Now she could bury any memory of that conversation underneath everything else in her brain. Pretending that nothing had happened helped to elevate her mood. Considering that Josef was also gone made things twice as easy. Comfortable in her sofa, she took hold of the paper, a habit she picked up from her gran. Nothing was better to do in the morning than have breakfast as you read the paper. Today it was different, as a couple of pages in Abigail nearly spilled the hot coffee into her lap over an article close to her heart. It was about a young Indian girl who had poisoned herself to avoid an arranged marriage. The news carried on how this young girl was promised to a 45-year-old Indian man who was now demanding his money back, despite the practice being illegal in the UK. Abigail had to be sure. Shaking she pulled out the phone and dialled Kirty's number. Someone else picked up.

'Hello, can I speak to Kirty please?'

A short sigh was followed with an aggravated response. 'Kirty is no longer available, she isn't with us. Who is this?'

'I'm a friend. I just wanted to catch up on how her wedding went and to wish her well.'

The man mumbled something in another language, but it sounded sharp.

'She is dead, OK, we have lots to sort out, she decided to poison herself to spite us, she brought shame on the whole family. Don't call again.' There was a beep in her ear and then silence.

Abigail was the only one that knew Kirty hadn't poisoned herself. Of course, it had been Josef.

It was the singing that took her attention. Dan singing to himself as he walked towards the sofa and planted a kiss on her cheek. 'You look like you saw a ghost!' he quipped. Regaining her composure, she proceeded to read the full article in detail. The family was completely slaughtered by the media. There in black and white in the middle of the article was the confirmation of her own involvement.

'The young female poisoned herself with a home-made concoction of monkshood. This caused her to have a heart attack and the death is being treated as suicide and no further investigation is to be carried out.'

A pang of guilt tried to creep into her heart but then seeing Dan singing to himself made it go away. She hadn't caused this. Having had enough of news for the day, she folded the paper and stuffed it underneath the sofa.

Knowing what Josef had said the last time, the clock had started to tick again – one done, eight more to go. Abigail opened her laptop when Dan left for the gym. Back to where it all began, she logged onto the Twitter chat. By now there were so many unhappy women chatting about how they didn't want to go through with their wedding. Who to pick from the endless list? Eventually she settled on someone called Joan. She had agreed to marry a guy out of pity. She'd been a little over the limit at the time he popped the question but then was too weak to back out once she came to her senses. She was a good choice because if she couldn't say no she wouldn't see any harm in speaking to a stranger or taking a posy from them.

Contacting her was easy as again this woman had left her profile completely open for everyone to see! She even advertised her home address. With no time to waste, Abigail decided to turn up at her house.

A person who couldn't say no was less likely to veto someone away. Monday she would call in sick. There had to be some theatrical performance also for Dan's benefit. Uncomfortable as it sounded she had to stick the end of a toothbrush down her throat only to claim that she must have eaten something dodgy on Sunday. All was prepared for her to turn up uninvited at Joan's home. Having all day spare mean that Abigail had plenty time to wait for Joan if she wasn't in.

Faking an illness with Dan worked well. The mobile flickered with a text back from her boss telling her to take as many days off as needed. The address Joan had given came up easily enough on the sat navigation system. She was only forty minutes' drive away. With some luck she would be home so Abigail could be done by lunchtime.

About twenty minutes into her thoughtless drive, one nagging revelation came to her. She had completely stopped caring what happened to others. She had utterly disregarded the life of another and lied to herself that all was fine. The reflection in the mirror confirmed that it was still her, even though inside she felt different. The sat nav voice announced a petrol station ahead. Maybe a nice drink would help to regain control. It wasn't difficult to park as the service station had plenty of spare bays. A bit of rubbish was flying about. Some suited men walked out noisily ignoring her waiting patiently at the door holding it open. Inside, as if her guilt was seeping out, the key words kept jumping up at her. "Monster Munch buy 1 get one free" – 'monster' an apt word to describe her. Funeral services, helping to deal with death notice for a local undertaker – the word "death": that's what she brought with her now. The queue for the coffee faced an advert that read "Guilt-free chocolate bar" – something she lacked: the quality of being guilt-free. Glad to finally be getting her prize of a hot drink she slumped into her car seat. She seemed heavier now as the seat gave a groan. She was about to take a sip before the engine started and she got interrupted.

'You have to make these difficult decisions. That decision gave you Dan. You can't back down now.'

Missing her mouth made the drink spill all over her legs. Yet again Josef was with her. He knew how to manipulate her, what her darkest secrets were as if he was her, he lived inside her.

'I don't want to do it anymore. I'm too tired for this, mentally and physically.'

He just sat there with a smug smile, not responding.

'I mean it I just can't do it anymore, I can't go on. This is lunacy, I'm never going to get away with this. I don't care what you think anymore but, in this world, they will put me in prison. Once I'm behind bars I won't be able to find or meet anyone for you!'

It was only about five minutes of conversation later that Abigail noticed the car next to her was occupied. A grey-haired woman watching her with puzzlement. Abigail frowned back with some verbal abuse. She'd had enough of arguing with herself or Josef, too weak to fight back. It worked as the woman turned the engine to move on.

The drink no longer tasted good, so she whizzed down her window and threw the cup onto the grassy verge. The sooner she made it to Joan the quicker she'd be back home able to deny this ever happened. With roaring engine, she merged onto the busy motorway.

The bad drivers kept her focused until the satellite navigation system told her to take the next exit. A short distance from the motorway was the estate where Joan lived. Abigail found it hard manoeuvre through this modern estate with its little lanes full of mini roundabouts. She spotted the right number. To make things better, she also spotted Joan right behind the kitchen window in her terraced two-bed house. The house was a new-built with its white wooden door and shiny red brick facade.

Joan's street was not yet fully finished as the builders were still putting final touches on the houses at the end of her road. The pavement still wasn't finished, which gave Abigail more space to park in.

The engine rumbled to a stop with a little jolt. Unsure whether the phone had jingled Abigail retrieved her phone out of the pocket. The screen lit up and Dan's photo appeared as the wallpaper.

It had been carefully chosen because Dan looked gorgeous in it, his blue eyes sparkling with one of his cheeky sideways grins. That's why she was here, why had to speak to this woman so that she could keep Dan. Putting the phone back into the pocket, she pushed the door open. Out of the car she made her way towards the door. A little moment later a chiming of the doorbell sent in the cheerful owner to open it.

'How can I help you? I must say I just bought this place, so I am poor. Not mentioning the money that will be spent on my wedding! So even if I would want the stuff you are selling I ain't buying.'

This was Joan, a friendly Labrador, wagging her tail when meeting new people. It was her 'I want to please' attitude that was making her go through with the wedding she didn't want. That was why she was in this situation. That was why she was chosen to be the second one.

'I'm Abigail. I spoke to you over the internet, the chat forum 'Unhappy Brides'. I just wanted to say ...'

The little pause wasn't nerves, it was just that Abigail had realized she hadn't prepared what she was going to say. Her words were lost like her voice box just gave up. She gulped like a fish thrown out of water.

'Ehm, I wanted to tell you you've placed your private data completely out there, so I wanted to warn you just in case the man you are going to marry reads it. You know he might get cross or something.'

Pink all the way up to her hair follicles, all she could do was just pull out her best puppy eyed expression. Joan took some time to digest her words.

'Well that's nice to hear someone worries about me. You see, I did that on purpose. I was desperate. I hoped he'd find it, so we can call the wedding off. I put my home address on it to make sure he knew it was me, hence having my mobile number on there too. I knew that I put myself out there for weirdos but if I get married this place will be sold. He doesn't like modern houses. I'd have to move to his crumbling cottage. Look, do you want to come in for a cup of tea? I just made myself one so the water's still hot.'

Abigail shifted from one foot to another, taking some time to decide whether to go inside. A little beep from her pocket gave her a minute to regain her confidence. It was Dan: 'I love you xxx' shone from the screen.

That did it. 'Sorry, it was rude to check the phone, but I have to because of work. Yes, I'd love to have a cuppa. I won't take much of your time; I must be on my way soon. Work won't wait.'

Trying to sound chirpy, Abigail chitchatted whilst Joan made a nice cup of tea in her U-shaped kitchen that fitted perfectly in to the compact space. Joan managed to squeeze into her lounge a whole double sofa, flat screen TV and a small coffee table. Abigail saw Joan had noticed her looking.

'I know it's not much, but it will do. Soon I won't need this anymore. My fiancé has all the things I do, so I must get rid of my stuff. This is all I have left of it.'

Curling her fingers around the hot mug, Abigail responded. 'Sorry to say this, but the guy you're going to marry is a selfish bastard. Why are you putting up with him? Surely just call the wedding off and tell him to sod off?'

Joan had a sip of her tea. 'I would love to, but I don't have the guts. I can't tell him that I don't want to marry him.'

Seeing her change, Abigail decided to go for the reason why she was there. 'Well I have to come clean. I did come here to tell you about your security, but also about something else.' She gave a slight pause to make sure to look sincere.

'I speak with those that have departed from this world to the next. I'm fully aware that some ghosts can change things. Now one has seen your sorrow and asked me to give you this.'

So not to lose this important moment, she held the posy right in front of Joan's nose. 'If you wear it on your wedding day you will get what you wish for. But the main thing is that you must believe. Without your full belief, it won't work.'

The sudden slump of Joan's shoulders, the face getting long, was all confirmation that Joan had had enough of the stranger in her home. Reading the body language, Abigail stood up and walked to the main door.

'Thank you for the tea, I loved it. I know it might sound strange what I said. That is why you have to do what you think is right.' Abigail gently placed the posy onto the sofa and made her way to the front door followed by Joan.

'I'll wear it on the day. I'll believe but only if you don't contact me ever again, please. I might be desperate, but I don't want to meet like this again. I don't feel that this is right. Goodbye.'

Abigail's nose just about made contact with the slammed door. If Abigail hadn't made her way quickly into the car to drive off, she would probably have been moved by the sobs coming through the door.

***

Joan did believe, and things did change for her. She wore the flower on her wedding day but never made it to the end. Josef was there to make sure her heart stopped beating right before she said, 'I do'. Instead of a wedding, Joan got a funeral. This time Abigail felt it as it happened, as if it were her holding Joan's heart, stopping it from beating. At the same moment, in her trance, Abigail's hand clamped into a fist until Joan's heart stopped beating.

***

No news is always good news. No mention of Joan, apart from her no longer being present on the chat forum. Others must be found, or Josef would be back.

'Honey, you've been lying to me.' Dan was waving around a small envelope like a fan.

'This came in the post today for you. I opened it by accident. You haven't attended any of your appointments in the last two weeks. What's happening, love? I know it worked because you're back to normal, but I don't want you to have another nasty episode. You must go back to finish the treatment!'

She snapped the screen shut so that Dan couldn't see she had found her third. She was a posh girl telling everyone how sad she was, how hard her life had been because she couldn't marry the man she loved, who, by the way, was one of their gardeners. Bless this child as she should marry some other aristocrat's son who wouldn't be her choice. Her parents were, by the sound of it, complete control freaks. Her mother was some professor or another and her father was a top-class cardiologist. Abigail was mid-way chatting to her when Dan walked in like a Victorian lady with hot flushes, fanning his face with triumph.

'Abigail, are you even listening?' The glassy expression didn't impress him.

'Honey, I'm tired. I'm listening. Yes, I haven't attended any appointments but I'm going back at the end of this week. I promise. I just feel so well. I was celebrating that I hadn't experienced these horrid visions for a while. I was worried that seeing the psychotherapist would bring the memories back which would bring back the visions. They always make you re-awaken these visions and guide you through them, so you can teach yourself a way out. They call it something psychological or whatnot and they bring back your worst fears. That is why I wasn't going. I was worried.'

She felt triumphant with her performance as Dan softly hugged her.

***

Contacting the posh girl was a little harder than the other two. It took a while of chatting up before she finally gave her name: Lynne Everleigh. After that it took some convincing before she agreed to meet up with Abigail. To try to entice friendship, Abigail had to pretend that all those designer things, clothes, handbags mattered to her. When Lynne mentioned she was going to shop for a handbag and Abigail asked if she could join her, thankfully Lynne agreed. The turning point was probably the photo she sent to Lynne of her current handbag.

Lynne took pity on Abigail for never having owned a designer handbag, so she offered to take her to the Dior shop on Oxford Street. It was little harder for Abigail to swallow her thriftiness. Sometimes she had to put her hand deep into her pocket. After all, she simply had to pretend to be interested in buying one of them.

Dan did not need much of an excuse as to why Abigail was going out shopping in London on Saturday. He was satisfied that she attended all her appointments and their relationship was finally warming up to be what it was prior the accident. The day before he'd kissed her goodbye, telling her to have fun in London, he had pressed a handful of notes into her palm.

'Darling, you're going to Oxford Street, so you must spend some of my money too. Here, take this and buy yourself something special. Maybe look there for some ideas for the bridesmaids. Have a lovely day.'

The train ride to London wasn't bad apart from some smelly drunk singing some unrecognizable tunes. The whiff of him carried across all carriages so everyone was pleased when they reached Paddington.

It took her some time to get to the Oxford Street. The London underground was a great solution to the bottlenecking traffic above. However, it was the number of people that used the underground that put Abigail off.

It was like an obstacle course dodging all the tourists and masses of human bodies to get to the Dior shop. It was a never-ending caterpillar queue from which occasionally people left or joined at different times. Abigail had expected to see a skinny, goofy little bespectacled girl with a very strong posh accent, but what turned up was a slender, young lady.

'I recognized you because of your handbag. You have portrayed it well, it's truly a ghastly thing. You need a replacement.'

Abigail faked a smile, holding up her handbag for the full view. 'I don't lie, Lynne. You are right about my bag. I can't even look at it anymore.' She extended her hand and shook Lynne's.

'Hello. I'm Abigail.'

Turning her nose up at the sight of the bag, Lynne gestured towards the shops. 'Let's go and buy you a proper thing. Mummy and Daddy are working so I have plenty of time to shop.'

Lynne did the typical girlie thing Abigail despised. She giggled stupidly as she put her arm over hers. Then she dragged Abigail into a shop full of snobs who sniggered and made remarks about her bag. The shop attendants tut-

tutted and had a long discussion on the latest fashion trends with Lynne. They clearly knew who she was.

A century later, Abigail walked out of the shop thousands of pounds lighter. 'What a bargain! Seventy percent off. You're so lucky,' chirped Lynne, completely relaxed and swapping her bulging bag into another hand.

'So many lovely bargains, Mummy would be pleased.' Abigail's head was spinning over the money she just handed out. Something had to be done before Lynne changed her mind and dived into yet another shop.

'Go on, Lynne, let's go to Costa for a drink. I'm tired from the travel. The train always tires me.' To give the right impression, Abigail squeezed herself into Lynne's arm.

'Oh my! You poor thing, did you have to take that awful train? We must sit down. I understand. Once I took a train by accident and afterwards Daddy had to pay for cognitive behaviour therapy as I had suffered claustrophobia! The journey was packed full of smelly people who sat on those horrid little uncomfortable chairs. Seriously, how people manage to use that train! Awful! I still get some flashbacks now! Come on, let's get a nice coffee.'

Abigail finally rested her strained shoulder once they entered the coffee shop.

If there aren't empty spaces, I will push this girl into the running traffic myself, Abigail thought. In the meantime, she scanned for a spare table. Just like any other coffee shop, it had some walls covered head to toe with Italian scenes of people sipping coffees on small dinky tables. All the seats were scattered as people pushed them there and back from table to table depending how many people sat around them. In between like bees around a meadow were the exhausted-looking staff tidying tables only to be claimed by new customers a moment later. Being a busy place, it had scuffs everywhere on the tables, chairs and even walls.

A couple vacated a table for two in the corner. Quick as a flash, Abigail ran to it, putting her coat on the puffed-up seat. Lynne joined the queue leaving her Gucci coat over the seat she claimed. Clearly Lynne's impression of 'street life' was a little bit like 'Teletubby land'. Abigail's purse squealed with displeasure of being opened again to pay for the coffee. Somehow despite the wealth, Lynne still expected Abigail to pay. The lactose-free skinny cappuccino Lynne asked for looked like it consisted of two ingredients: airy fluff and muddy water. Trying not to shake too much, Abigail placed the tray down with the tip of her tongue out.

Lynne didn't need to be prompted as she was still going on about fashion, which made Abigail tired. Over the verbal fashion diarrhoea, Abigail put her hand out after she yet again counted that Lynne only took three breaths in what seemed like five minutes.

'Sorry to stop you there Lynne, but may I ask one question? About that man, you're in love with, the gardener, did you think about trying to manipulate the situation, so you can have him?'

Lynne's lashes butterfly fluttered underneath the large spectacles. With her pursed lips she looked like a strict teacher at a private school for girls.

'That's impossible. There is no way I could have him. Mummy and Daddy won't allow it. I tried to convince them a bit but there is no chance. Daddy even said that he will not let anyone without a proper degree near me. That means this gardener has no chance.'

Lynne's lungs expanded as she closed her eyes for a brief pause.

'He is a most handsome gentleman. I believe that people are here for reason. You see I am little mad like that. I believe in reincarnation. I feel this man, whose name is Simon by the way, was an aristocrat in the past. Shame, I cannot trace his origins, I bet I would be able to prove his blue blood heritage. Do you believe in reincarnation?'

Abigail didn't waste a second.

'Reincarnation is real, Lynne.' To add more secrecy, she leaned towards Lynne to whisper. 'And what's even more interesting is that I have something for you. I know it might sound strange, so bear with me. I had a dream, you see, that I must pass you a posy. In the dream you were a princess, in a previous life. I really think that should you have this flower with you on your wedding day as if you do, you will get your gardener!'

Lynne placed her delicate slim hand over her open mouth.

'Oh Abigail, we are like the spiritual sisters! You really think I was a princess in my past life? How wonderful, I always felt it within me. I always felt that I was destined for more things; that I was somehow related to the Royal Family. Bless you, Abigail.'

She jumped at Abigail to give her a squeeze. Abigail was smiling into their hug because it worked. This spoiled brat really believed that she was re-incarnated princess. Knowing to keep her thoughts to herself was her survival, so to keep them where they belonged Abigail triumphantly took a sip of latte. The victory kept her going, despite Lynne reverting to fashion. Her 'Daddy' arrived, so, posy pinned to her Gucci, Lynne waved frantically, full of smiles as she was driven off in a limo. Good riddance, Abigail thought, but the words escaped her lips. She walked towards the underground talking to herself.

'I would kill her myself, stupid mare. She so deserves it.'

The busy landscape full of sounds drowned her words. Nobody took notice of a mumbling female in the busiest street in London.

'This is the end of it and I will never see her again.' The feeling of being completely incognito was shattered when she noticed Lynne's father eyeing her up in the mirror, but she pulled her coat tighter, picked up her pace and chided herself for talking to herself in public, drawing attention. And then she pushed the sight of the man to the very back of her mind.

***

Lynne noticed how her father was eyeing up Abigail.

'Daddy, are you OK? I had such a lovely day with her. Her name is Abigail, by the way.'

Her father turned towards his daughter.

'Darling, it's nice you had a good day, but you know my opinion. I don't like you to mix with those sorts of girls. They are no good for you. They are too common and will only lead you astray. Particularly … did you see how her mouth was moving? You sure she isn't mad?'

Thankfully Lynne had a good handle on her father and managed to weasel out of the uncomfortable conversation. With the wit she always had, she moved the discussion onto how the day went. Somehow, she managed to keep quiet about the bit about having Simon. She knew perfectly well it would aggravate him badly to even mention the gardener's name. She had always been the perfect little daughter doing whatever her parents asked for. She even enrolled herself onto one of her father's studies of cardiac rhythms in a normal life scenario. She was given a heart monitor to put on her anywhere she went, and she even had to sleep with it. This bloody monitor was permanently attached to her. Each time she got excited the rhythm of her heart was recorded on the machine. At least it was light, miniature in fact, nonetheless it was a nuisance. Her records would be scrutinized by researchers who worked for her father. Her mother would be there cooking only what was on the list of foods that wouldn't interfere with the study.

She hated the fact that she was their little free-of-charge gerbil. Her parents had such control over her. They even argued when she said she wouldn't wear the machine on her wedding day. Her father was adamant she couldn't jeopardize the study because of life getting in the way.

'You have to wear it. It's important as you will be under a lot of pressure. I need these recordings!'

Lynne knew how they reacted each time Simon was around, being interested in what the readings where particularly when they had their evening tea in the garden. She had many dreams about making love to him in their garden underneath the moonlight. She kept thinking of one of those steamy dreams of Simon repeatedly but was too ashamed to tell anyone.

Neither was she going to tell her diary, just in case. Her father would be most worried if he knew that she carried these ideas in her head. She usually recorded everything into her journal, but this was one thing that she couldn't have the heart to write down. She closed the journal at the recording of handbag shopping with Abigail and the interesting discussion they had.

'Abigail is a strange but interesting girl who will help me.'

How little she knew of her parents' obsessive need to control her life. Her mother knew everything about her, even those naughty thoughts that she had. One day her mother discovered her journal whilst trying to clean her bedroom.

***

The wedding drew near, and with it the culmination of the cardiology study. Lynne's father needed this last recording of her heart rates. For years they had been tracking cardiac rhythms, which had remained stable with just the expected fluctuations on days of distress. Her heart was strong and healthy.

On the day of the wedding, Lynne's father sat in the front pew, his wife by his side. Their elbows touching, their spines tall, both a little sad and happy for their only darling daughter was now a grown woman. As a proud father, he tried to hide his red eyes under the excuse of hay fever. His strong proud wife shed no tears, but he knew she was emotional. It was just the years of practice to hold her stance that helped her to control herself when their daughter walked past to the altar. He had a flashback of Lynne putting herself into her mother's ballroom dress. She had looked like a pumpkin with a tiny head. The poke in the ribs was unexpected.

'Do you know anything about that?' his wife whispered. He followed the finger and saw a small, dry, unattractive posy pinned to their daughter's Vera Wang wedding dress. All he could do was a little nod of 'not sure'. Huffing, his wife turned to find the wedding planner. He knew that look well and was pleased this time he wasn't on the receiving side. Someone was about to have a bomb exploded in their face: his wife was very particular, and this was out of scope of the colour scheme. What stopped her from scanning for the wedding planner was the thump and ring of a vase shattering into thousands of pieces on the floor around Lynne. The girl lay collapsed on the floor.

'Arthur, what's happening?' were the words he heard from his wife as his medical mind sprang to action and he pushed his way to his daughter. Nonetheless, the police had organized a doctor to come to the scene, despite Arthur wanting to treat Lynne himself.

His wife collapsed as his lips let out his diagnosis: cardiac arrest. The whole family was outraged, and from the hospital, Arthur called for his friend, the psychiatrist, to pay a visit to his wife.

***

'That's preposterous!' Lynne's father pounded his fist onto the mahogany desk in his study, causing the tea tray to rattle and the teaspoon to clatter to the ground.

'I've seen the recordings!' His hands trembled.

'My God, I've been studying her cardiac rhythms for years. This is impossible!' By now he'd been looking over the preliminary findings for days without finding anything conclusive.

'Darling.' Lynne's mother, who had brought in the tea a short while before, rested her head in her hands. 'Darling, I must tell you, I finally gathered the strength to read her journal.' She sighed.

'The last month of her life was normal apart from that trip to London. The day she said she was going shopping for a handbag, remember? You saw her that day. Do you remember her meeting anyone?'

He turned towards his wife.

'Why would that be interesting? What difference is that going to make? It will not bring her back to life. I just cannot figure out why she collapsed. I have been over the results dozens of times, yet I cannot find any reason why she should have had a heart attack!'

He sat down and placed his head on the desk strewn with paperwork full of cardiograms.

'Well, it might interest you if I read you this.'

She raised the diary and started to read:

'I had a lovely time in London with Abigail. She is such a fun girl to be with. Abigail is such a good listener. She agreed with me on so many fashion ideas. She also agrees that there is more that can be done about Simon. I took the posy she gave me. I know what I must do. If I do this one thing, I can marry Simon. We had a celebratory drink. Abigail is a strange but interesting girl who will help me … Mummy is coming, I will write later.'

Lynne's mother finished reading. The tears were now streaming down her face. This time she stood up and gently placed a small dried posy onto his desk. He picked his head up, puzzled, the tips of his fingered examined it.

'She took some flowers from this person! What if she's been poisoned? Who is this girl, this Abigail? She has poisoned my daughter!'

Lynne's father digested the information. Was there a possibility that a compound of this flower might lead to cardiac arrest?

'It's possible. Let me see.' He grabbed the diary.

'I saw the girl, Sybil! Lynne waved at her. This girl was poor, I could tell. It could be someone jealous of our status. She spoke to herself as she walked. Dear God, my darling, you are right she must have been poisoned!'

Lynne's father picked up the phone and dialled the police. Nobody wanted to really listen to his pleas. Thankfully being a rich man means having contacts. He had treated many top brasses in the police. One of his patients was the current police lieutenant, who was the man who listened to his reasoning.

He was correct with his choice: the police lieutenant, Derek Jarvis, gave him his full attention.

'I need to make sure that the post-mortem is done properly. I strongly believe my daughter has been poisoned. Please ensure the pathologist doesn't miss a thing. I need the forensic team to look closely at any plant-based material they find. She was poisoned! There isn't any other way why her heart would give up like that.'

As he put down the receiver he knew time was running out. And if he didn't find out what he needed he'd have to go to the papers.

***

Jarvis was aware of the predicament. He knew the family would insist on keeping the investigation going, whether the coroner ruled natural causes or not. He knew his crew too well to be able to guess whoever he asked to investigate more, he would be moaned at. None of the younger recruits would be a good choice as they were too fresh around their nose to be able to look too deep. They were too keen to close things up as quickly as possible. What he needed was someone with many years of experience behind his belt. Someone, who was old school and wouldn't question the reasoning too much. Furthermore, he knew the current sergeant in charge and who he would prefer for him to choose. He pondered on this a little but at the end called in Detective John Hendon.

***

As soon as John saw Jarvis in his doorway he knew this supposedly open-and-shut case was to prove otherwise. He knew his boss's manager was cosy with the victim's parents, so he expected to be told to re-open it, even though he'd just finished the paperwork. Though much older, Jarvis had that type of retired army man look. Basically, you would avoid messing about with an old fellow like him. Even though his paper-pushing time had given him a slight belly, he kept fit and was able to break bones with one blow. John approached with caution.

'Some new evidence has come to light, suggesting poisoning. I want you to consider this possibility. Have you managed to get the full pathology report?'

John slumped into the small chair for visitors, its wheels squeaking with displeasure. Arms crossed leaning back focusing on the ceiling, John exhaled.

'Sir, I haven't got the final papers, but I don't need them. This isn't a case for us, it's just like any other medically related death. She just plonked, that's all.' By the pulsating vein on the older man's forehead John could see what Jarvis thought of this.

'I am sorry, detective, but this stands. I won't be arguing with you, it's been all approved with your sergeant, so I suggest you do as you're told.' Jarvis stood up and faced the window making it difficult for John to gauge how angry he was.

'Sure, consider it done, but I have the car robbery to sort out. And then I give it my undivided attention.'

With that he left the room. He knew that the atmosphere was very explosive, so a fast retreat was best.

When he returned to his desk he was most surprised to find a large orange sticky note attached to his computer with the words 'Call pathology immediately'. Maybe he'd been wrong. He dialled the number.

'Hi, it's Detective Hendon, what have you got for me then that's urgent?'

'Detective, there is something strange after all. You see, all tests are normal, cause of death cardiac arrest, open and shut, etc, etc. Only thing is, when we looked at the posy that came in with her dress, we found it contains some odd flowers. Upon closer inspection we noted they were common wildflowers, but they have strong poisonous properties if ingested. I'm not sure if this is valid for the case, but we did the tests and there was no poison in her blood or stomach, but it's strange that she had them pinned to her wedding dress. Could be relevant.'

John gasped. 'You're darn right that's relevant! Email me the photos ASAP. Got to tell the boss. The family just called to say that she's been poisoned, so we keep this quiet for now, OK.'

That wasn't all the pathologist wanted to say. 'Look, detective, I know I might be an old woman and don't do well with gossip or superstition, but there is more. You know me, right, you know that I won't say something unless I feel it's relevant. You see, the thing we found, that little posy, isn't the only one.'

John frowned. 'You mean that there were more on her body? More poisonous plants?'

'Not hers, the others. I had two more young women brought to me and the only thing that was the same is that posy. It had the same bow, the same content, all perfectly dried the same way. The first one was Kirty Patel, whose family said she'd poisoned herself. She had that posy tucked in her sleeve when they brought her in. She was also a bride, but the strange thing is, though no poison was found in her bloodstream she had the same obscurities that Lynne Everleigh had. No poison, but what's strange is that all the three girls had unique chest bruising unlike any I've ever seen. It's as if someone was holding their hearts. The bruising on the heart has five points as if there are finger marks. I know that's not possible but what are the chances that within the space of three months I have three women who are to be married, die from heart attack on the day of their wedding and all have the posy in their possession? The same posy?'

John felt as if a huge bucket of cold water had landed on him.

'What women, how many, what are their names? You gotta email me ASAP all the details, right now. I need to go to see the boss. This is huge.'

'It's Kirty Patel, Joan Wallace and Lynne Everleigh. All are between twenty-five and thirty-five, all had the same cardiac episode, and all had the same posy. I'm emailing you my preliminary finding sheet now.'

With that the call ended. 'Shit,' swore John underneath his breath.

He was still swearing on his way back to see Derek Jarvis. The man would not be pleased. It didn't look like John was going to do that car robbery at all.

Jarvis was reading something as he walked in, so he knew he had to be quick.

'I think you might be right, sir.'

Jarvis looked up, eyebrows raised.

'Just had pathology on the blower, and there is commonality between that Lynne girl and two other girls. All young brides, sir.'

Jarvis put his head into his hands. He emitted a slow whistle through his teeth.

'OK, I'll need to call the parents now. I'll tell them you'll go around to do some investigations. I will need to tell them they might be right about the poisoning but please keep this quiet. We don't want panic on our hands. No journalists! I'll pass the robbery to someone else, so you can concentrate on this case. I will also speak to your superintendent that you now report directly to me about this only. Be thorough, Hendon, no mistakes!'

Keen to see the email, John marched back to his office. He had a feeling about this, that it was going to be huge.

Chapter 9

The evening started to cast shadows all around the lounge when Abigail finally got the time to leaf through the paper. The pages kept swishing around as she frantically flipped through. The dimming light made her squint slightly until, wide-eyed, she found what she was after. There was it again. 'The Bride Poisoner' was the article beaming up from the page. Somehow, they got the posy right to the last daisy. Dry mouth, pulse racing in her neck Abigail dragged her finger down the column of text, scanning, scanning for the name Joan. Nothing. Abigail let the air out of her lungs in a big whoosh. Maybe they hadn't made the connection after all. Gingerly she took a sip of the now lukewarm coffee but then nearly spat it out as another name jumped out: Abigail! The words felt like a punch to the gut:

'The family has asked that someone called Abigail get in touch as they wish to speak to her.' It even offered a reward! And then the description: 'A young thirty-something female, medium build, brown mid-length hair, medium height, named Abigail'. This was too much!

Thankfully she looked so ordinary no one would bother to say, oh yes that's her, Abigail. If they did, there would be plenty more people doing the same thing. Nevertheless, the secrecy somehow was tainted. It was concerning that that the police was involved. Abigail didn't remember Lynne's father seeing her. Scrunching the page in her palms she did a baseball move and lobbed it across the lounge. What if Natalie's parents read this and started wondering whether their daughter was also killed? What if Joan's boyfriend started asking? Abigail rushed to her computer and wiped the history clean.

The dusk set in but somehow Abigail felt scared to turn

the lights on in case anyone was watching. Her laptop, now closed and turned off, lay on her duvet in her bedroom. The curtains were shut, muffling the noise from the outside. Picking up the laptop and hiding it underneath the bed made more sense. As she peeked from between the small opening between the curtains, her racing pulse slowed. Nobody was there standing looking up at her window. Walking through the lounge she stamped on the balled-up newspaper as if that would make it disappear.

The ball bounced back, casting a small shadow on the wall. As she cleaned the lounge only that morning, the ball was a sore point. It had to go. Picking it up she made her way to the kitchen and turned the gas on. The satisfaction of seeing it burn brought relief to her shaken body. When there was nothing but charred remains, Abigail dusted the remains into her palm and flushed it down the toilet. Pacing around the flat did the opposite to calming. Before Dan returned she had to pretend nothing had been happening. Running to the fridge she retrieved a nice chilled bottle of white. Back in the bathroom, she turned the taps on full, so the steam heated the whole room. Thankfully there always were some nice bubbly bits and bobs to throw into the water. Once it was all milky with bubbles nearly tipping over the edge, Abigail turned off the taps. Wine and bath usually calmed her nerves.

Once inside, the warmth and alcohol made her sleepy and she sank into a dream. Skin tingling with chilling air, swishing pine trees behind her made it clear she was back at the lake again. Only this time her toes were freezing as they were touching the edge of the water. The only illumination was the white bridal dress floating on the surface closer to Abigail. Eyes closed, the bride faced Abigail, with her floaty dress tickling Abigail's frozen toes. The Bride's face was in a grimace, as if she had been mutilated. The pulsating vein in her forehead made the skin twitch. The lines underneath her eye sockets were full of wickedness, then she opened her eyes, which were a large hollow dark empty socket.

'Now you are mine! I have no choice. You must come with me.'

She pulled Abigail towards the middle of the lake. As she dragged Abigail into the lake the cold water ran up to her body. Though Abigail wanted to run away she couldn't. She was stunned, like a pigeon hitting a window. Without any choice, without Josef being there to help, she was being dragged in deeper. As the chilling water came up her neck the Bride spoke for the last time before submerging her.

'This is retribution for your greed.'

Abigail was being drowned but couldn't do anything about it. Furiously she tried to fight the pain in her lungs as she took what felt like the last breath in this world. It was agony, but finally her body gave up.

Under water Abigail's eyes fluttered. The bubble bath stung. Though she was just barely out of the dream, it was just enough for the horrid truth to register: that she was drowning in her own bath. Yet her limbs were powerless and numb, paralyzed once more. Even her heart seemed paralyzed, and her lungs.

Then the light dimmed. A shadow hovered over her. Dan? Yes! The next moment his hands were gripping her shoulders as he pulled her out of the water and she gasped.

***

It took some convincing that it had been only drunken passing out but finally Dan accepted it was an accident. He was distraught as it brought back all the memories from what happened to Natalie. He wasn't happy at first when the GP said it was nothing, and insisted Abigail saw her shrink immediately.

That was why she was back, in the bleached hospital corridor, again waiting to see Dr Passan, in this hospital she was now familiar with. When finally let in, Abigail took the seat in the navy-blue chair, its metal digging into her back. Dr Passan was scribbling something into his notepad, only briefly pausing before he gave her his full attention. A dove took moment to rest on the outside window sill which was well overdue a clean. The whitewashed walls were grey, crumbling at the edges. His desk had some varnish coming off, yet it was a solid piece of furniture. Dr Passan said something, but the dove distracted her. The doctor harrumphed and knocked on the desk.

'Abigail …' shaken back to full attention, and with cramped fists she leaned onto the desk so that there was no any confusion over her sanity.

'Dr Passan let's just be honest here, I'm not a crazy person. I already told you, it was the Bride! I told you about that dream before, I told you about the Bride who comes to my dreams. It was her that dragged me under! I can also say that I started seeing Josef again, as he still hasn't received what I promised. So now I have two things trying to kill me. What doesn't help is that you keep insisting I'm a crazy lunatic! I know I must do something about it and I've already thought of a plan but for that I need you to stop bothering me. Just give me pills. I'll take them and that's it!'

Dr Passan was not moved by her speech whatsoever. Like a psychologist who had heard it all before. Gently tapping his pen onto the notes, chest gently rising and falling, he finally spoke. Putting his pen down, he knitted his fingers together to make a ball with his hands. He rested them on the paperwork, one eyebrow raised.

'That is interesting, Abigail. This is first time I see that you truly opening to me. You have lots of anger, which we can work on, but pills can only do so much.' Picking up his pen again, he scribbled something down. 'I need you to start attending regularly as we need to work on this issue together. Can't you see your problem is escalating? It's not helping that you're fighting with me.' Calmly the pen again rested on the table as his eyes locked onto Abigail's. Temples pulsing, she shuffled in the chair, bearing the pain in her back, trying to gain control.

'Do you get a hard-on trying to make your patients squirm? Who the hell do you think you are? You play god with patients' lives, but I won't let you mess about with mine. I'll take the pills, but I won't be needing your services anymore.' She stood up so rapidly the chair to tipped over with a thud. Dr Passan twitched a little with the movement but then remained unmoved as if in trance.

Abigail grabbed her handbag stomped to the door and flung it open. 'Goodbye, Dr Passan.'

***

After the door slammed shut, Dr Passan took off his glasses, closed his eyes and massaged the bridge of his nose. He hadn't anticipated for Abigail to go off the deep end like that. He'd been thinking she was at a turning point. Instead, she'd been roaring in the opposite direction. Maybe it was time for the next step: admission.

The records showed the clear degradation of her mental state. First, she only saw the man she called Josef; later this vision became more realistic, but then she denied that he existed.

Now it had escalated to the new vision of what she called "the Bride". Dr Passan ran a hand across his scalp. It was a little puzzling when she said she'd found what Josef wanted. Why then the new hallucinations? From the case history he knew the hallucinations had been plentiful and went back years. Even as a child she'd had "invisible friends", but now there was this nefarious presence, this Josef. What was that she said he wanted from her? Maybe that was the clue.

He rustled through the paperwork until he found it. 'Ah.' There it was. He mumbled to himself as he read the statement: 'has to find unhappy brides for Josef'.

The doctor pondered the issue a little bit longer as he watched the birds chirping away outside of his window. What an odd thing to create in one's mind, he thought. Yet Abigail would have created these brides to please vision number one, this Josef.

So, it made sense that she had to create more characters, these brides, until one took on a more prominent space in her mind to the point of now becoming "real", like Josef. Dr Passan considered what to put in the report recommending admission, if it came to that.

***

A week later he was sitting in his kitchen at home, once again massaging the spot on his nose where the specs pinched. He was mulling over Abigail's case, annoyed that she seemed to be following him in the manner of the ghosts she complained of. He replaced his specs, took a deep breath and let a rush of air out of his mouth. It was the weekend, dammit, and his wife was cooking him eggs and her special spicy tomato concoction.

As he dabbed the napkin to his lips after the meal, his wife poured him a cup of coffee.

'What a sad story,' she said as she sat down and pulled the newspaper towards her. 'Really, the things they come up with these days to get people to buy their paper.' She shook her head. 'Darling, you see this, look!'

She held the newspaper under his nose. He had to push it down to the table to be able to read it at all.

'Look,' insisted his wife, 'they say that someone is killing young brides.' She tapped her finger onto the article. 'What gets me is that the first was some Kirty Patel.' Letting her finger off the page so her husband could see it in full, she spooned some sugar into her tea, clinking the sides in a chime.

'Apparently, she was killed, *poisoned* in fact! Look, darling, at this drivel. The family of the white girl are saying that apparently some girl contacted their daughter and saw her some time before the wedding. It gets better! This girl that contacted them most likely contacted Kirty Patel too.' Stopping the chime, she tapped the paper again exactly in the bit where it was written.

'... Look here, they say how both had some posy on them when they died.' Throwing her arms in the air, she snorted. 'Now they blame flowers! Oh, and now apparently some Natalie might be the one who was first killed before these two were! Where do they find these stories? Those are the real patients, my dear, these are the people you should treat as their imagination is way out of this world.' With that little outrage, she took a sip of her tea as she pushed the paper closer to her husband.

'This is ridiculous, Pranil, don't buy this awful paper again. After all you are a proper doctor, a specialist. You can't afford to have your mind filled in with such, such ... drivel.'

Dr Passan was about to agree with the ridiculousness of it all when it hit him. It was the flowers that intrigued him. He pulled the paper closer, wiped away the toast crumbs and read the story. And that's when he had a flashback to one of his conversation with Abigail. The things she'd told him about brides, unhappy ones ...

He removed his glasses. This time he laid them down on the table with a sigh and closed his eyes with both hands. He shook his head and mumbled.

His wife shuffled over with a hurried swish-swish of slippers. 'What is it, Pranil? What is it now, it's as if you see a ghost?'

'Oh, Mruna, it's just about a patient, something I realized I should do.'

She clicked her tongue and swish-swished away, mumbling. 'Always on duty ... never any rest for either of us ...'

He opened his eyes and stared into the black swirl of coffee in front of him. As if that would help. And then he closed his eyes and rubbed him temples. Should he? But what about patient confidentiality? Yet … there were boundaries. If you thought the patient might harm another person. He sighed, lifted himself from the kitchen chair with a groan and walked over to the telephone. This was his duty. With a grimace he picked up the receiver and dialled.

Chapter 10

Detective Hendon was sitting at his desk, drinking tea, when his secretary walked in. 'I have a call for you. It's some shrink who says that he has some details that will help our enquiry. I checked him out already, he is genuine. He quoted the Data Protection Act, which is why he won't speak to anyone apart from the policeman in charge. Oh, his name is Dr Pranil Passan.'

John was just looking forward to a cup of tea as he mulled over how to find the girl who might be the key. Now this call came in and interrupted his thoughts. It better be good.

'I am ready, put him through. Hello, Detective Hendon speaking. How can I be of help?'

A slight Indian accent came over the line.

'I have vital information which I can only pass onto you. However, I must omit patient details.'

What a strange way to put it. 'OK, carry on.'

'Well, a patient of mine, female in her thirties, has been having visions. Her vision consists of a man that asked her, insisting she find him …'

The man on the other end inhaled sharply as if struggling to come to terms with what he was going to say next.

'It might sound strange. I do feel awkward telling you this as I am completely embarrassed to say it, but she says …' There was a pause in which John could hear chirping of birds in the background.

The doctor began again. 'She says that a man keeps asking her to find him unhappy brides. There you have it.' A woman's voice sounded from the distance. 'Hang on Mruna, I am speaking, let me finish.'

John cleared his throat. 'OK, Dr Passan, carry on, what other information do you have?' He twisted the phone cord around his finger.

'It was my wife that pointed it out to me in the paper, you know, the article and it sounds so like what the patient is experiencing. She has potentially tried to take her life, but she is linked to the incident where her own best friend died in the same way the girls in the newspaper did.'

John stopped fidgeting with the phone line and shot up in his seat. His ears were virtually on fire.

'OK, Dr Passan, there is nothing to be embarrassed about. This is interesting information. Can you give me her contact details? We will need to speak to her.'

There was an intake of breath on the other side of the line. Dr Passan was probably already at the end of what he wanted to say.

'I don't think that I am able to. I have the duty to keep my patient's data private. I am ...'

He was interrupted by John. 'Sir, this is a potential murder investigation and you must provide that data. It's up to you. I know your name, and where you work, so I give you the choice to give me that information or I will turn up with a search warrant. It's up to you.'

While trying to control his voice, John pumped his fist and started tapping his feet under the table in the beginnings of a victory dance. He had to contain himself and have the conversation end in a professional manner despite him wanting to shout out loud 'we're back in business!' Unwillingly and pressured, Dr Passan caved in and provided him with the home address John desperately needed.

'Thank you, Dr Passan. I really appreciate your co-operation.'

The doctor stammered a moment. He was cornered, and he knew it.

'I do not expect I will be needed anymore. I will ensure my secretary has the paperwork ready. But I think I gave you enough.' And with that he ended the call.

As John let go of the receiver he twirled in his office chair. He had a lead.

***

The news travelled at the speed of light. When it reached Vavřinec Terberk, the old detective was enjoying breakfast in the early sun of his garden. He nearly dropped his croissant onto the keyboard of his laptop when he read the headline. At last!

It had begun.

There was working to be done. The work Terberk had been waiting for was not something for public consumption. This explained why Terberk had had the secret stairs to the basement installed. Past the wall of lockers, Terberk made his way to the Faraday cage, beside which his main desk rested. Behind the desk was a large pin board buckling underneath all the papers pinned to it. Too many to go through, not enough time.

Slowly he sat down behind the solid oak desk. His fingers got working on the keyboard. Trawling the internet was a key part of his investigations. Those he was looking for could pop up almost anywhere in the world. His moustache twitched when he came on an interesting lead. Being a retired police detective from the Czech Republic police force, he knew exactly what he should be discarding and what was interesting. Experience had taught him that sometimes there was more to things than just what people scientifically believed in. Being old fashioned, he liked to read certain things off the paper, so as he pressed print, he waited for the machine to spit out the document. Waiting gave him opportunity to engage into some more thought. Surreptitiously he giggled underneath his little black moustache at the knowledge how baffled the professors of the world would be if he ever chose to present his findings to the world.

He cast his gaze around the basement. Those little lockers, the kind you found at gyms and swimming pools, held a different type of valuables. A small symbol some might wear on a lapel would be stashed in one locker beside another holding a priceless little polished stone. Some items might be made of precious metal or carried some but mostly they were just normal objects holding no value at all. There was also the occasional meteorite fallen from the night sky – the moldavite they called it, though he knew very well that it's not just meteorite.

It so happened that one of these lockers had one particularly large moldavite with mind-reading ability. In the wrong hands this would cause great harm. Still he toyed with the idea of using it for his benefit but knowing that those that used to own it had died in unnatural circumstances had made him to lock it up for good. All these little lockers, all these banal items had one thing in common – murder.

They all related to murderers that trailed through time, so they could kill repeatedly through centuries. Their negative energy, the wickedness itself embodied into materialistic things. Those who came through time to kill over again used the weak-minded to do the deed.

There were lockers though that puzzled him as he didn't fully understand. That was why Terberk had to keep them secret. The simple war-time swastika made of cheap metal and worn on the lapels of Hitler youth gave him grief. Recently Terberk realized that he had a replica. But it led him to the question: if these murderous souls dwelled in material objects such as jewellery, gemstones and trinkets, if an object was copied exactly, could it be that the soul of the murderer could split itself between more than one object? If the answer was yes, then what use was Terberk's locker system? The idea was to remove "possessed" objects from circulation, thus curbing the murderers who dwelled in these objects. But if objects could be replicated and remain potent in terms of black magic, the whole world might be in peril.

These questions were why he carried on despite being retired. He was the only one ready to investigate the unimaginable. That's why he set up and kept his private investigator's website going. And so, the local police kept knocking on his door with cases they had trouble understanding.

The key to these items was that Terberk had to find the person in the current world who possessed them. It usually was the link between the living and the dead that would then lead him to the murderer which only then could be contained by hiding the item keeping his door opened to the living. Terberk placed the cold swastika tingling in his palm back into the locker. He was about to finally move on with the Nine Crosses massacre. The swastika had to wait, for now.

Back behind his desk he began the work. First, he found the clippings and unpinned them from the board. Next, he pulled out from his filing cabinet the folder marked *9 Crosses*. This morning's newspaper article left no doubt. The monster of Devět Křížů was again at large. Now it was up to Terberk to find the item that had been keeping him alive. And time was of the essence. The object, the monster's talisman, was what Terberk was after. Find the object, lock it up, and the monster's power was controlled.

Terberk smoothed one of the clippings with the palm of his hand. He knew all the photographs, could see them in his sleep, but again he searched them for clues. What was the object? It must have been something, a token, that was near the murderer when he died.

So many years, more than one fine-toothed comb investigation of the site, and still he could make just an educated guess. However, seeing as the newspaper had showed him the current events were taking place in the

UK, the item had made its way across Europe. Thus, the object was small and easy to transport.

Usually the items are those nearest to the murderers at the time of their gruesome deaths. Buttons, brooches, goblets, mirrors, rings, chains ... Most often, the items were enduring, of this kind, but sometimes the magic would hide in organic matter. Flowers, for example. Organic matter would decay and disappear, but the effect could be recreated if one went to work very precisely: a specific combination of certain flowers, for example.

And so, opening the nine crosses file, the first things he scanned for were flowers, posy, wedding ring, dress, necklace, button. The one item surely had to be one of these. He scanned the news article. So far there were two brides who had died the same way: heart attacks right before the altar. 'Both were healthy young women linked to potential poisoning,' it read. Only two deaths? Terberk had no doubt there would be more. What caught his interest was that they are looking for a young girl who might have the answers.

'Aha!' A young girl. He would have to find her before anyone did. She was the key. Find her, and he'd find the one thing he'd been looking for all these decades. He doubted the police would be interested in listening to him. How would he find this girl before anyone else did?

He took a break from his computer and walked up the secret stairs to ponder these matters in his garden. He pulled off his slippers, and barefoot he walked over the sun-warmed patio. It was the typical Bohemian summer, very hot indeed.

The parasol was a good purchase as it shielded the sun just enough to be comfortable to sit outside. He loved this garden overlooking the wheat fields. In the time of the harvest the combine harvester came right up to his wire fence, the shaking of the machine just about tipping over the bollards holding the wire. The grain was in full growth, golden, swaying in a gentle summer breeze that was in a short supply. Mice were frequent, unwanted visitors to his garden and used the large pine tree as a climbing frame. They did that to get to the birds' nests. These hungry pests loved to eat fresh eggs. Occasionally he could see the squirrel chasing the naughty mice down the tree. He enjoyed watching them running up and down.

He sat down onto his garden swing and gently rocked. Then his tranquillity was disturbed by the ringing of the landline. With a huff of disapproval, he made his way back into the house. Nobody called here unless it was work related.

Well, that was not strictly true. Ivana Barvova, the girlfriend he met in the winter of his life, called sometimes. Ah, he hoped it was her.

He rushed to the phone. Perhaps Ivana wanted to take a walk along the meadows. 'Or to the lake,' he said to his black cat. The creatures usually appeared in the garden to sunbathe with him. By the time he grabbed the phone at what was surely the last ring, he was out of breath. His greeting escaped his lungs in a whoosh.

'Hello? Vavřinec Terberk?'

He sighed, rolled his eyes. The voice too young and tinny to be Ivana, and of course Ivana would never reduce that "ř" to a weak, English "r".

'I am very sorry to be calling out of the blue, but I need help.' A girl's voice.

'I was Googling … Looking for a private detective. Specifically, in Bohemia.' She cleared her throat. 'I need your services. I have so many questions. It's about a specific case in your area. I believe – as it shows in the article I have here – that at the time you were a young detective. I need you to help me. Tell me, do you know anything about the Nine Crosses?'

Terberk nearly dropped the phone. 'If Mohammed doesn't come to the mountain, the mountain must come to Mohammed. Good heavens, I was looking for you. You are having visions?'

An incoherent mumble came over the line, a shaken jumble of emotions and words completely mixed up followed by a brief pause.

'You see him!' Terberk shouted. 'And you are scared, wondering how to stop it?' Now Terberk needed a little pause needed. His veins throbbed in excitement. After all these years, this! 'What is your name? Where are you, I must meet up with you.'

After a moment's hesitation, the young voice spoke again.

'Abigail, I am Abigail. I might be losing my mind but yes, I am scared, and I want this to stop! I have a deadline, you see, I am going to be married but I can lose him.'

The sobs drowned her next words. After some sniffling she spoke again.

'They thought I was suicidal, but I wasn't. It was her, the Bride, you know, she wants to kill me!'

Her breathing sped up to the point of hyperventilation.

'Calm down, I can help, but you must be strong.'

As if he had just said the most magical words, in between sobs the girl said,'Thank you so much, I knew as I read up on the internet about you that you would have the answers. I saw you in the old newspapers. I also know why. I know the story, I just can't find the answers. That's why I need someone like you. Someone who knows.'

'You are right. I have the answers you are looking for. But we must meet immediately. Time is running out! Give me your telephone number and an address. I'll come to you.' Terberk wrote the information down neatly onto a piece of paper. He wasn't a modern man, he still needed his piece of paper to place information onto.

The goodbyes behind him, he strode to first the basement and then the bedroom, where he stuffed the key necessities into his suitcase for a three-day stay in a foreign country. The main necessity was his folder. This he placed neatly into his suitcase, whereas the socks, boxers, spare shirt, shaving kit and other bits he simply flung in. Despite the initial messiness, once it was all in the suitcase, he was very particular in how things were packed.

He was grateful to be just an hour from the airport, and thanks to the internet he booked the flight from Brno to Stanstead in minutes. Initially he thought it was in London but when he looked at the map it was miles away. He had always been fond of the Royal Family, so he hoped to get the chance to see the majestic Buckingham Palace, maybe even catch a glimpse of the Queen. Well-mannered, beautiful, smart girl she was. Now it was obvious it wasn't going to happen. London was way off course, and time was short.

That brought the thoughts of his girlfriend back. Addressing the cat, he said 'I should call Ivana, Mourku, and ask whether she would like to accompany me.' He turned to the black moggy that had leisurely placed herself on his bed, watching him pack. But he discarded the idea. Hardly a pleasant trip for Ivana, given he was there to catch a ghost. He decided to give Ivana a quick call to inform her he would be unavailable for walks for the next couple of days as he was away on police business. Thankfully she was used to attending to his cat when he was away and knew where to find the house key.

On his way to the airport he called Ivana from his mobile and thanked her for taking care of his property when he was away, promising to take her out as a treat. He tried to be chirpy, but his mind was elsewhere. How many brides were dead? What would the girl be like? What was the current state of the Bride? She had certainly turned dangerous, but where was the murderer himself? His whole life Terberk had been waiting in the shadows to solve this one. This opportunity he wasn't going to miss. He had a duty to close this one off.

***

The weather in England was, as expected, rainy. It drizzled with large clouds hanging in the sky like stuffed sheep. Terberk thought of home and of the dumplings he would have once he returned. He only been gone a couple of hours, yet he already missed home. He certainly didn't like this weather much.

The poor taxi driver tried to pronounce his name out of politeness but gave up on his second attempt. Terberk didn't hold that against him. Not many speakers of other languages would be able to say his whole name without any stutter or the occasional pronunciation error.

The hotel he had booked had the old English Tudor design with plenty of old-fashioned feather pillows. The downstairs entrance, through the old pub, had somewhat claustrophobic low ceilings with broad beams everywhere, with all sorts of stuff hung off them: an old ski, just gathering dust, some horse brass with a couple of painted horseshoes and an old rake in the corner, plus many other things all over the place. Terberk noted that the skis were in very good condition. In his country they would be battered or at least well used.

No time for unpacking: Terberk was ready to go to meet Abigail. There was much to do in a short space of time. Each moment wasted was time where a girl may be in danger. Down the stairs he went, past the bar into the dining room. He had already texted Abigail his address; she was on her way. He sat down and ordered a beer. By the time he was on his second, Abigail turned up. He recognized her voice from the phone. He noted her white skin and messy hair, lack of self-care. Skittish, scanning the crowd she locked onto Terberk watching her. He raised an eyebrow in greeting. Hesitantly she stepped toward him.

'Ah what a lovely evening. You must be Abigail.' Terberk held out his hand to shake hers.

'Now sit down and I shall order you a drink. What would you like?'

Sheepishly, Abigail sat down, handbag on her lap clasping the handles so tight her hands went white. Leaning in, she whispered, 'Not here. Can we go to my place? I don't want to be anywhere apart from home, where it's safe.'

This girl was certainly troubled. A rabbit in the headlights.

'OK Abigail, let me pay for the drinks. Wait for me outside if that makes you more at ease.'

Outside they didn't speak apart from some hand gestures from Abigail as she led him to her small battered car.

The journey back was silent, despite Terberk trying to prise out information. He was beginning to wonder if he had the right girl. The only thing she said was that they at least would be alone to talk freely once they were in her flat.

***

When the young woman parked her car, Terberk followed her to her front door.

'Could I make you some coffee?' Abigail asked as she turned the key in the lock.

'That would be lovely, though I am little hungry as I haven't had my dinner. Are you sure there isn't a restaurant we can go to?'

She turned to him with widened eyes. 'I can't, I can't go out. She's there waiting to kill me! It's her or him, both want to kill me.' She began to sob.

He took pity on her. She obviously was under some treatment as normal sane person could explain certain things that were happening to her.

As the girl put her hands on her face, Terberk's heart leapt as he spotted something that didn't fit. This girl's clothes were drab, non-branded basics and her shoes were well worn. So how could someone like her afford that gleaming gold ring? She wasn't married, so it couldn't have been a wedding gift.

'Abigail, that ring!' Was this the thing he was after? Was this co-incidence? Is it yours? Was is always yours?'

Abigail took her hands off her face. 'That's nothing to do with you. It's mine, nobody else's!' She spat the words.

'I know,' he soothed. 'I'm not taking it away, I just want to talk. You want my help, you called me, remember. I can help you, but we must be completely honest. I will show you the full story but now you need to give me some information. I am the one who has answers. For years now, I've been after a man who has been hopping through the centuries finding brides to kill. I am here to solve the mystery, to stop him for good. I know his modus operandi: finding someone just like you, possessing them, making them believe that he is going to change their future. You are his, aren't you?'

Abigail stopped sobbing, dropped her arms, mouth still open, unable to speak. Gulping, she fanned her face with her hands. 'You know about HIM? You must know how to be rid of him, you must know how I can get my life back, tell me now, tell me before Josef comes back! Before she comes back to try to kill me again. He will be back to torture me! He will be back for Dan!'

Ah! Finally, Terberk had the man's name: Josef. Nobody had ever recorded the tyrant's name.

'This Josef, does he speak of the Bride? Is she ever present in the same place as this man you spoke of, this Josef?'

Abigail closed her eyes. 'This Bride you ask about, this woman I saw many times. Her name is Anna as it was revealed to me in one of my dreams.' Forgetting the coffee, she and dragged Terberk into the lounge. Even before he sat down, she started spraying information at him like machine-gun fire.

'I know why she died, I know because she has let me see the whole story, she has come into my dreams to tell me, to warn me of Josef. I didn't listen! And now she's returned to my dreams, and now she is different. More dangerous, blatantly says I must die! She was the one that was going to kill me.' She clutched her head in both hands.

'I listened to Anna's nagging, to Josef's constant abuse, demands, which is why I had to do something. Seeing my love, my dear Dan in pain, in tears by watching me with worry what I might do next was a wake-up call. He has gone through so much, he deserves better. He deserved Natalie. It is only now I see how wrong I was about her. She was true, she was vain but honest-hearted. Anna is right, I have to end this!'

Terberk pondered his next move. This was a defeated young woman. He could see no future for her beyond a life of self-pity. Choosing his words carefully, he pointed at her ring.

'There might be a way, Abigail, there just might. I think what we could try is to go to the place of where it all began. Now, tell me, is that ring yours? Where did you buy it?'

She slumped into the sofa so hard it creaked at the seams. 'The old woman, the gypsy.' As if her head was spinning, Abigail leaned against the sofa. 'It's not mine, I bought it in Brno, from an old gypsy, who went a bit mad saying thing I didn't want to hear, but she said that if I take it I will belong to him.'

Terberk nearly jumped from his seat. 'Yes! I think it all makes sense to me! It's the ring that has kept Josef alive, to help him to through the centuries to continue sowing hatred and death. We must go at the right time, to the place where the Bride, Anna, will be as she always is on her wedding day. We must go to these woods and try to expel Josef from you, to leave your body. He has a great hold on you, like a virus, he has permeated all the cells in your body. There is no simple way to rid yourself of him.'

Abigail jolted out of the sofa so fast that it made Terberk twitch. 'If it's the ring, I just take it off, I do it now and we don't need to go anywhere!'

Reaching for her finger she gently tugged at it. Each tug was like an invisible rope around her throat, tightening. It only budged a single millimetre before she passed out blue.

Terberk jumped up and kneeled beside her as she came to. 'Silly girl, if it was that easy I would have told you over the phone, or at least in the doorway as soon as I noticed.'

Now that her arms were by her side, no longer working at the ring, her colour returned to normal.

'We must make him leave of his own will. Trying otherwise will only make him kill you.'

Terberk pointed at the little photo in its silver frame on the coffee table.

'Oh, the picture?' she said. 'My boyf— my fiancé, Dan, and I took it the first week when I really believed that things were turning for the better.'

'You don't want to die. You want what's in that picture, so be strong. Thankfully what I know is that he leaves for just one day of the year, to do what he did those many years ago: he attends the wedding. That's our only chance. Only then can you, must you take the ring off your finger and hand it to me.'

The girl took the photo and hugged it. In between sobs, she pleaded, saying she would do anything for this Dan.

Terberk patiently stroked her hair. 'I know it's hard, but you must come with me to the place where this began. We must attend the scene of Anna's wedding day massacre.' Abigail's sobs changed to a high-pitched squeak.

'You mean have to go there to see what I dreamed about?'

Terberk peeled the photo frame from her chest only to press it under her nose. 'If you want this, you must. I am not talking about time travel. The local people know that one day, each tenth year, the wedding occurs as the moon is high above the woods. At midnight, the locals hear the faint sounds of a wedding song as the procession goes through the woods, the children running, chattering.'

Silent, Abigail put her hand against her mouth. 'And the Bride, will she be there?' Terberk lay down the photo. Facing Abigail, he gently squeezed her shoulder.

'Yes, the locals do say that you can hear the wailing of the Bride, the laughter of the evil one, the screams of the others who were also slaughtered on that day. If you believe, then you must pack now. Are you ready to have a go at being rid of Josef forever?'

Abigail was near tears. 'Why are you trying to help me? I am a murderer, I killed those innocent girls.'

Terberk felt his back straightening. He grabbed the girl by the shoulders and shook her. 'Abigail, how many? How many did you give him?'

She didn't break eye contact. 'I gave him three. That's why I know he will be back. He usually comes back right after if there isn't one waiting, with me having passed on a posy. I have killed my best friend! I am an awful human being.'

Terberk released her shoulders. 'Ah, so there is time: only three, but the madman always wants nine. We have time. Go quickly, pack, do it now.'

Abigail sprang to her feet, running to her bedroom as Terberk followed. One skip on her chair and she retrieved the small suitcase she kept on top of the wardrobe. Frantically she threw in clothes, underwear, a hairbrush.

'I must be rid of him, if he is gone then all is well. I can't fail Dan, I must go with you. Let's do this.'

Terberk spoke: 'Don't forget to tell this boy of yours you are going to be away for couple of days.'

And then the doorbell rang.

***

The last person Detective John Hendon expected to open the door was this character resembling a Victorian teacher, neat moustache and all. If the man had been wearing a bowler hat, Hendon would have thought he'd gone back in time.

'Hello, I am Sergeant John Hendon and I need to speak to Ms Abigail Small. Is she present?'

From the passage the girl's unbrushed head popped out. Her eyes were exhausted, her T-shirt was dirty.

'Hello, Ms. Small, I presume that it's you, you are Abigail, is that correct? May I come in? It's urgent. We can talk here, or I can take you to the station. Your choice.'

It was the old man that spoke. He extended his arm. 'Hello, nice to meet you. I am Vavřinec Terberk. Detective, I am here to help Abigail to resolve certain issues she is having. Please do come in and sit down. We can talk.'

The man closed the door behind John and ushered him to the sofa. The girl quietly slipped down into the chair opposite. Nobody spoke as John's stomach gave a grumble. It had been a rash decision to turn up at her flat as soon as Dr Passan passed him the information he needed to find the girl.

'As I said, Abigail, can I call you Abigail?' The girl nodded. 'This is urgent.'

The moustached fellow nodded. 'Yes, important things to be discussed.'

What the hell was this old man doing here? And what was that accent? Russian, John decided.

With that name and accent, John would have expected this Terberk to have a couple of scars and an old KGB logo tattooed on this arm. Yet, he wouldn't trust the man's genteel appearance. Anyone who had been a policeman during communist times must be as hard as nails.

Then Terberk cut through the foggy silence.

'Hello Detective Hendon, it is nice to meet you. There is a lot we need to talk about, but I must ask you to be openminded if you really want to understand what is happening. Firstly, as my name is hard to pronounce, you can call me Vava, which is short for Vavřinec. Surname is Terberk.' He passed John his business card.

**

When Terberk opened the door, he was surprised to see a blotchy-faced man in his forties. White hair, miserable looking face. After the introductions, the detective that spoke next.

'OK, Vava can you tell me more?' The man immediately took to the shortened form of Terberk's name.

'I don't have much patience as I really need to interview this young lady. Why are you here? This is a serious, private discussion.' He cleared his throat. 'I'd appreciate if you'd make yourself scarce.'

It was Abigail that finally spoke. 'Mr Terberk isn't going anywhere. I employed him. He's my private detective. You can talk in front of him.'

Terberk gave her a grateful nod. The detective pulled a long face and rolled his eyes before he spoke. 'OK, OK, fine, I get it, whatever you want. Abigail, I need to speak to you about your friends, the ones who all mysteriously suffered an unfortunate demise right before the altar. Is there anything you would like to tell me?'

This time, instead of speaking, Abigail turned to Terberk and nodded. Terberk pointed to the bag lying at his feet, at which the English detective picked it up and pulled out a single folder. He opened it in the middle to reveal a picture of a young dead Bride with the same posy in her hand. Hendon's hands shook; his pitch rose and sweat rolled down his forehead. Wide eyed he pointed the photo towards Terberk, tapping on it with his index finger.

He shuffled closer.

'This is it! This is how we find them! The same way. Who is she, when, why, what, who?'

Terberk looked at him. 'This woman died twenty-five years ago.'

Detective Hendon went back to the picture. One could tell by the bridal dress that it was a little outdated, but twenty-five years was a long time ago. He would realize that young girl opposite them was too young to have been involved in this.

'Does it mean the murderer was never caught and charged?' The detective's voice shook so he had to repeat himself. He closed the folder with frown before reaching down for another folder, hurriedly opening it.

'I don't understand any of the writing but the dates ... is it a year, wait, 1500? This is dated as 14.08.1500. Am I reading this right, what the hell is this?'

Eyebrows raised, Terberk tapped his hand.

'Don't worry, Detective, I shall soon explain everything to you, just be patient. What I need you to understand is Abigail and I must travel outside of England. If you want these murders to stop you must let us do that.'

Hendon's stomach grumbled as he flicked his eyes from Terberk to Abigail and back again. 'Where is the posy from? The poison, how does it enter their bodies?'

Terberk took the lead again.

'Detective, why don't we get something to eat? We can speak so Abigail can pack. She won't run away, you can trust me on that. She will not leave my side.'

Abigail slowly nodded.

***

Terberk was pleased with the outcome. The detective wasn't throwing him out neither was he walking away. There were some worries but thankfully the man had made the right decision.

'Alright, let's get some fish and chips. You can tell me all about what's in that magic bag of yours. Call me John, by the way. If I call you Vava, we can spend less time pronouncing names and get down to business.' He turned to Abigail.

'You, young lady, have no chance of running away. I know your name, I can find you anywhere. I will catch up with you tomorrow.'

Terberk winked at Abigail and softly patted her shoulder. 'Don't worry. Soon it will be over. Now rest. Tomorrow we travel. Call your fiancé to make sure he isn't worried while you're gone.'

With that, followed by the English detective, he left. He took the sergeant to the hotel where he was staying.

'Oh, fab, I know this place. They do an excellent fish and chips.' They found a quiet corner at a table for two and Hendon stepped away to order beer.

Terberk was aware of the strange English dish called fish and chips. The fish was battered, and chips, which are pomme-frites to a Czech man, were usually covered in some aromatic vinegar. He was certainly disappointed with the Yorkshire pudding: not a sweet dish as expected but a bland pastry to be eaten with gravy.

Hendon came back grinning with satisfaction that Terberk couldn't share. He placed a pint in front of Terberk.

'Try this one, called a Fursty Ferret. Really nice beer made in Dorset.'

The discussion about beer came up: a favourite topic to any Czech male citizen, especially as during the discussion one had to taste the nectar.

When the food arrived, Terberk was not impressed. This "fish and chips" meal should have come with a health warning: high-fat calorie bomb. Still, once he tasted it, he was hooked. A truly wonderful, addictive concoction of salt and fat.

About five Fursty Ferrets later, Terberk had brought Hendon up to speed with the case that had followed him through his life. He explained how he had failed to get the full understanding of the people in charge at the time he was a policeman in the Czech Republic. Hence eventually he had to resign as a chief constable.

By the time he got to the point of murders re-occurring, Hendon was sitting there like a statue.

'So, you are saying there are two of them, one is the killer who skips through time and the other is the Bride? Why did she kill the … the footballer? The one in the newspaper? How does he fit in?'

Terberk closed his eyes and somehow transferred himself to the past. In his mind he was again leaning over the football player, dead on the ground. It was the time of mullet haircuts.

'John, I was there, examining him as he lay there on the ground. Heart attack, they said, most likely from a shock. The Bride didn't want to kill, she wanted to raise awareness, to warn us all. Otherwise she would have killed me too.' John leaned in, whispering.

'Are you telling me you met her?' As if they were discussing a conspiracy, leaning in face-to-face, whispering.

'I did, she was there, watching me from behind a tree in the shadow. She was weeping, warning me. Only I could see her, nobody else. I thought I was mad, that the stress of the job was getting to me, but I wasn't. After investigating further, I met with the town folk and those who meddled in the things we don't understand. That's how I met Ivana, a strong woman who speaks with the dead. I listened to her and thanks to her I know there is more than meets the eye.'

Terberk's throat had gone dry. He took a swig of the beer. 'At the time I was going to be promoted but I just couldn't let this case drop. It didn't fit. It was the village people who gave me the eureka moment. The story about the Bride worked like a juicy worm at the end of a fishing hook, reeling me closer to the truth. After many years of secretly trying to crack all the theories I managed to get hold of the Benedictine archives from the time of the massacre. They were the most vital information as they pre-dated the wedding but also gave full account of the actual story and what followed.'

Hendon's chair creaked as he leaned back with force. 'Are you telling me the Bride is the key to the whole mess?' His frown deepened. 'Because if I remember the discussion earlier, you confirmed it was this other guy, some murderer, who is killing all the brides.'

He tapped his chubby finger on the file on the table. Terberk noted how condensation rings from years of beer glasses had eaten into the varnish. 'All this, this makes sense, the story, the old photographs and sketches. Who the hell the killer is, and how they come back, is beyond me. Although now, for the first time, I have a name. Josef, she said.'

'Josef?'

'Yes, that's what the girl called him.' Terberk leaned in to the folder and opened it. Retrieving a little picture, he passed it to Hendon.

'This is how they connect.' Hendon stared at the photo of the little posy. It was the same one he had seen in his own file; the same one his pathologist was most concerned about.

'I can see from your expression it's jogged some memory,' Terberk said. Then he pulled other photos and started laying them like cards to play solitaire, lined up before John, showing multiple young women, all dead brides. One little circle in different sides of the photo made it easy on the eye to spot the posy. There it was in all the pictures going back from the earliest era of photography. Then when John expanded each pile, they lined up. For the year 2000 there were four pictures of dead brides, each with a posy. The other line had six from the year 1991 with similar scenes and another set from 1982. Then

Terberk pulled more, a lot of smaller folders with 1955, 1923, 1887 and so on. They didn't contain many a picture but snippets of information and copies of an old text from town chronicles.

'And here is the last folder, which relates to the Bride sightings and accidents on that small part of motorway D1.'

This is where Hendon retrieved the photo of a young man in his football shirt smiling at the camera for the local newspaper interview. The same newspaper had a photo of the footballer's death announcement.

'Is this you?' Hendon pointed at the small moustache figure in one of the newspaper photos.

'Look there, that's your name, right?'

'John, I know it's overwhelming, but you must listen to the evidence before you. I have no time! I must take Abigail with me to Czech. That is where it all started. That's where it can end. I must take her tomorrow as time is running out. We only have that one day only to sort this out!'

Arms crossed over his chest, Hendon entered a staring contest with Terberk. Shifting in his chair, not breaking eye contact, Terberk felt that he could see steam coming out of the man's ears. After what felt like a century, Hendon uncrossed his arms.

'A murderer comes through time and does what he is best at – he murders those he chooses, not the Bride. She is just collateral. He comes through time using those with weak minds who have desires which makes them controllable. So that's why Abigail is linked, she is the one that passes on the token, the posy. Then he comes for them.' Unaware, John mumbled to himself, 'Explains the strange bruises on their hearts …'

Terberk tidied up all the evidence, replacing everything into its folder, shuffling the papers around. 'Yes, that's why you can see it on their hearts, because that's his handiwork.' Surprised he had been heard, John's ears burnt.

'You know I can't let you go alone with her? I haven't checked you out yet. How do I know you're genuine? You can only go if I can go with you.'

Terberk passed John a file called Copies. 'There it is for you to read. You will need it to explain to everyone, show evidence of what has been happening. I shall meet you tomorrow 8 a.m. sharp, with Abigail.'

As he got up to leave the table, Terberk spoke the last word. 'The bride is the key to resolving this issue. She's the one that can lead us to how to end this evil.'

With the idea of getting some sleep, Terberk went to his room. As he stood in front of this bathroom mirror he thought of how he had kept the Englishman in the dark about the ring. He *had* to have it to lock it up with the others. It would only confuse Hendon if he knew. And he couldn't risk the man confiscating this talisman. It would lead to disaster! It had to be locked away.

No, he had to keep this one secret under his hat. His underground store was built especially for safeguarding items with evil, ghostly presence attached. All these things carried evil, hoping to be released upon the unbelievers to take over their beings. These unsuspecting targets would have their life sucked out them. Terberk had seen the proof too many times: the dead returning for revenge. No, he didn't say anything to John. He, Vavřinec Terberk, had to take this ring and lock it away forever.

***

The morning was full of birdsong. The English made a pastime feeding these little critters, who then visited regularly to feast on the well-stocked bird-feeders.

That would never work in Czech, as people wouldn't spend money on food for wild birds. He felt embarrassed about how the Czech treated their garden birds. He would do more when he returned as he did like their song in the morning, their chirruping happiness.

'We do feed the wild animals in woods though!' he told one of the birds that landed on the window ledge.

'Yes, we do, we collect conkers, acorns into large sacks to give to wood keepers who give to the animals in the winter months. Yes, we are not that heartless.'

Terberk breakfasted in the garden, after which Hendon and then the girl turned up as scheduled. They left for the airport.

***

Uncomfortable, Abigail made more toilet breaks than usual. She knew it was time to listen to that strange foreigner. He was the first person who knew more than she did, and he was ready to help to get her out of this mess.

The time was running out, that was obvious as the Bride was once again infiltrating her dreams, floating above Abigail as she lay paralyzed on her bed. Dan was there to shake her awake, but she wasn't safe anymore. Thankfully Dan was so withdrawn that before she was ready to tell him where she was going, he came up with the news that he was moving back with his parents for a while. To clear his head, he said. But it worked well. No need to explain her trip. It was hard to ignore Anna standing behind Dan, her black eyes bleeding as she whispered commands of suicide. As Dan was leaving the flat, she could remember the words, as if they were being said repeatedly into her ears.

'You have no choice, Abigail, you must kill yourself because you'll end up in hell no matter what, you might as well end up there with dignity. If Josef won't do it, I will. I've had to kill many over the centuries to stop Josef. I stood on the side of those who were wronged. I talk to your friend, Natalie, and she isn't pleased. Through eternity she'll learn to hate you and your kind just as I did.

My hate is against those weak ones who are so easily turned by him. Just like you, they are people who value their own needs above the lives of others. I have taken life and enjoyed it too. You have no choice, you must come to my wedding. Don't miss it if you wish to have a chance!'

That was why it was the right choice to go, that's why it was a great stroke of luck finding the old private detective.

Somehow, though scared, Abigail felt excitement. This was her chance to turn this around, to have Dan back again. To have Dan to hold so tight that his heartbeat merged with hers, that his lungs took in the same air as she did. Those were all the things that were worth dying for. For love, one was ready to do anything what was required. At the airport, Terberk gently squeezed her hand in encouragement.

'Are you ready to attend the wedding?'

Abigail squeezed back. 'I am.'

Chapter 11

Abigail wrote the outline of Dan's name on the airplane window. The third time she ran her finger across the big D, Detective Hendon interrupted.

'Abigail, can I please just ask, how many girls? How many altogether? I don't believe in any mumbo jumbo stuff, but you are scaring me now. Until now I have been very open to new ideas. This is taking it that little bit further for my comfort. Are you aware that you have admitted to being involved? You are speaking to a police officer that has a crime to solve. Do you know what it means?'

Abigail shifted slightly as despite the whispering, some words escaped to the passenger in the front of her. The man now took a quick turn to check her out with disapproving frown.

'Only three,' she said after the passenger returned to his seating position. The detective darted up to pretend to stretch his legs, only to sit down immediately. It was good luck the seat next to him was empty; if someone had been there they would have got the elbow in the face.

'Only three? ONLY? Are you grasping of the seriousness of the situation here? Are you thinking of the destruction you have caused to people's lives?'

As he whispered this to her, everything in his face got blacker.

'I don't appreciate this, Sergeant Hendon, do you think that I don't know myself? Don't you think that wanted this to happen? I want the man who controls me gone.'

Abigail got closer to his nose. 'All you have is a confession from a psychiatric care patient. Now, be reasonable and listen to the only person that is making sense.' She pointed at Terberk.

'He is the one that can stop it.' With this the flight went on silently apart from the nosy passenger who on occasions turned to check them out again. Abigail had her head turned towards the window, watching the small drops of condensation sliding down. At no point was she going to turn to face detective Hendon. It was clear from his clamped jaw and stiff lip that he didn't like the situation or sitting next to her.

***

Terberk noticed the tension between them but wasn't ready to join the conversation. He was pleased to be on his way home. Though the flight wasn't that long he didn't enjoy being squished in a plane body on body, with no leg room. To make it bearable, he kept thinking of how lucky he was, how lucky he was to have Ivana. In his mind this woman was all he wanted. He had been devastated when his wife died, of course, but life must go on. It took him a long time before he started to think about having someone else. His wife's death really affected him. All happened at the same time of the death of the young footballer. His wife was one of the victims in a fatal car pile-up on that atrocious part of the motorway.

Ivana appeared as if from nowhere, giving a helping hand when needed with explaining the blanks he had about the footballer's death. She was a chair member of a society of mediums, some of whom were the real thing, while some others were simply masters at guessing.

This whole thing of Nine Crosses thing bothered him now. He knew that one way or other he would have to get the ring. Abigail was on very thin ice. He was relieved she had immediately agreed to come. Time was of the essence. He had shared all relevant information, though he wasn't sure of everything. But how could he admit to the fact that he didn't know how things would work out? He couldn't cause that level of alarm!

Maybe Abigail wasn't going to make it after all. His gut was telling him the ring wouldn't come off her hand easily. It would want something in return, or someone. That was what he felt deep in his heart, although it was just a hunch. He remembered how, on leaving home to meet with Abigail, he had said to his black moggy:

'Let's just hope it's only a hunch,' as he stroked her between the ears. That's what he was thinking now. 'Let's hope that I'm wrong,' he mumbled as the plane made its descent for landing.

***

Detective Hendon had a different set of worries rattling about his brain. Though he had an open paper in front of him, he didn't pay any attention to the words. It worked as a distraction from not being interrupted unless necessary and it bought him some time to collect his, now chaotic, memories. It was completely out of his character to just jump at the whim of a weird foreigner. It was even weirder that he would let his prime suspect out of the country. He was certainly completely out of his comfort zone with his mind firing off one theory after another. The thought that he would try to save someone who was a murderer was ludicrous. What next? Going through prison, asking all the mass murderers 'Were you possessed recently? If so, can you state, the name and date of birth of your possessor and if available can we also have his status? Jack the Ripper? No?'

He could imagine what the discussion with his superiors would be like. It would be more like an early asylum retirement than a revelation. Thankfully Abigail sat facing the window, so he didn't have to speak to her.

He found Abigail awkward. It was clear she was disturbed but was there was a chance she was playing everyone. This Terberk's idea might be true but was this one of those things, where Abigail was using it to her advantage, so she could get away with what she had done? How could she murder the victims? That was impossible to work out without Terberk's theory.

It was clear Abigail was nowhere near the women when they died. He had been asking anybody present and willing to speak to the police about whether they seen her there on the day.

His good old police nose was trying to make sense of it all. He gave up pretending to read the paper. The rustling of the paper made Abigail shift a little on her buttocks, but she remained facing the widow. It was only on the descent that he noticed her reflection.

He was interested to see what the Eastern European airport would look like. He wondered if it was like one of those harsh concrete communist blocks from a Bond movie. To his surprise they landed in one of those building projects that happened thanks to the Europe Union money flooding into Eastern Europe. Still it seemed that more money left the UK than was coming in. By the look of it the Czechs hadn't had much of a budget as the old airport building was still standing there, in its own communist beauty: old ugly concrete, shapeless eyesore as he was expecting. The modern part of the build looked like a modern extension on an old gothic building, it was ridiculous. All of them remained silent as they walked down the plane stairs directly onto the tarmac. The weather was very hot, the sun beaming so much that the surface was cracking up, melting under the heat.

Detective Hendon noticed Abigail teetering towards him. They walked side by side, silently like two strangers. Two strangers heading for the same destination.

***

Terberk followed soon after for he was all the way at the back of the plane. He never was one to stand up immediately as soon as the plane stopped. Almost everyone did that at the same time, trying to go through bodies to run out. It made no sense, so he usually sat until the plane was half empty. He knew the airport well. You could spot it between the fields immediately as you turned off the motorway, past the junction with many tall trees on each side of the road. After passing these trees the road snakes around and then the whole valley opened before you. You could stop by the side of the road before getting to the airport and watch planes land or just enjoy the country view.

That was exactly what Terberk did every time he had to pick someone up from here. It saved him some money and it was enjoyable to see the buzz before him. He enjoyed watching the people coming in and going out; the buses driving past with planes in the distance landing. Terberk disliked to pay the car park fee, so with his binoculars he waited for the right plane to land. He would usually watch for the right flight airline logo which then with quick internet check confirmed which plane carried the visitors he was waiting for. He knew he was a little tight in doing it and that Ivana would find it embarrassing. He couldn't care less, people would mistake him for a plane watcher not someone who is too tight to pay the car park fee. Once the right plane landed he would wait further ten minutes before he got into his car and drove the last half a mile to the airport car park. It doesn't not cost anything if you only stay for less than fifteen minutes. However, if you park there for longer than the charge was ludicrous. At least he didn't need to worry about how he was going to get to Brno where he planned for all of them to stay.

Terberk spotted Abigail getting her suitcase and walking through the sliding door that separated the arrival hall from the baggage hall. Then it was Detective Hendon who got near the conveyor belt to get his bag. Terberk was a little puzzled as to why Detective Hendon was grumpy. He put it down to being nervous just as he had been ever since they met each other. Terberk would catch the killer he was chasing years; Detective Hendon would have a some explanation for his unsolved crime and Abigail would be free.

'Bloody daylight robbery,' mumbled Terberk to himself as he dropped the heavy coins into the parking meter which swallowed them with a clunk. Outside the weather felt tropical, very heavy to breathe. As Terberk drove an old Peugeot he bought many years ago it didn't have functioning air conditioner. He was used to it now, so it didn't seem to be relevant to him despite Ivana nagging him to get it fixed. The air vents worked, so did the car. There wasn't a point to replace perfectly working manual solution. No need to throw money about, for he had just put a fortune into the parking meter. The car slightly leaned as he sat into the worn suspension and with a whistle he started the motor. One handed with a jolt it unwillingly moved towards the exit whilst he turned the handle to open his window. Once the exit gobbled up the ticket the car let a large cloud behind as he accelerated.

'Does this thing have at least any air con?' Hendon interrupted with distaste. Terberk, taking the corner too fast to join the motorway, just nodded.

'Use the handle and get winding.' At least Abigail, who was fighting to wipe the beads of sweat from her forehead, got it and was already halfway winding down her window. Like a dog she poked her face out.

***

Once on the motorway she noticed a sign that seemed like they just left Brno rather than going into it.

'Aren't we staying in Brno?' Terberk stopped whistling.

'No. We are going to stay at Nine Crosses.' With that he glanced at the rear-view mirror at Abigail who was trying to keep up her pose of pretending of not being scared.

261

'When are we to arrive? I need the toilet.' At the same time Terberk put the signal on, which was ticking away until they took the turn.

'We are here.'

'Yes, we are turning off but how far from the turn is the ...' She hadn't finished the sentence because right before them was a T-junction with its crosses three metres high. They stood tall, creating shade as if playing with the strong rays of light.

'We arrived at Nine Crosses,' said Terberk.

Abigail remembered this place from photos from the internet. She leaned closer from the back seat to the front to get a better view.

'Well I think you got that wrong,' chuckled Hendon, pointing at the crosses. 'There are only eight of them, only eight of them.'

He was pointing this fact as if he had discovered a naughty magazine his father was hiding under the bed. Terberk grinned back at the detective.

'You are right; there are only eight.'

He turned the signal on again at the T-junction only to immediately turn right into a small gravel track, what seemed like a car park. He stopped the car and got out.

'Abigail let's see if Detective Hendon is correct. So, there are only eight of them, you say.'

Terberk walked towards the crosses confidently like he knew something they didn't.

'One, two, three, four, five, six, seven, eight ... nine.' Terberk counted, followed by Detective Hendon walking by his side.

'There is the ninth; it has fallen onto the ground,' remarked Abigail as she stepped closer to the fallen one. To be closer she had to come down the little bank that obscured the view of it lying on the ground among the wildflowers and long grass. Crouching down to the cross she run her hand across the weathered wood. The whole area was covered with wildflowers. There was monkshood, daisies, foxgloves, hemlock, buttercup and many others.

'Why did this one rot and not the others? It looks like it was only replaced recently. It is the same new wood as the rest of them. Typical council botched up job.'

Abigail had started to find Detective Hendon irritating but thankfully Terberk replied. If she did it wouldn't be that polite.

'There might be another explanation. What everyone knows who has lived in these parts for many years, is that no matter how many times you replace the cross, no matter how thick the wood is, it will always rot from underneath and fall before any of the rest of them will. It is because of the rotten soul buried beneath that sends all of us a message that he is here, still with us.'

Rotten soul? This was the place where Josef was buried? Abigail retreated from the cross as if it were a poisonous snake. Spine chilling, she shook with cold despite the heat. 'This is where he is?' As if snake just gone to attack her, she jumped away from where the cross stump was. She then lurched herself towards it digging her nails into the dry ground. As she worked the earth, her nails splitting, she dug deeper still like a dog in search of a bone.

'Stop, Abigail, it won't help.' Gently Terberk pushed her away from the disturbed earth.

'I have to get him out, get that bastard up and burn whatever is left. I must obliterate him from this world.'

With a saddened expression, Terberk worked the dirt off her hands. 'This won't help, you know that what lies beneath is nothing but pile of bones.'

It was Detective Hendon that changed the discussion onto a different subject.

'Why is he here with the others? If someone killed your family, why would you burry him so near them?'

Terberk answered with less enthusiasm. 'It is a long story and it's tough to keep track of all information that I gave you, I get that. I am hungry, let's go to the motel. It will be dark soon. Nobody is safe here in darkness in the summer. Who knows what can come out of these woods at night?' He pointed to the dense woodland right behind the crosses.

Abigail didn't want to leave. Already bored, Detective Hendon made his way back to the car. Terberk did the same only pausing to nod towards her that it was time to go. She walked slowly towards them, taking a last glance towards the fallen cross.

Was her mind playing tricks or was there a hand clasping the cross from beneath the ground? Turning to take a better look, Terberk shouted.

'Come on Abigail, dusk is settling. We have much to do.' Twisting her head back from the car to the cross, she saw it no longer revealed the hand but a small ray of sunshine looking like fingers streaked across it. Shaken, she took her leave, but looked back as they drove off.

There behind one of the standing crosses a hand held tight to one, with a small head peeking through it, looking as a child who peeks through the door to see Father Christmas. Abigail squinted to try to make out who it was. The distance made it impossible, but the shadow was there. Someone was standing there, watching them.

***

The motel was very basic: no niceties, only a clean bed with a bathroom. The reception room was dull with nothing to look at. Even the carpet resembled something between a dirt track and a cleaning rag.

The receptionist was so displeased to see them that Abigail expected to be spat at as she was handed the room key. Thankfully this place had a small restaurant serving the home-made basics. The food was wonderful considering that the restaurant resembled a public toilet.

Terberk repeated the whole history though Abigail didn't need much reminding. She read it over thousands of times, but by the look of the detective, there was a critical need for a refresher. That night Abigail fell asleep thinking of Dan, her phone shining on the pillow next to hers, with his picture on.

***

It was in the morning that a knock on the door woke her up. Her lips were sealed as if she'd been drinking glue. She was desperate for a good coffee. That was the one thing this place didn't do right.

'I can't wait to get a proper stuff when I get back home,' muttered Abigail at the breakfast table. The words might have been said to the table, as neither Hendon nor Terberk were listening. They were engaged in a whispering argument.

'Are you telling me there actually isn't a real plan? A step by step procedure? Are you raving mad?' Detective Hendon pushed his cup with such force that the contents spilled all over the table.

Calmly Terberk retrieved a napkin to wipe it all off. 'The plan now is that we have a nice turn about the town, see some scenery until the dusk for when we begin to work. Unless you want to sit here all day.'

Abigail noted how calm Terberk was compared to Detective Hendon, who was explosive like a volcano, spitting his all lava around. 'Fine, I will play along but by tomorrow I am getting her little backside back to England's finest police jail for investigation..'

Abigail didn't like the way he was pointing at her. She decided to avoid talking to him for he was useless, he knew nothing and was just a liability. When in Brno, she recognized the alley where she bought the ring from the gypsy. Hopeful, Abigail tried to extend her neck to see as far as possible to find the gypsy. In between the crowd she tried to spot the familiar face. Instead the only familiar face glancing back at her was Josef. In the distance he was pushing through the bodies to get closer. Then his face turned into a crow that flew directly at her face. Detective Hendon managed to catch her as she tripped over the cobblestones.

'Careful here, you nearly cracked your head open. It's just pigeons; they won't hurt you.'

Terberk wasn't fooled as he was checking out the crowds. Happy, with nothing to worry him, he took Hendon's attention before he was going to ask more questions. 'I must show you a brilliant church. It has only one gargoyle.'

After a day filled with touristy things such as buying presents for relative or just taking in the scenery, the day hours run short to the end. Their little pretence could have fooled passers-by but not Abigail. She could tell that they were all tetchy as hell. Each shadow was checked, each corner checked before proceeding. The more the day wore on the more tired her feet felt so she appreciated it was time to make their way to the recommended restaurant. The place looked completely insignificant on the outside but inside it had the cosy country kitchen feel. The tables were dressed in red and white chequered table cloths with basic condiment sets in the middle with a little simple bud vase. Even before they made themselves comfortable in their chairs, pints of beer spilling out of the cold glass were placed before them. They just magically exchanged glances with Abigail as if they were asking who ordered them. Terberk already had foam on his moustache, smacking his lips with the large gulp he took.

'There is nothing better than a good cold beer in summer.' A young good looking blonde Eastern European girl came in with the menus. Abigail noticed that Detective Hendon was blushing a little when the waitress winked at him. Like a love-struck teenager, looking after where the waitress left, Detective Hendon asked.

'Do they serve fish and chips?' Terberk turned over to inspect the menu.

'Unfortunately, no but I am sure you can find something other that's tastier. Look, you can have whole salmon that slowly cooked in butter with lemon.'

Abigail had a reasonably cloudy day, the way Detective Hendon reacted to the waitress made her little warmer as it took the dark thoughts away. After some time Detective Hendon requested chips as a starter followed by goulash.

***

Terberk ate his meal quietly. There were many things going through his mind. One bother was Hendon, as he was a man hard to convince of anything that was not England. The thoughts were coming in fast from both directions like cars on a motorway, speaking to each other.

Why couldn't he stay at home to enjoy his retirement? Why did he get muddled up in these things? Wasting his time and money for some young women that he will never meet and most likely never save. He stopped and paused for a second at the sight of Detective Hendon.

Just look at that man, this so-called detective from England. That should be someone very young and incredibly fit, so he could fight with all these strong criminals and murderers. He should be man of steel, not an advert for Dunkin' Donuts who is gobbling his food like a dog that was not fed for days!

Shaking his head, he waved for another two pints to be delivered. When they arrived he placed one before Detective Hendon.

'I must say I'm warming up to this place. Simple but delicious food, beer to die for and the women, well ...' Detective Hendon smacked his lips as he checked out the waitress again. 'Well, the women, they are something else.' Terberk didn't appreciate Detective Hendon's blatant breast staring.

'I am sure that it's not the women, beer and food you came in here for, right?'

Terberk dived down to his feet to get the laptop bag he had been carrying with him all day. He pulled out the same folder that Detective Hendon and Abigail saw they day before and ran through the story again, though this time he came clean.

'There isn't much of a plan really, there never was because nobody has attempted to do what we will tonight.' Pointing at the map, he circled part of the woods.

'This is approximately where the old footpath was, so we need to be here and find the time when the wedding party appears. Nobody recorded the spot, so we need to walk the path once we find it and find them.'

Hendon snorted. 'You're telling us we go to woods in the dark and look for what used to be a path and walk that all night until we find some spooks?' Eyes rolling, he tipped the beer down his throat.

'What am I going to do?' asked Abigail sheepishly.

'You will need to keep up with us, then watch for the man you now recognize as Josef. For when you see him he will be out of your body, that's when you take the ring off and give it to me.'

Detective Hendon whacked the glass onto the beer mat. 'Ring? What ring? Nobody said anything about a ring?'

Abigail hid her hand into her pocket.

'Don't tell me, I can see that you two have a hush-hush situation going on. I no longer care because tomorrow, you're coming with me and I am just tired of this garbage. Let's just pay and get on with it so I can go to bed.'

Abigail appreciated the gesture as she wasn't ready to start explaining the ring, nor to speak that it was now giving her some serious bother. It was so hot that it was burning deep into her skin.

***

The dusk was shedding its darkness between the trees on the ground as they drove back to that small car park area by the crosses. Abigail followed Terberk who set the pace followed by Detective Hendon. They entered the woods with the sunset falling behind the horizon.

The evening chorus of the birds was the only sound apart from detective Hendon who had a face of thunder mumbling to himself like an Alzheimer's patient.

Abigail took the bird song as a victory anthem. She was full of hope of being free to get on with her life with Dan. The deeper they got the darker it become until it cloaked them completely, turning the surroundings jet black. Unable to make out the surroundings she gave her trust into Terberk completely. Surely, he knew these woods, he knew where they were heading.

Detective Hendon walked past her to tap Terberk on the shoulder. 'Are were there yet?'

Terberk said nothing just put a finger to his lips, pointing to go forward. What was he listening to? Abigail fell behind a couple of steps as she tried to prick her ears to listen. A little crunch came from around her and a small twig beneath her feet tripped her up. Then as she fell the skin on her back prickled with bumps. An icy hand ran up her spine. Picking her body off the ground she turned 180 degrees trying to make out what was surrounding her, whose icy hand was running up her back. Straining hard, screwing up her eyes, she wondered whether it was all just in her head. It was dark, yet the moonlight managed to come down through the thick of the trees to provide some help to see but it wasn't enough.

It was like the dream, each step the same as those in the nightmares. The smell of pine was overpowering yet wonderful. The twigs snapping with each step, carefully making sounds that disturbed animals running away from the hedgerows and bushes.

Two silhouettes way ahead were most likely Terberk and Hendon. Trying to listen to their voices so she could pinpoint the way to get to them, Abigail saw that the two shadows parted and now there were four. A breath hit her ear lobes, whispering burst all around her. Turning around to see better, the shapes were coming up from the ground floating to circle her. One, two, three, four ... The fifth wasn't a tree, there stood a figure.

Unable to work out, Abigail was filled with dread. Moss lying motionless on the floor began to grow from beneath until a figure emerged from the hedgerow. All the figures gathered to walk away in the opposite direction. As the figures floated slowly away, Abigail whispered into the darkness.

'Terberk, Detective Hendon, this way. I think I can see something!'

She took some steps towards the hill where the figures disappeared. She skipped over tree trunks and bushes and God knows what else as she could barely see the tip of her nose. Twigs snapped at her face, leaves brushed past her hair.

Struggling through, trying not to lose the figures. Somehow it didn't worry her that the figures weren't walking but were floating over any obstacle in their path. Her feet got wet as she stood in puddles of water, cutting her ankle on one raspberry bush as she ran past it. Soon additional light came through as the trees became less dense and she was near up the hill from where one figure stood watching her to struggling to make her way to it. It turned its head towards her, waiting.

'Who are you?' Abigail asked as she pushed past yet another set of brambles, that were scratching her face like hands of an old witch.

The figure didn't answer, it just stood there silently, head faced towards Abigail. The light behind the figure was so strong that it was hard to make out whether it was a man or woman. Abigail was tired now from making her way to the top of the slippery mossy slope. Little by little she made it to the top despite it all.

At the top of the hill, Abigail no longer had to ask who it was. She stood the edge of the woods from her dreams facing grassy plane and beyond reeds which grew by the lake that shone like a mirror. One side of the lake was open, free of reeds and the moonlight skipped off the water, shining and dancing in patterns. Though the lake was only half a meter away, it was still impossible to make the figure out. Slowly it floated towards the lake only pausing once it reached the edge, as if trying to bathe its feet in the warm summer night. As it turned it dawned on Abigail that it changed form into a figure sporting a floating dress rather than the trousers the figure in the woods had.

Unsteady, Abigail took a couple more steps towards the lake. She had to face her to ask for her forgiveness to tell her that today it all would end. She walked slowly across the smooth moist grass. A sound from behind startled her, afraid to check what it was, Abigail stopped walking.

It was most likely Detective Hendon, as he was the clumsier of the two. Gently turning around, she grew braver, hopefully she was going to greet at least one of them. More than ever did she need somebody with her when she was meeting the Bride. Instead what she turned to was someone completely unexpected.

There it stood, right in front of hers. The memories came flooding in, who was it, she knew her, it was, it was … 'Joan!' she gasped. Joan's nostrils enlarged, the air rushing over Abigail's cheeks. From behind her walked out Lynne followed by Kirty.

They stood there saying nothing, staring at Abigail furiously. An atmosphere full of sickness brought a dark cloud over the moon and they were gone for a second. As soon as the cloud passed, they reappeared. The moonlight bathed them in an eerie glow.

'MURDERER! MURDERER! MURDERER!'

The whispers came from a familiar voice, right behind Abigail from beyond the lake. She felt it on the back of her head, the little puff of air falling across her neck as the words were spoken. Not wanting to turn back, she had no choice, she had to face the Bride. As she turned the hair rose on the back of her neck.

'MURDERER!'

Turning back, Abigail faced another figure, this time there wasn't the need to search through her memory of who it could be. There before her stood Natalie. Through her clenched teeth came the hoarse whisper, 'MURDERER!'

Natalie sounded like an angry viper. Through her teeth spitting out words like daggers aimed at Abigail.

'You are conniving bitch! I saw you as my sister, I loved you like one but all along you were a selfish, greedy witch. You're going to pay like everyone who does such a thing, who has taken life away for their own greed. These woods are full of those who paid for it as you will. They will be here soon to watch you die! She is coming!'

The wind picked up. The tall pines were moving side to side batting against each other. More whispers came within the woods followed by song. To both of her sides more shapes appeared by the edge of the woods, standing lined up just like soldiers waiting for a command. Unable to hold the view, Abigail averted her eyes so that she doesn't need to see Joan who now stood closer, leaning towards her ear.

'I hope she will gouge your eyes.'

In the other ear, Lynne added, 'or pull out your dirty tongue,' then Kirty had her say: 'I hope she will rip your heart out for you to see.'

Breaking free, Abigail ran towards the nearby wheat fields. Her hair was pulled, face scratched, she got kicked and punched by invisible forces in all directions who were chanting.

'Witch, witch, you selfish witch!'

As she struggled through the reeds which blocked the footpath to the field, the chanting stopped. Song coming from the woods replaced it.

'The woods! I have to run to the woods!' screeched Abigail as that was where she had to take the ring off. That's where Terberk was with Detective Hendon. Abigail jumped into the woods like a hunted deer.

The brambles were dense, the song got louder. A beam of light was like a lighthouse guiding Abigail through the dark forest. Detective Hendon and Terberk had torches, it had to be them.

'I'm here!' she shouted as the light got sharper.

The footpath that ran through the wood was alight but not by man-made light but by ghosts. There were many of them walking in a neat row, following the ones at the front. Children were running past, playing. In the front was Anna, the Bride holding a man Abigail didn't recognize.

Behind them were more people. Anna's sister, Nela was also there.

'Josef must be here, where is he?' Abigail pleaded with Nela who just floated past her. From within her own throat came a hoarse voice that wasn't hers.

'I am here, I was always with you, I never left. I am you. I am Josef and I am Abigail.'

A brief glance at her own hand revealed the whole puzzle. For her hand multiplied, as if a second skin started to peel away but like shadow, it moved the same way. Abigail was one body, Josef the second, together joined.

'That's how you read my thoughts, you were always inside me, using my body as a vessel to control and take over.' Disgusted, Abigail clawed at her own skin.

'Get out!' Instead of feeling the scratches, Abigail felt the coldness of steel. Both hands she held shiny antique guns which she now raised to fire. Then, as all froze, she run at the figures with daggers retrieved from the belt stabbing anything that was near. This repeated action was done with lust, laughing madly with the pleasure of it. The more blood was spilled the better it felt.

Then, it went black. Ice came all over making the leaves shine with frost and the Bride, bleeding stepped towards Abigail who could feel her breath upon her forehead. Abigail bowed to avoid her like a naughty school girl for she couldn't look her in the eye. The Bride raised her hand and pulled at Abigail's chin to make her to have and eye contact.

The Bride had nothing but two empty sockets full of dark blood, her mouth was gravely black, and her skin shone pure white. Her hair was full of wildflowers bearing a wildflower headband made of same wildflowers as the posies were. Her hair was swept up in the breeze as she opened her mouth.

'Just see what you caused? This is your fault. See those bodies lying on the floor? You have killed them by your greed. Was it worth it?'

Anna pointed towards the mayhem. Abigail peered at where she had pointed only to avert the Bride's hollow eye sockets.

The bodies were no longer strangers. They were not the people from the ghostly procession, instead on the ground lay Natalie with the whites of her eyes shining in the moonlight, her hands spread out just like when she fell at her wedding. She lay there on the cold ground on her back.

Next to her was Kirty with her dark black hair covering nearly all her face. She lay on her side like a peaceful child, sleeping on his side cuddling a soft toy.

Then it was Joan with legs bent at her knees, lying sideways leaning onto Lynne, who lay on her front. There was one more person on the cold ground: a man

'Why a man, I haven't killed any man. is it Josef?' Abigail blurted out the words with pleasure, because with Josef finally vanquished, she could take the ring off and be rid of him forever. The Bride laughed wickedly.

'You silly girl, you think that's Josef? You think it's him lying on the dirt track by those that you killed? You really think that you're free of him? Oh, do come and look, I am most intrigued!'

The Bride floated towards the figure, kneeling by him, reaching for the head to turn.

'Who do you think it is?' Toying with Abigail, she grabbed the hair on his head. She moved her eyebrows as if questioning, teasing Abigail to step closer. Then she pulled and snapped the head clean off the body. The crunch made Abigail shake. She held the head and wafted slowly back.

'Do you want to see? To be sure, to know who this is?' Teasing, twisting the head there and back to reveal the face.

'Just show me now!' shouted Abigail.

The Bride came closer and as she was near enough she threw the head at Abigail's feet where it turned on its face. 'Dan!' cried Abigail, near fainting, her breath came in ragged gasps.

'You bitch, I'll kill you, how dare you touch him? He's mine, mine, I own him!' Abigail clawed at the her with left hand as she stabbed her with the right. As soon as the metal plunged deep into her body, the blood started flooding out of the hole. It was not hers; it was Abigail's for it was her chest that was bleeding.

It wasn't her doing the stabbing. It was Josef, who had come out of her at the same moment she took on the Bride. Unable to speak, Abigail clutched at her chest as Josef stood there with glee.

'I love the feeling, I love the ownership of life of another I love ...' He didn't finish, as the horseman, Martin, came running from behind a tree, wielding a large knife. He stabbed Josef over and over. He clawed at his face with the knife, stabbed it into the lifeless body as if it was a pin cushion only turning the dagger upon himself, pushing it deep within his own chest. Once he fell upon the cold ground, within seconds, he stood up as if nothing had happened, looked around until he found what he wanted to see – Anna. They embraced as soon as he got close to her.

'Finally, the year has come again, the only time I can see you my darling, for all eternity I am happy to wait to have this one night of embrace with you, my dear. I will die many times over only, so I can have you in my arms again.'

They kissed passionately as Abigail bled nearby. Then the place lit up again by the presence of ghostly bodies. Abigail hurt badly but the pain got worse when she noticed Natalie, standing there, holding Dan's hand. Josef rose from the place he fell.

'How dare you! How dare you let her trick you, how dare you die! I shall find another, one that will give me what I need! You will see, this isn't the end!'

Gasping for air, unable to answer, Abigail lay there like a fish out of water. Lungs shutting down, with Josef being furious but like magic being pulled away from her. An invisible force dragged him away into the darkness beyond.

'I shall be back! I am not finished I am never finished!'

Natalie stepped closer, kneeling before Abigail, ignoring Josef and his behaviour.

'I love Dan. He is mine. He was always mine.' She stood up ready to leave with Dan by her side. He knelt to the same height with a saddened face.

'I never guessed you would be so cruel, that you would do such a thing. Josef came for me, that is why I am here, he came to my home as I ate my dinner with my mother. He ripped my heart out. I now know what Natalie felt, how painful it was, how she suffered because of you. For all eternity, I shall never forgive you. I have never loved you. I hate you!'

He stood up, embraced Natalie and both walked away into the distance, side by side. Everyone turned around to do the same as if the curtain came down. In agony, gasping in shock all alone, Abigail noted that someone was running towards her.

'Abigail, Abigail, are you OK? What's the matter?'

It was Terberk and Detective Hendon.

***

Terberk was the first who sprang up for action once everyone gone. Tugging at Detective Hendon's sleeve, he made his way towards Abigail whilst Hendon was half frozen in shock. Terberk let go of his sleeve as he caught Abigail falling backwards. Her eyes rolled slowly towards the sky.

'I loved him more than anything! More than life itself.'

A small tear rolled off the tip of his moustache onto Abigail's face. He knew Abigail wasn't going to live another minute. He felt rotten to ask, to think of it but he had this one chance only to ask for what he needed to hide from the world.

'Abigail, will you give me the ring, the one on your hand? Will you give me Anna's wedding ring?'

With a gasp, Abigail reached for her finger and took if off. As she did, she was gone. Terberk held her lifeless body closer to him, while Hendon, open-mouthed, wide-eyed just stood there like a statue. Terberk kneeled there clutching Abigail's mortal vessel with his tears streaming down her face.

***

Abigail saw it all, Terberk crying, clutching at her lifeless body, then Detective Hendon frozen on the spot. Then she took an unsteady step towards where Natalie and Dan had gone; hoping she could catch up with them, hoping she could be with Dan in the afterlife; hoping to be near him for all eternity.

Chapter 12

As Terberk woke up it came to him that finally it was over: he had caught him. With the help of Ivana, he performed the ceremony in locking the spirit into the ring, so that if it remained under lock and key, untouched, it wouldn't cause harm. It wasn't an ideal situation but for now that was all he had. So far none of the items had been destroyed: he didn't know how. Each time he tried he failed. That was the goal, to find the way to destroy them, annihilate them.

Once the metal lock clicked into place, he gently tapped the box. 'Finally, under lock and key. For now, not forever.'

Shuffling to his desk to finish the report, the ink on the final summary dried on the sentence 'Though the end was not ideal as it cost a human life.' He exhaled.

'Poor Abigail.' He put down the pen. Leaning back to try to find the positive from the whole mess, apart from having the ring in a safe place for now, was the knowledge that there was another detective in the world who now had a different way of thinking. Detective Hendon. The poor mad had been impossible to calm once they got back to the hotel room. He was still hyperventilating for a long time after.

The next day when they visited the pathology department to say their goodbyes, Hendon was mute when handed the paperwork to take to England with him. The memory of the pathology visit was still fresh; the sterile room, smelling of sickly-sweet death, an end of a human life. Terberk could still smell it on his skin. The odour of death hitting his nose, assaulting his nostrils as they walked in. The room, so clean and tidy, like the path to heaven shouldn't be spoiled. The hospital bed placed in the middle and the hunched pathologist over his paperwork contemplating what should be written in the notes.

After extensive search, the pathologist found no cause of death. Terberk kindly brushed Abigail's cheek like a father would to his daughter to pay his final respect; to say a final goodbye. It was the sob that made his presence clear to the pathologist.

'Hello, you old fool! I hadn't seen you for a while. Retired or still in the force?' The surprise in the pathologist's face was that of a friend, happy seeing an old acquaintance. The pathologists lined forehead was like freshly ploughed field.

'Like you, my old friend, I dip in occasionally to top up my retirement fund.' Terberk tried for a smile which was returned by his old acquaintance, Doug Jones, an expat American married to a Czech girl. He met his wife in the US as at the time their school got permission to travel, but on their way back, the iron curtain closed, and she could never return. A young lost 19-year-old in a strange world without the family. Thankfully the agencies were helpful, and she met him in university where their love blossomed. After thirty years of not being able to see her family, be there for her father's funeral, she was able to return. That's when they decided to move back in, as Jones had mastered the language well. It was Jones that disrupted Terberk's trip down memory lane.

'So how do you know the deceased? How long have you known her? You don't need to pussyfoot around, I have known you for a long time Vava, has it been twenty years? Thirty? She is one of your cases, right?'

Terberk nodded; the tear on his eyelashes slowly fell to the ground. 'I have failed this one, I had hope that I wouldn't see her like this.'

Jones gave his old friend a look of pity. He threw his arm over his shoulders as he pulled the white sheet over Abigail. Jones's boots squeaked as he shuffled Terberk away from the table.

'Well as she is one of those you couldn't help then nobody else would have been able to. If she was your case it would explain why I cannot seem to find the cause of death. Why I am cracking my brain in trying to figure it out. I never will, will I, because my reasoning is purely biomedical thinking. Therefore, I am missing out all the other non-scientific factors. So, I shall never know how she died apart from sudden death syndrome? Broken heart?'

Terberk was ushered close to Hendon who so far remained silent by the entrance door, unable to move closer to the table where Abigail lay.

'Here, stand by your friend here for a second.'

Jones walked back to the desk and pulled the wheelie chair away, so he could shuffle in between his papers to retrieve what he was after.

'Ahh there it is, preliminary report to take back to England.' Turning the main beam of light above Abigail on his way back, Terberk noted that he carried two folders rather than one.

'Here you go sir, take this back to England to give to your guys. Good luck in trying to explain what happened here, as what I can tell, anyone that meets Terberk ends up regretting it.'

Chuckling at his joke, he turned back to Terberk.

'Here, Vava, this is for you. I will call you later as I want to discuss the other case you're working on. I have been examining the other girls. The one that was buried alive was probably awake when it happened. Look, go home and I'll call you in couple of days and we will discuss it, OK? For now, take a break.'

Terberk felt the gentle shove in his back. He knew Jones well: it was the sign to disappear. Tapping gently Hendon on the shoulder 'Come on John, let's go to a pub and have a beer.'

Last glance towards the table, the crystal white sheet over Abigail, Terberk turned around and walked out of the doors that slowly with a gentle thud closed behind him.

***

Now you know the whole story of what truly happened. You now know why I am here, in my own hell, paying for the need, the want, the greed of having the man who was never destined to me. My own hell consists of walking through these woods in a country that is strange to me. I am unable to speak to any of the other, walking lost souls such as me. I can see those to whose death I contributed. Joan is here with Lynne and Kirty. Each time I want to say how sorry I am they cannot hear me.

I cannot speak, I cannot make contact, I can only see. My hell is continuous as I see Natalie with Dan in passionate embrace. They are happy, finally together for eternity.

I am forced to watch this day in, day out, infinitely until my debt is paid, if it ever will be, as I have taken the life, the right of living from the innocent. No one is interested that it was not my hand that killed them, that I was a tool; that I was as used as the others who are in the same situation as I am.

In their minds, it was my greed that guided the killer, therefore I was the killer. I am here walking bare footed in this never-ending woodland so far from my beloved home. Each step I take is a step among sharp needles digging into my soles causing me a great pain.

This is me in my private hell. So, next time you are travelling on the motorway past Brno, turn off and try to count how many crosses you see. But don't get too close. You mustn't disturb the dead souls who will suffer for eternity to pay their debts of love, hate and malice. I can bet that the ninth cross will be rotten from the ground just like the soul lying beneath; the soul whose name is Josef, the one that is finally gone.

But if you are intrigued, go and visit on the day of the wedding massacre, the day that made Josef. Turn up at dusk when the gorgeous summer sun is setting in the east, go and venture in the woods to see if you can hear the singing of a wedding song and sobbing of the Bride.

You might hear my sobs too if I would be able to express my grief. Do come but be aware, should you disturb the dead could come back to haunt you.

Do come the wedding! The wedding song is so beautiful, so enchanting. If you attend, you will feel a presence near you. That would be all of us, the lost ones, who will stay close to you, so we can try to get into your body, to use it for our own. We want you to be our vessel, so we can pretend that we can live again.

Do come, sing with us, listen. I shall be waiting.

THE END

Historical facts

The village of Nine Crosses (Devět Křížů) lies at the turn of the motorway D1 towards the second largest town in the Czech Republic, Brno city. It was at the Nine Crosses village where the story used in this book occurred. This story, told across generations, is about a horseman who fell in love with a local girl who was given in marriage to another. In a drunken haze this horseman approached a stranger and agreed to pay him to stop that marriage from happening. This stranger went mad at the wedding and murdered nine people as the wedding procession was on their way to the church blessing.

Questions have been raised as to why so many accidental deaths have occurred there since the wedding massacre. The local people blame the apparitions of the Bride and the murderer for the accidental deaths. Therefore, every ten years, the local monastery monks place some holy water upon the crosses where the victims were buried. Throughout the centuries, the local monastery replaces the old crosses as they break or rot away beyond repair. Yet, no matter the amount of repair or replacement the ninth cross always rots from the bottom. The rot is due to the rotten soul that lies beneath, as the murderer was buried there by accident with the victims.

The St. Jacob Church (Kostel svatého Jakuba) was erected in 1460 by a bitter architect. Before finishing the church, he was told by the members of society funding the construction to stop work on St. Jacob Church, as he was showing up the architect who was working on another church in the more affluent side of Brno. The stonemason was a well-known joker, and after agreeing to stop the work he asked to finish off the last window on this church.

The stonemason carved a man, who from below looked like an angel, with his buttocks pointing directly to the other church. What is not immediately obvious is that not only it is a man who has been carved, but also a woman beneath him locked in an intimate embrace. When they realised what he had done, it was too late to do anything about it.

The story of the bent tower in the Old Town Council began in the sixteenth century, when a master stonemason from Prague was asked to build hall for the Town Council that surpassed all others. Back then a payment was given up front, but the stonemason started the work without seeing a penny. Half way through construction he approached the town council for a deposit that was due to him and his workmen. The town council did not agree and said that they would only pay when the whole work was completed. The master stonemason finished without payment but built the middle tower twisted, just as the town council had been. The Town Council tried and failed to get the stonemason to return and fix the tower – to this day it still stands twisted.

The stories of the crocodile and the large wheel is also unknown as to where their origins began. There are many theories, but both can be seen in the walkway to the old Town Council which is found between the Freedom Square (Náměstí Svobody) and Green Market (Zelený Trh) in the Town Council Street (Radnické ulici).

The Ninth Cross

The Ninth Cross